FATH

(NEVER TOO LATE BOOK 4)

Aiden Bates

© 2017

Disclaimer

the reader's pleasure. Any similarities to real people, places, events, living or dead are all coincidental.

Chapter One

Oliver checked himself out in the mirror. The new haircut was a good one. It showed off the slight waves to his hair instead of fighting them. His shirt emphasized his narrow waist and his slender body, while the print brought out the best in his eyes and his skin tone. He looked good, damn it.

Then he threw his hairbrush down. What the hell was the point of any of this? He looked good. Fantastic. The well-cut shirt, which hadn't been cheap, would be hidden under a lab coat for the day. The hair could be well cut, or it could be bowl cut, or it could be shaved. No one was going to see it. No one who mattered anyway.

What good was working with a bunch of alphas if the one he wanted wouldn't even look at him?

He stripped off the pretty shirt and replaced it with something cheaper. The nice shirt was wasted on Detective Nenci, and he didn't give even half a crap if a table full of lab samples thought he had a nice ass or not.

He raced toward the door and barely remembered to grab his lunch on his way out. He didn't want to forget that; he hated to leave the lab once he got into a rhythm, and things had a way of building up enough that he found it difficult to leave.

He unlocked his bike from the rack in the parking garage and wheeled it out to the fresh air. He could drive to work. He did that if the weather was bad, or if he had a lot of stuff to bring back and forth. He would generally rather get out and enjoy a little bit of fresh air and exercise and restrict the amount of pollution he dumped into the air if he could. He only lived a twenty-minute ride away from the lab, for crying out loud.

The air was beautiful at this time of year. It hadn't gotten to be too hot yet, and all of the flowers that he passed gave off amazing scents that helped to ease his mood on his way in to work. Okay, so Nenci wasn't interested. He'd had time to get used to it. He could just avoid him, right? He loved his job, and the guys that he worked with were fun and respectful. Maybe it wasn't the kind of sunshine and roses life he'd imagined when he was a young teen, but he helped people every day and he could feel pretty darned good about that.

He waved to Rebecca, the lab's receptionist, on his way in. His workstation looked deceptively calm as he approached. There were no brightly colored sticky notes on his monitor, at least. That counted for a lot. Three huge file folders had been dropped into his inbox already, but that didn't mean a whole lot. Each file was a case. He might have a lot of analysis for each case, or he might have to run one DNA sample. There was no way to know.

He settled in, stowed his helmet and his lunch, and logged into his computer. Most of his emails were pretty bland and boring. He got the usual round of agency emails, to include the one that went around in mid-June or so every year reminding people about uniforms and standards of professional dress. Someone in Human Resources had taken to sending around weekly examples of Staties "doing good," in response to the recent dirty cop scandal. Oliver deleted that; he knew they were doing good, just by doing their jobs. He didn't need to be pepped up.

Then he started to dig into the nitty gritty. The dirty patrolmen, and the dirty folks in Organized Crime, weren't the only scandal facing the state troopers. The Crime Lab had its own issues. Oliver had those scandals and issues to thank for putting him in the position he was—a senior analyst, at only twenty-five. That wasn't too shabby at all. Unfortunately that good fortune meant a lot of extra work. The Crime Lab had been forced to let a lot of people go very suddenly when they'd found out about some of what had been going on. And all of that extra work got a lot more scrutiny than it would have only a few short years ago.

He opened his first real message. This one was from Ryan Tran in Abused Persons. He wanted an analysis of injuries reported from one particular neighborhood in Springfield. He could build the program to do the statistical analysis, that wasn't a problem, but he needed data to run the program from. Was that something that Oliver could get for him?

Oliver tapped his pen against his teeth for a moment. He could get some of the information without a problem. Of course, so could Ryan. Teachers, principals, and school nurses were all mandated reporters. Sergeant Tran was a smart guy, and he'd have already thought of that. He needed something more.

Oliver accessed data from local hospitals. He couldn't see specific patient data; that would be illegal. It would be up to Sgt. Tran to go out to Springfield and talk to people, which was why he was a senior detective and Oliver was a technical analyst. If Oliver had to guess, Tran was working on something involving human trafficking; he did a lot of work with human trafficking. Well, good luck to him.

The next email came from Ray Langer. Oliver knew perfectly well which case Langer was working on. He had a thirty-year-old case involving a murdered child. Everyone knew that he had the Reyes case. He was in the news at least once a week, thanks to the Reyes case. *Any word on that rope, Oliver?*

Oliver sighed and scanned down the rest of his messages. The results should have come from the machine overnight, but they hadn't. *Sorry, Detective Langer. The machine is still processing the data. The good news is that there's something to process. You'll be the first one to know.*

That wouldn't make Langer all that happy, but out of all of the alphas on the Cold Case Squad, he was the most reasonable to deal with. Oliver made a note to revisit that and make sure that the machine was still processing that request, and hadn't malfunctioned, and moved on to the next request.

"Hey." Wheels spun as Oliver's nearest neighbor slid his chair around the cube wall and into Oliver's space. "You got any plans this weekend?"

It would have been easy for Jake and Oliver to compete. They were both good at what they did, and as omegas they both had something to prove. What was more, they both had something to prove to the same man. The main difference, and what kept them from being at daggers drawn with one another, was that Oliver was trying to prove something to the only man he would ever want for his alpha.

Jake was trying to prove something to his father.

"Nah." Oliver looked up from his computer. "I figured I'd come in here and get caught up on some stuff. You?"

"Nothing too serious. I figured maybe I'd go into Cambridge and hit a club or two. You want to come with?" Jake lifted his eyebrows and smiled in invitation.

Oliver squirmed. He'd never been into the club scene. They were all about pickups and hookups, and he didn't want that. "Thanks, but I've got a lot on my plate here."

"Hmm. Yeah, I know those guys over in Cold Case are running you kind of ragged. But you know, you're never going to find someone if you let them use you like that. Come out with me tomorrow night. You can come and pick me up at my place." Jake dropped his voice, so no one else could hear them. "I'm pretty sure my dad will be home."

Oliver's cheeks blazed. "Jake!"

Jake clapped his hands and laughed. "Oh, man. You should see your face. You look like carbon monoxide poisoning, dude."

Oliver glowered. "That's not a good thing!"

Jake toned down his response just enough. "Oliver, man, I'm mostly messing with you, but come on. You have to know that it's a great opportunity to let him see you out of the lab coat."

Oliver slumped in his chair. "You're joking, right?" He shook his head. "It's been years, Jake. If he wanted to see me out of the lab coat, he would have by now."

"Okay, so come out and meet someone who isn't literally old enough to be your father." Jake rolled his eyes. "Trust me, it's a life changing experience."

Oliver straightened up. "Some other time. I have this rope thing for Langer, and then once I've got that done you know he's going to want to run a test on the DNA under her fingernails. There's the room reconstruction, too. Plus, Robles is working on the kid they found in the Blue Hills, and Tessaro's got that forty-year-old shooting and someone needs to identify the remains for him."

Jake jabbed him in the arm. "You mean the good folks at NAMus?" He shook his head and scooted back toward his own space. "Look, buddy. The only way to know for sure that you can't have him is by not trying, okay? You know that. You have to know that. If you want to spend the rest of your life knowing that you didn't even reach out for what you wanted, then be my guest."

Oliver huffed out a bitter little laugh. "Yeah, okay. I'm sure he'd be all over an omega just strutting up to him and saying, *Hey, baby, my place or yours?*" He checked his messages. "He's pretty old fashioned."

"Maybe he'll be so bowled over by your good looks and charm that he'll forget that he thinks fire is an innovation." Jake chuckled and retreated entirely to his own workspace.

Oliver got up from his desk. He was the go-to analyst for the Cold Case squad, but they weren't his only constituents. He had a load of soil samples to run for an arson investigation up in Haverhill and six rape kits to run, just as part of the overall project to get the backlog down. He didn't have the time to sit around and moon over Detective Nenci.

He soon lost himself in the rhythm of the work. Lab work was precise. It required his full attention, all of the time. He needed to know exactly what he was doing. The soil samples came in unlined, clean paint cans. He heated the cans and used a charcoal plug for the vapors, and then he heated the plug to inject the vapors into the chromatogram.

He did this for six samples taken from the scene of the crime. Oliver could do this all day, but the process only took a short time. He'd worked on a lot of arson cases when he first started, and he'd interned at the fire marshal's office during his undergraduate days. He could run these tests in his sleep, and he could even interpret them before coffee.

He collected the results and brought them back to his desk to examine them. From the looks of things, the heaviest concentration of the accelerant used—kerosene, contaminated by what looked like evaporated wood oils—was found in a spot near the front of the house. A small concentration of kerosene was found near where the front door would have been. Samples that had contained wood, labeled as having been from the second floor, showed that the kerosene had been splashed liberally upstairs too.

He wrote up his report and sent it to the detective in Haverhill. If he wanted to talk about Oliver's findings, he would be available. Until then, Oliver had rape kits to work on.

Once Oliver had gotten that depressing task out of the way, he started work on projects for the Cold Case crew. He checked on the rope in Langer's case, and found that the machine had finally finished analyzing the sample provided. He set it to work on the DNA from under the girl's fingernails and wrote up a report for the detective, but he knew that Langer wouldn't read it. He put a hard copy into a file folder and put it into his outbox so he could walk it over later on.

He might have given up hope of actually being with Nenci, but he could still catch glimpses.

He'd just started working on the few non-human artifacts found with the skeletal boy found in the Blue Hills when his boss walked over to his lab workstation. "Hey, Oliver," said Nina. Her bright blue eyes burned into Oliver. "Lock that back up for a while, would you? I need to speak with you for a little bit."

Oliver nodded and obeyed, but inside his entire body trembled. Was he about to be fired? He'd have hoped that they would give him more notice that this. As far as he knew, his performance was more than satisfactory. Had Nenci complained about him? He thought he'd been subtle and not at all overt or obvious, but maybe he'd gone too far. Maybe Jake had said something to his father, and Nenci had complained to Human Resources.

Maybe they were transferring him to the lab in Sudbury or in Maynard. Maybe they were just sacking him outright.

He followed Nina into her office, which was about as orderly as a government employee's office could get. The stacks of paper were neat and weren't threatening to take over the room, at any rate. "Is something wrong, Nina?"

Nina smirked. "Wrong? What could be wrong? We're down ten lab techs thanks to that scandal, we don't have the money to replace nearly enough of them, and do you think that means that they're asking less of us?" She snorted. "Have a seat. Nothing's wrong with regards to you. On the contrary, everything's just fine. No, I asked you in here because I'm giving you an assignment that's a little bit outside your normal comfort zone. It's going to involve actually getting out of the lab."

Oliver frowned. "You mean like collecting evidence at the crime scene?"

"Well, maybe." She winced. "Your friends at the Cold Case Squad have decided to re-open an investigation into an arson and murder that happened up in Salem some fifty years ago."

Oliver tilted his head. "Well, that's kind of their job, isn't it?"

"Right. I mean yes, it is, but here's the thing. This case, it's not going to be like other cases that they work." She tapped her fingers on the desk and glared out her window. "It's different. So much of the case is going to be built on physical evidence, and they don't really understand the science behind how all of that works. Lt. Devlin asked that we put you on the case in a more hands-on kind of role, to make sure that the data is interpreted correctly and that the detective on the case is able to use the information correctly. I wanted to give you the heads up before we go into a meeting with them."

Oliver's insides clenched. "Do you know which detective will be assigned to the case?"

She shook her head. "No. I know that neither Nenci nor Morris has a specific case assigned to him right now. Say the word and I'll make sure that bastard Nenci stays far away from you."

For a brief moment, Oliver considered saying it. Nenci's feelings about having omegas in the field were well known. He didn't want to put himself through that kind of torment. Then Jake's words came back to him. This could be a good opportunity to show himself in a good light to the alpha of his dreams. To be sure, Nenci still wouldn't love him, but he might be more open minded about omegas. Maybe the next omega would have a chance.

"That's okay, Nina." He forced a little smile. "It really doesn't matter to me which detective I work with. They're all great guys, good professionals, and I can work with any of them."

***

Sam finished typing up his report on the Vecchio homicide. He remembered when the case was new, and Sarah Vecchio had only just been killed. There had been a manhunt for a mysterious "black male assailant," with thousands of Bostonians being stopped and searched and all sorts of things because they fit the description.

Sam had been new to the force back then. He hadn't been a detective. He'd just been a regular trooper, but even then he'd been suspicious of the husband. He hadn't been the only one. Too bad it had taken another dead wife to prove it.

He ran the spell-check thing on his report, decided that it didn't know what it was talking about after the third time that it implied that he didn't know the difference between "your" and "you're," and hit *send*. Devlin would forgive any real spelling mistakes in favor of not having to puzzle through his handwriting anymore.

Today was a busy day around the Cold Case squad room. Langer had one of the biggest cases of the century, in terms of visibility anyway. The Reyes case had been an absolute scandal when it hit, with the poor little girl at the center getting completely lost in the lurid accusations against this family member and that family member. If Sam was any judge, and he was, Langer was the right guy for the job. He was smart, sure, but he was also the gentlest alpha Sam had ever met. He could handle the case and keep the victim in mind.

Robles was working on some kind of mess in the Blue Hills. They'd found a body, the body of a young adolescent boy. The finding of bodies in the Blue Hills wasn't all that unusual, unfortunately. Some "businessmen" had seen land that eventually became incorporated into the Blue Hills as an excellent dumping ground. Most of those bodies had once belonged to adults, however. This one had not, and finding out what had happened to him seemed like an impossible task.

Robles could handle it. He didn't have a lot of imagination, but he was diligent. He would explore every possible avenue until he got to his answer. He'd follow the procedure right down to the last letter, and that would be the end of it.

Then there was Tessaro. Tessaro's case was messy. How someone could have been shot forty years ago, in full view of five people, and still be a complete unknown was something that Sam couldn't quite understand. Something fishy was going on there, but Tessaro would get to the bottom of it. The case was messy, but Tessaro was messy, and they were well suited.

Sam and Morris had just finished up cases. Sam's had come to a satisfying conclusion. Morris' had been a little bit less satisfying. It had been a case of self-defense. None of them thought that a jury would see it that way, though. They'd given the suspect the number for Langer's omega, who was a damn fine defense attorney. If he couldn't sway the jury, the poor lady was hosed.

Sam shook his head at himself. Since when had he become the kind of guy that gave a crap about what happened to suspects? The woman had killed her husband, and then she'd concealed the crime for twenty years. Self-defense didn't matter. At least, it hadn't mattered, for a long time. Now it did, and he wasn't sure that he liked the change.

The change had happened, though, and he couldn't pretend that it hadn't. Oh well. There wasn't anything that he could do about it now but shake his head at himself.

The door to Cold Case opened, and two people walked in. The first was Nina Burton, who ran the lab here in

Framingham. The second was someone Sam didn't need to open his eyes to recognize.

The first time that Sam had met Oliver Wesson, he'd gone tearing down to the nearest health food place to sniff at each and every one of their essential oils until he could identify the exotic, enticing scent that emanated from the handsome, slender omega. When he'd finally found it, he'd almost passed out. Myrrh. He'd never met, or even heard of, a myrrh scent for an omega. And he wanted more.

Of course that scent would be attached to the omega whose workstation was next to Sam's son. Why would life be any easier than that?

He kept his eyes strictly on Burton as the pair disappeared into the conference room with Lt. Devlin. He didn't want to stare. He didn't want to give the impression that he was some kind of creepy old man, even if he was.

Tessaro scratched his head. "Did Oliver get a new haircut or something?"

Sam shrugged. "I have no idea." It wasn't a lie. He hadn't looked. He didn't want Oliver to have gotten a haircut. He'd had enough fantasies about running his hand through that hair, gripping it tight—

"Nenci!" Devlin poked his head out of the conference room. "If you'd be so kind."

Sam choked on his own tongue. Tessaro and Robles snickered under their breath, but Langer just gave him a sympathetic glance. Sam ignored them all and grabbed a notepad and pen. He didn't want to go in there. He didn't want to be in such a close space with Oliver Wesson, not if he couldn't touch.

He dragged his feet, but he walked into the conference room.

Devlin closed the door behind them. The scent of myrrh was overpowering, but Oliver's eyes were on the file in front of him. Nina Burton, though, glowered up at Sam while he took his seat. "Detective Nenci," Devlin said. "How much do you know about the Cooper Block Fire in Salem, Massachusetts?"

Sam snorted and accepted the folder that Devlin passed to him. "I know that it was a little bit before my time, sir. I'm not actually fifty yet, and that fire happened more than fifty years ago."

"Two points for Nenci." Devlin grinned. "You do remember it, then. Mr. Wesson, maybe you can fill us in on some of the details."

Oliver cleared his throat and glanced around. Whose bright idea had it been to stick an omega in a closed space with two alphas? The poor guy's heart had to be beating a mile a minute. "The building, while it occupied several different lots, was really just one large building with multiple entrances. It had a single owner, multiple retail establishments on the ground level, and approximately fifty apartments on the stories above. It was replaced with a similar establishment, with better sprinklers, the next year. That structure partially burned in 1992."

Sam frowned. "Was that fire also arson?"

"It was, and it was also fatal." Devlin spoke up when Oliver looked down and away, pink coloring his high cheekbones. "The first fire killed fifty people—one for every apartment, although they weren't quite so evenly distributed. Thirty of the deceased were children. Some of the doors had been barred to prevent escape. The building's owners, the Coucher family, initially faced charges for that obstruction, but it was shown that the doors were blocked from the outside and hadn't been before the fire.

"The fire in '92 was similar. It had a lower death toll because of the improved sprinkler system. The Coucher family apparently learned from history, because that system had been upgraded within the past five years. Security cameras around the building showed a masked figure attempting to seal the building shut, but the camera feed was cut not long after that. Ten lives were lost that day, to include two firefighters attempting to save children."

Sam bowed his head for a moment of respectful silence. "I remember that one, at least. I was new to the force then. My kids were still new, too. My omega, Chris, was horrified by the whole thing. He was terrified that something would happen to me on the job." Instead, something had happened to him. Sam wasn't going to mention that, though. He wasn't even going to think about that if he could avoid it.

"The thing is," Sam continued, scratching at his beard, "this seems very…" He frowned. "This seems very strange. It seems like someone has it out for the family, like an old-style vendetta. Is the property still in the family's hands?"

"No." Burton shook her head. "It's on the ghost tour though." She rolled her eyes. "They sold it to the City at a loss after that, and the City built some offices on the site and used the rest for a park. The Coucher family left Salem, both in terms of business interests and personal property. Their commercial properties have continued to suffer from a spate of fires, not all of which have been proven to be arson. Under the circumstances, though, I think it's a safe bet."

"We can't bring charges for safe bets, or admit them as evidence in court." Sam scowled at her. "So let me guess. We're re-opening the cold case, because we think that we can get something from the old evidence."

Oliver cleared his throat again. "With all due respect, sir, we can. We didn't have the GC-MassSpec in 1967. We didn't even have it in 1992. It existed, but the technology has improved and it's become much more accessible. Forensic evaluation of arson scenes has come a long way in the past few years. Even the invention of the Internet has improved things tremendously, because consultation with a specialist or details about a similar fire or case are simply a click away." Oliver's silver eyes gleamed for a moment. "Arson is never *easy* to solve, but it has become so much more solvable in the past ten years alone."

Sam made the mistake of meeting those silver eyes, just for a moment. He wanted to reach out and touch that smooth skin. "Okay, sure," he said after what he knew was a moment too long. "But the thing is, Oliver, there's so much more to proving it in court than chemical formulae and emails to professors."

It was the wrong thing to say. Burton turned to Devlin. "Are you sure that we can't get Morris on this case instead?"

"Morris is available to help out, but he's not going to be the lead on this case." Devlin ignored Burton's comment. "It's a difficult choice to make, but I think that Nenci's the right man for this job. I happen to agree that this has all of the hallmarks of a vendetta, and he's definitely the one who has the patience to tease out the little connections between the crime scenes. He's also the one who's going to find the crimes that are retaliatory. It would be unusual, to say the least, to have someone kill fifty of a family's tenants without any kind of retaliation whatsoever. It's pretty much unheard of to have someone kill fifty of a family's tenants and then kill eight more, without there being anything in between to spark that second killing."

Sam's mouth went dry. "Are you suggesting what I think you're suggesting, sir?"

Devlin nodded. "This is going to be an unusual investigation. Arson investigation is tricky, and Oliver's our best arson investigator. He's got a lot of great contacts at the state fire marshal's office, thanks to his work there, and he's a very gifted investigator when it comes to the analytical side of things. You and he are going to work together to get to the bottom of this feud and arrest everyone responsible."

Sam scowled. "He can't actually arrest anyone. He's not a detective. He's not a cop. He doesn't have a badge. He doesn't have a gun." He looked directly at Oliver. "Do you even know how to use a gun?"

Oliver shrunk into himself, and Sam felt like he'd kicked a puppy. "I've had adequate ballistics training, sir. I know how to aim and how to fire, how to load and how to check a gun to see if the gun is loaded. I haven't explored beyond that and I don't care to."

Sam threw up his hands. "Sir, don't get me wrong. Oliver's fantastic in the lab. I wouldn't trade his work for ten thousand lab techs. I just think that it's a big mistake bringing omegas out into the field. Bringing omegas out into the field who don't have any kind of field training, who can't protect themselves if things go bad and who might make things worse, is just foolish. Sir."

Oliver hung his head. "It's true. I don't have any field experience or training. I haven't sought it, either."

Burton snarled at Sam. "You're even worse in person than the rumors suggested."

Devlin held up a hand. "You know, Nenci, I understand what you're saying. I do. You're concerned about Oliver's safety, and of course your own. No one's suggesting that we give him a gun, and Oliver's shown plenty of good judgment. He's not going to go grabbing for a gun and looking to play hero."

Oliver managed a sad little grin. "Not my place, sir. I'm here for science. That's all."

Devlin folded his hands on the table. "The fact of the matter is, Detective Nenci, that if we want to solve this case, we're going to need a lot of science to back it up. We'll need more of a hands-on approach from the forensic team than we ever have before. Oliver was chosen for this task because of his consistent display of good judgment and because of his extensive arson experience. You will work with him, and you will get the conviction. Do I make myself clear?"

There was no wiggle room. There was no getting out of this. "Crystal, sir."

Devlin stood up. The others stood with him. The meeting was over. "Excellent. Good luck; keep me posted."

Burton and Devlin left the room. Oliver hung back for just a moment. His perfect pink tongue moistened his lips. "If it's any consolation, sir, I didn't ask for this. I'm sorry they forced me on you." He scurried away after his boss.

Sam hung his head again. Oliver clearly thought that the problem was him, instead of the situation. Sam could understand why. He'd shot his mouth off again, and now that beautiful and delicious-smelling omega looked almost ready to cry. That was on Sam.

Well, it was better that he thought that Sam was an asshole. It was better than thinking that Sam was some kind of pervert. He sighed and got up from the table. He had a lot of prep work to do before they could get started on the project.

Chapter Two

Oliver stared at the screen before him. It had taken him a week to come up with this data, although maybe it shouldn't have. Nina had taken some of his lab duties away from him for the duration of the case, but not all of them. Oliver still had to do the work for the Cold Case crew, and nothing short of a major disaster was going to get him out of processing rape kits to help whittle down the backlog.

But he'd carved out time to do his own digging, since the case was on his plate and he'd received no communication from his partner. Whatever issues Nenci had with him, or with omegas, or with arson cases, or with the moon being in Sagittarius, someone needed to resolve this case. If it wasn't going to be Nenci, it was going to have to be Oliver.

It seemed logical to start with Coucher family properties. Oliver didn't doubt that the Coucher family were participants in a feud, just as Nenci had said. After all, Nenci knew all about the darker side of human behavior. Oliver didn't. He knew about science. He knew about logic. The Coucher family might have been equal participants in the fight but Oliver didn't have any clues on where to start with their opposite number, so he would have to treat them as victims for now.

He'd have plenty of data to keep him busy, that was for sure. Not all Coucher properties were easily identified in public records as such. Oliver had been forced to dig deep to find them. Some of them were owned under real estate partnerships, or as part of a limited liability corporation with a weird name. Most of those were fine. As a general rule, the more obscure the connection to the Coucher family, the safer the building was. More of the properties owned under that type of hidden pattern of possession seemed to have come into the family's portfolio after the year 2000, which prompted Oliver to take a look into the family's personal records.

Just as he'd started to suspect, there had been a major death at about that time. Albert Coucher, the *paterfamilias*, had died in his sleep. The family and its fortunes had passed to his son, Bill. It must have been Bill that had chosen the new tactic of hiding the family's possessions. It had been successful. There had been ten fires in the two years leading up to Albert's death alone. There had been two fires in the first decade after Bill's accession, and only one after that.

Fires were only one source of property damage, however. On a hunch, Oliver had done a search for floods. There had been plenty of floods in buildings that were owned by the Coucher family, caused by "faulty" pipes. Oliver could see just from the pictures that the pipes had been sabotaged.

Another expansion of his search found more damage. "Faulty" wiring caused electrical accidents that led to the deaths of four men, seven women, and two children. Carbon monoxide leaks led to hospitalizations in four different buildings, and three deaths. Gas leaks resulted in two explosions. Cars slammed into two buildings, resulting in structural integrity issues.

Oliver sighed and shook his head. The crimes had taken place over the course of fifty years. Everything had passed unnoticed under the eyes of state authorities and the police, possibly because they happened in different jurisdictions all over the North Shore.

Even the Couchers hadn't said a thing. If it had been one or two accidents, Oliver could understand that they might not even realize that there was anything deliberate about what had happened. The way that things played out, though, even a goldfish could tell that this was criminal. That alone told Oliver that the Couchers were up to something bad.

Jake craned his head around the wall separating their cubicles. "Hey, buddy, what's up?" He glanced at the morass of tiny print on Oliver's monitor. "Dude, what the hell? That's like something one of the actual cops would come up with. Not, you know, part of our job."

Oliver squirmed. If Nenci could see this, he'd flip his lid. Oliver wasn't a cop; he shouldn't be trying to do a cop's job. "I know, I know. It's just that this case needs to get finished, and I don't know if there's been any progress on it. So." He waved his hand at the screen. "I mean it's easy enough to zoom in on a section, if some of it's looking too small for your geriatric eyes to see."

Jake scooted his chair over. "I'm like a few months older than you, whippersnapper. Don't get all uppity on me now. You've done a lot of work on this. What've you found?"

Oliver stretched his neck back. "It's more like what haven't I found. I haven't found the other half of this equation. I haven't found who the Couchers are feuding with. I haven't found who they've got such a beef with that fifty people get killed in one day and it just keeps on going from there. And I haven't found out what sparked the whole thing." He massaged little circles into his temple. "I have found that owning a whole bunch of property apparently makes you a target. And that digging into this stuff is duller than watching the GC-MassSpec work."

"Ouch." Jake chuckled and then nudged Oliver out of the way. "You know, I don't actually mind this sort of thing."

"You don't?" Oliver couldn't help the look of disbelief he gave his friend.

"Nah. I wanted to be a cop more than I wanted to breathe, actually. Wanted it like burning. I figured that I'd be a detective, just like my dad." He shook his head. "He was having no part of it, of course. You know how he is. My other dad got killed when an omega cop was supposed to be watching him, and now all omega cops are flighty irresponsible tools. I'm surprised he didn't block me from getting this job, just out of spite. But hey." Jake's lips twisted upward in a kind of grin. "That's not the point. The point is that I don't mind doing this kind of digging. So I'll trade you. If you'll handle the blood spatter analysis on this crime scene for me, I'll see what I can make out of this data you've already pulled out, and see what I can't get for you too."

"Deal." Oliver shook hands on it. They drew up the necessary documentation and signed off on it, and Oliver got to work right away. He'd spent a week digging into insurance files and public records. He was pathetically grateful to Jake as he took up the analysis. He liked blood spatter analysis. He was good at blood spatter analysis. A man knew where he stood with spatter analysis. The drops either matched the witnesses' story, in terms of velocity and gravity, or they didn't.

In this case, Oliver didn't take long to figure out that it would have been impossible to have one donor leave blood in that pattern, in that room. He ran another analysis, this time accounting for two different people in the room. Then he ran a DNA analysis on the samples, both from the larger initial pool and from the samples taken from the second spatter cluster. The results, when they finally came through, gave him two different donors just as he'd expected.

More specifically, the donor of the smaller sample was already in CODIS. By the time he was done cleaning up from the DNA analysis, quitting time had long since passed. Oliver just laughed and wrote up the report. He sent a text to Jake as he got ready to leave the lab, and then he hopped onto his bike and rode back to his apartment.

For a moment, he thought about taking advantage of some of the building's amenities. It was late, and he was lonely. A few people were hanging out and watching the game in one of the lounge areas, and he wouldn't mind just being around other people for a while. Right now probably wouldn't be the best time, though. He smelled like the lab, like chemicals and sweat, and no one wanted to be around someone who smelled like a lab. He locked up his bike and trudged up to his own apartment, where he scrubbed himself down and fixed himself a quick bite to eat.

Sometimes he wondered if he shouldn't think about moving. He knew that part of what he was paying for with this place was the "social living" aspect that the developers touted, and he could only rarely take advantage of it. The building did have some amenities that a guy like Oliver, with weird hours, could make use of though, and it was one of the safest living situations a single omega could find for the price.

He'd never thought he'd still be a single omega at his age. He hadn't counted on unrequited, unrequitable, love.

He slipped between his sheets. His bedroom, everything about his apartment, was neat and clean, the way it should be. He'd make a good omega for Nenci. He'd even gone on vacation to Florence with Jake last year for a cooking school holiday experience. They'd sold it to Nenci as Jake's idea, so that Jake could learn the *food-ways of his ancestors* or some such thing, but in reality Jake had just been indulging Oliver.

It hadn't done him any good. He was still alone. He could probably find another alpha, if he put his mind to it. Most alphas liked them a little bit younger, but Oliver was only twenty-four. He'd give good, intelligent children. He was attractive enough, and he was still a virgin. Most alphas liked that, too.

If the thought of giving himself to an alpha who wasn't Nenci didn't turn his stomach, he'd have to consider putting up a personal ad or something. Maybe someday.

He stretched and tried to get comfortable enough for sleep. The only thing that worked was imagining himself sheltered in the arms of his alpha.

The next morning, he headed downstairs to use the omega-only gym before he showered and got ready for work. Maybe working out more would help him to focus more, and get over Nenci. Then he hopped onto his bike and headed into the office.

Jake thanked him for his spatter analysis efforts with a huge iced mocha, complete with chocolate whipped cream and a chocolate drizzle. "Because you're the sweetest," he declared. "Also, I've found a kind of pattern to the madness with your mayhem people there. The people that are attacking them aren't being at all subtle, are they?"

Oliver shook his head. "With some of them they are, sure. I mean they seem to have made some effort to disguise the plumbing *accidents*, and as near as I can tell I'm the first one to raise the alarm about the cars crashing into buildings. But for the most part, no. I mean barricading the exits when you torch a place is not considered subtle behavior."

"No." Jake grimaced. "That's something we've got to bring up with my dad, bro. I mean he's got to hear about it."

Oliver froze. "I mean Jake, I'm not sure that your dad has been interested in the case. I haven't heard from him since the case started."

Jake rolled his eyes and shook his head. "Okay, buddy. If this were any other cop, and I mean any, would you stand for that kind of thing? Even for half a second?"

Oliver shrunk in on himself. Then he straightened his back and threw his shoulders back. "Hell no. I'd march right down there to Cold Case and tell him exactly what he needed to know, whether or not he wanted to know it." He picked up the report that Jake had printed out for him.

"Damn straight you would. Now, all of this is stuff that Sam Nenci needs to know. At the end of the day, he's just a detective. Just a man. You just walk down there, like normal, and you give him the report. If he balks, you leave it on his desk. With witnesses, so he can't throw it away." Jake put a hand on Oliver's shoulder. "Our job is to give information. So go give it, tiger."

Oliver marched down the long corridors to Cold Case. Their admin gave him a cordial nod; she was used to seeing him around the place. Langer spotted him and gave him a wave. "Hey, Oliver. I haven't seen you around much."

Oliver swallowed. He hadn't counted on having to be around all of these alphas. There was Robles, and Morris, and Tessaro, too. And of course, there was Nenci. Beautiful, forbidden Nenci. Oliver could feel Nenci's gray eyes burning a hole into his skin.

"Sorry about that. I got pulled off of most of my cases to work on this case with Detective Nenci. I'm still working on your cases, of course, when something comes up." He cleared his throat and turned to face Nenci. "Here's a report on all of the property crimes that took place at Coucher family properties between the 1967 fire and today. The people attacking them aren't just restricting themselves to fire, sir. There've been too many incidents, all with clear-cut signs of sabotage."

Nenci stared at him, unmoving, and Oliver waited for him to explode. "Figured all of this out by yourself, did you?" Nenci finally asked. His voice was dry and almost hoarse.

Oliver narrowed his eyes. "As a matter of fact, yes. I knew what I was looking for, so it wasn't difficult." He snatched the paper report out of Nenci's hands, ignoring the way he jumped in astonishment, and flipped through it. "You see here? Insurance investigators determined this to be a case of decayed pipes, but the pipes were only twenty years old and pipes don't decay in perfectly straight lines. You can see where it was cut, for crying out loud.

"And here." Oliver flipped to another picture. "I have a picture of the damage to the stove that caused the gas leak. That's very clearly been tampered with. You can see the marks left by the wrench, clear as day on the photo. It took a lot of digging, into a lot of insurance records and crime scene reports, to find this information. If we're supposed to be working together, Detective Nenci, it would go much more smoothly if you didn't throw evidence away out of hand because it comes from an omega's lowly hands." He turned on his heel. "And by the way? Your son helped with the final analysis. He printed out the report you just sneered at. So when you sit there and turn up your nose at omegas, it affects all of us." He left the squad room.

Once he was out of sight, and away from all of those alphas, he found the nearest bench to sit down on. His legs wouldn't hold him up any longer. He was shaking too badly to move. He'd just ripped into his alpha. If he'd still had even a snowball's chance in hell with Nenci, it was gone now.

What was worse, there was no way that Nenci wasn't going to file a complaint with HR, or with Nina. Oliver had never been much of a drinker, but maybe he should start.

***

Sam went home a little early after work. He'd been working on the Coucher case during the week too. Part of him kind of resented the unstated implication that he hadn't been, but it was a small part. He hadn't shared his work with Oliver, or with Oliver's supervisor, or with anyone else who might have passed it on to the guy he was supposed to be working with.

He'd clearly been in the wrong there.

Not that anything else that Sam had been doing was wrong. No, he'd been doing good work and getting solid information on the case. He'd gone back through the original case files. He'd walked around. He'd talked to people—actual police work, the kind he'd been doing for close to thirty years now, thank you very much. He'd learned a lot, too.

For one thing, he'd learned that the Couchers hadn't been the only family to want that building, before it went up in smoke. No, there had been three other real estate groups looking at it. Salem was looking at an economic rebound, and everyone wanted a piece of it. The Couchers had somehow gotten a leg up on the other bidders, even though they'd bid less than three of the four others. Because that wasn't shady.

Looking at the pile of data that Oliver had dumped into his hands, though—all written up clearly and cleanly, in a way that Sam didn't have to try to puzzle out—he could see that there was absolutely a greater pattern to everything. It wasn't just about this property. Someone was absolutely out to get the Couchers.

Maybe, just maybe, Sam could have been walking and talking to dig into that, instead of just digging further into one transaction.

The front door flew open, and Jake came storming in. Sometimes Sam couldn't believe his own nose. There was no way that this kid, with his personality, could possibly be an omega. It just wasn't feasible. He smelled like an omega, but he wasn't one. "Hey, Son." Sam looked up from the report he was still reading. "How's it going?"

Jake's lip curled. "How's it going? Oh, it's going just fine. By the way, my supervisor has declared war on Cold Case, and sent Oliver home early since he wasted a week's worth of work on something you clearly gave no hoots about, but you know what? Life's just peachy, Dad." He stomped into the kitchen.

Sam glowered after Jake. "I don't need that kind of attitude from you. I don't tell you how to run a DNA sample, you don't tell me how to do police work." He stood up and followed Jake into the kitchen. Sure, he'd handled the thing with Oliver poorly, but that didn't give Jake the right to come in here and give Sam attitude about it.

"Actually, Dad, you tell me how to run a DNA sample all the time. That's why Oliver got stuck dealing with you alphas down in Cold Case. He's the only one who doesn't want to punch you all in the throat. Or more to the point, he's the only one who could be trusted not to punch you all in the throat." Jake got himself a glass of water and gave Sam a tight, unpleasant grin. "Of course, you shot yourself in the nuts with that too."

Sam shook his head and waved his hand. "Oliver's a professional. He's not going to go getting his panties in a bunch because of one bad interaction." He frowned. He knew that wasn't true. Oliver might be a professional, and sure he wouldn't be pushed off by one negative interaction, but it hadn't just been one bad day and Sam knew it. "He can't possibly think that I didn't appreciate what he did. What the two of you did," he added, because Oliver had made sure that Sam knew Jake had been involved with this.

Jake almost spat out his water. "You said it in front of witnesses, buddy. One of whom went running down to Burton to apologize, so she wouldn't take Oliver away from Cold Case."

"Langer." Sam clenched his hands into fists. "Langer needs to keep his mouth shut."

"No. No, he does not. Oliver Wesson deserves better than that. We all do, frankly, and that's why we won't work with you jerks anymore, but Oliver especially deserves better than that. You do get that we're not living in the Middle Ages anymore, and that omegas don't have to just bow their heads and get treated like crap because of how our genes express? There are laws about it and everything."

Sam pushed away from the counter. This wasn't about omega rights. This was about policing, and detective work. "Don't give me that crap, Jake. Your father certainly never had a reason to complain. I treat you fine, I treat every omega I come across just fine. You're just bitter that you're still single. This isn't about how I treat omegas, this is about getting the job done."

Jake laughed out loud. "It's got everything to do with the way that you treat omegas. And I'm not *still single*. If I wanted an alpha, I'd have one. You do know that I've had three offer to claim me, right?"

Sam turned to face him. "What? Then why haven't you taken them up on it?" He shouldn't get distracted, but the fact that Jake had been keeping this kind of secret from him threw him for a loop.

"Because I'm not willing to be treated the way you treat omegas. Don't get distracted. It's entirely about the way you treat omegas. The entire case is going to ride on physical evidence. You were ordered to work with Oliver on this, you already practically broke his heart when you lashed out in that meeting, and now you're mocking the work that he did in front of witnesses."

Sam scowled. "Well it's not like he's exactly innocent there. No one asked him to look into any of that. I'm supposed to be the lead investigator. He should have waited for my authority, not done it on his own initiative. Who the hell ever heard of a lab guy just going off on his own to investigate something?" Damn it, why was he getting defensive here? He'd been in the wrong; he'd misspoken himself, why couldn't he just keep his mouth shut?

"Probably the people who decided that he would be the one working the case." Jake's voice was absolutely flat. "My God, you're willing to let a serial fatal arsonist walk because you think that an omega acted out of turn."

"It's got nothing to do with him being an omega." Sam crossed his arms over his chest. He knew why he was getting upset now. He couldn't make himself justify his behavior to his son. He was the father; he had to maintain his authority here.

"Show me one instance when you've lashed out at an alpha or at a beta who showed initiative like this." Jake shook his head and walked toward the hallway.

Sam followed him. "Show me one instance where an alpha or a beta has been in the same position, to step out of line like that."

Jake snapped his fingers. "The Vecchio murder. Tessaro independently investigated a tangent related to your case."

"That's different." Sam tried to fight back his irritation. "He's part of the team."

"So even though your boss, and his boss, *put* Oliver on your team, that doesn't count."

"No, it doesn't."

"Why not?"

"Because he's not!" Sam exploded. "He's not, because he works in a lab. Which is a perfectly good place for an omega, so long as they don't stick their noses into real police work. I'd honestly thought better of Oliver. He doesn't belong doing this kind of thing; it's stupid of him to even try it. And yeah, I'm angry that he didn't wait to be told to do it."

Jake stepped into Sam's space. "Omegas aren't pets, you dinosaur. We don't sit around and wait to be told to act. He was pulled off every other job so that he could work on this. With you, not for you. Not as your coffee boy, but as your partner. He's got a goddamn master's degree and lots of experience, so maybe you could lose the attitude and treat him like an actual professional person instead of like an infant?"

Jake walked away, and Sam grabbed his arm. "Don't you walk away from me. I am your father and your alpha until you find one of your own. You will treat me with respect while you live under my roof."

Jake broke out of his hold easily, a look of utter contempt on his handsome face. "There's an opening in Oliver's building. I'm putting a deposit down right now."

"The hell you are. Omegas can't live on their own. It isn't right." Sam scoffed. "It isn't safe, either. You're staying right here where your father can watch over you."

"An attempt to keep me here would constitute kidnapping." Jake met his eyes. "I make enough money, and I've saved enough money, to live on my own. I've been staying here for you. I'm not anymore. Call me when you get your head out of your ass." He disappeared into his bedroom.

All Sam could do was to watch in stunned silence as Jake emerged from his bedroom with a suitcase. He stood rooted to the floor as he watched Jake walk out the door, and still didn't move as he heard the car start up. This was it. He was leaving, forever. Sam had already lost one son to his own temper and ideals. Now he'd lost another.

He forced down a wave of panic. This wasn't twenty years ago. Many omegas lived safely alone. Pretty Boy, Robles' omega, had lived on his own just fine for a long time before Robles came along. Of course, Pretty Boy had guns and lots of them. Morris' omega, Pete, had lived on his own as a civilian, and he'd done fine too. Well, until he'd wound up on the wrong side of a bank robbery, but living at home with his mother wouldn't have stopped that.

Lots of omegas lived alone. None of them were his son.

What should he do? Should he go chasing after Jake? Should he call the uniform guys and say that he'd been acting erratically? No. It was tempting, but no.

He picked up the phone. He'd gotten Oliver's number when they'd been assigned the case together, but he'd never used it. He didn't trust himself, and he'd been right. Right now, though, he couldn't think about that stuff. He hit "dial" and waited for Oliver to pick up.

Oliver did, but only on the fourth ring. "Hi." Oliver's voice usually had hope. Now it only had wariness. The change was like a knife to the gut.

"Hi, Oliver. It's Sam. Sam Nenci."

"I know. Caller ID." Oliver paused. "Not to be rude here, but I'm not sure that we've got a lot to say to one another at this point. What can I help you with?"

Oh God. He really had shot himself in the foot. Who knew that one little sentence could unravel a life so badly? Sam had wanted to avoid letting Oliver know how much he wanted him, but not like this. He hadn't wanted to give Oliver a bad impression of him, for crying out loud. "Listen. Jake took off from here a little while ago. We had an argument, we were both pretty heated. He hinted that he was heading in your direction. I don't suppose that you've seen him?"

Oliver paused again. "He's here. He's safe."

"Oh thank God." Nenci fell into the chair, his whole body limp with relief. "That building—is it safe?"

Oliver snorted. "It's safe. I've lived here for three years. There's not a lot of turnover. Each apartment has a panic button. There's security, and there are omegas-only facilities for residents to use. They're keyed to the resident's key, so no one can go sneaking in."

"Really?" Nenci sat up. "You don't think it can be broken?"

"Any security system can be broken, by a determined enough criminal. But it's a pretty good system." Oliver hesitated. "You're welcome to try to break in, I guess, but I'm not explaining it to the cops when they show up."

Sam snickered in spite of himself. "I'll pass, thanks. I'm sure I don't need that on my record this close to retirement. I want my pension, thank you." Oliver didn't laugh, and Sam remembered how badly he'd embarrassed himself in front of the man on the other end of the phone. "Anyway, if he's safe, then I guess I won't bother you anymore."

"Have a good weekend, Detective." Oliver's voice was cold when he hung up.

Sam leaned back into the couch cushions and looked out over the lake. He could just see it from where he sat, even more beautiful at sunset than it was the rest of the day. Chris had loved the view.

God, what must Chris think of him? Chris would have made him sleep on the couch after that fight with Jake. Of course, if Chris were alive, that fight with Jake wouldn't have happened. Hell, Jake would probably have an alpha of his own, and Oliver wouldn't be mooning around over Jake's best friend like some kind of creep.

Furthermore, if Chris were still alive Sam wouldn't have carved out Oliver's heart today. And Oliver wouldn't have turned around and carved Sam right back. He'd forced Sam to look at his work, and he'd done it in front of other people because he'd come in with the assumption that Sam wouldn't listen.

Sam had to take a good, long look at himself. It didn't show anything he liked to see.

He didn't have a problem with evidence processed by omegas. He didn't. He could see why he came across that way. He hadn't even lost his temper about Oliver acting on his own initiative until he'd been fighting with Jake, looking to defend his own behavior. Sure, he did feel that way, but only a little bit. It hadn't been at the forefront of his mind until anger churned it up.

So what was his real problem? He had some very old-fashioned views about omegas, sure, but not as bad as what his son attributed to him. That was something else that he needed to address, and sooner rather than later. His bigger problem, though, was that he'd gotten too used to responding to everything with sarcasm and nastiness. He'd gotten too used to lashing out at people. Initially it had been his grief and his pain that had allowed him to behave that way, and people had let him get away with it. Then it had become habit.

He needed to get better. He needed to change his behavior. He had no idea how.

He turned his head to look at the portrait of Chris. It had been taken just before their claiming, when Chris was probably about twenty. He'd been dark skinned and devilishly handsome, the kind of guy that you wished someone had warned you about. He smelled like roses, and Sam guessed that was about right. Roses were gone in an instant too.

What would Chris want him to do here? Well, Chris would tell him to stop being a dick. But what would Chris want him to do about Oliver?

That was harder to figure out.

Chapter Three

Oliver sent up a quick prayer of gratitude to any deity that might happen to be listening for granting him the foresight to buy a pullout sofa when he moved into this place.

His apartment was a one bedroom. That was fine for him. He was a single guy, and it wasn't like he spent a lot of time at home anyway. When Jake showed up on his doorstep, Oliver couldn't offer him a separate room or anything like that. Jake signed a lease for a one bedroom of his own, but he couldn't move in for another three weeks.

Fortunately, three weeks wasn't forever and Oliver had the pullout couch. They could work out a schedule for the bathroom. Jake agreed to keep any hookups to outside locations, just because of the lack of privacy, and that was that. They would be fine.

Jake sat in the kitchen while Oliver scrounged together what food he could to fix a quick dinner. He needed to go grocery shopping; maybe he'd do that tomorrow. He hadn't shopped for more than one before. "I probably overreacted," Jake sighed, after Nenci's cryptic phone call. "I mean, I meant it, I don't necessarily regret anything I said or did, but I probably flew off the handle. I definitely could have phrased things better, you know? I was just so pissed off."

Oliver focused on browning some chicken in a skillet. "These things happen. Parents bring them out in us, you know?" He hadn't seen his own mother in years, not since his sophomore year of college, but he still remembered how tied up in knots he used to get around her.

Jake chuckled. "Oh, don't I know it. I mean he's a good dad, you know? Don't get me wrong. He took great care of us after our father got killed. He's just… you know. He's old fashioned, and he's super paranoid about a lot of things because of what happened to Papa." He picked his head up. "Oh, crap. I should call Joey and tell him where I am. Er, are you going to have an issue with an alpha you don't know showing up?"

Oliver blushed and shrugged. "Joey's your brother, right? No. I shouldn't have a problem with that. Do what you need to do, Jake. This is your home, until your place comes through."

They spent the night just hanging out and drinking a little wine. Oliver tried to hide his shock and disappointment in Nenci. He knew that he shouldn't take it too seriously; he was only getting half of the story. Instead, he supported his friend and drank wine with him, and went to bed.

The next morning, he washed their wine glasses and put together a shopping list. Jake was still asleep, so Oliver left him a note on the bathroom mirror. By the time he got home, Jake was up and able to help with the groceries. That counted for a lot. Jake had also made coffee, which officially made him the Best Roommate Ever. Oliver wondered if he could get him a trophy or something.

They got the groceries put away and made a schedule for dinner prep, and then Jake warned him that Joey would be stopping by in the afternoon. "It's cool," Oliver told him. "I'll just head out on a bike ride or something."

"It's okay, man. Joey actually wants to meet you. He wants to know who I'm staying with, in case there's an emergency or something." He shrugged and blushed. "He's not into all of the alpha posturing or that stuff, but he can be kind of a stereotype about some of it. At least it's the good parts, right?"

Oliver laughed and made sure that they had cheese and crackers ready.

Joey showed up at around two. He brought beer. He would have been Jake's identical twin, if it weren't for the scents. He smelled strong, like sage, and looked around himself and nodded before shaking Oliver's hand. "Hi. I'm Joe Nenci. You must be Oliver."

Oliver blushed. He couldn't help it. "That's me. Oliver Wesson. Can I get you anything? A drink? We've got some cheese and crackers over here." He led the way into the living room, where the sofa had been folded back up and the bedding discreetly stashed.

"Thanks. If you guys are having a little wine, I'll have some too." He smiled, just a little, and sat down on the edge of the couch. "So Jake, come on, man, what happened? I thought you'd never move, I thought Dad needed you to stay too badly."

Well, that was interesting.

"He pushed too far this time. He might be able to keep me from doing what I want to do, but he can't keep me from living the rest of my life the way I want." Jake rolled his shoulders and plastered a huge grin onto his face. "That's not the important thing right now, Joey. Did you see much of the building? Did you like it?"

"It seems nice enough. Are you really keen on living alone, though?" Joe tilted his head and stared at his brother. "I mean good for you, if you are, but it's not something you're used to."

"Well, it's not like I'm going to be in some cabin on the edge of a mountainside, dude. There are a lot of social spaces, to include social spaces set aside for omegas only. It's a safe building, and it's close to work. Plus, I've got Oliver here. We don't see nearly enough of one another at work, you know." Jake batted his eyelashes at Oliver.

Oliver laughed and brought the wine over. "It's true. We don't. That cubicle wall is insurmountable." He passed out the glasses and sat down. "So what is it that you do, Joe?"

Joe tugged at his collar. "Actually I'm a firefighter."

"That's right. My brother's one of the best, too. And Oliver here did his master's thesis in arson investigation." Jake grinned. "Isn't that a coincidence?"

"Not really." Joe smirked and shook his head. "Our family tends to attract fire in one way or another. It's dad's charming personality. It tends to have people reaching for the accelerant."

The twins laughed, and Oliver grinned along with them even though his heart wasn't truly in it. He was still disappointed in Nenci, but he couldn't quite shake his affection for the older man.

Joe stayed for dinner, something Oliver didn't object to. Later the twins went out to a club while Oliver stayed back; clubs weren't his scene. He spent his Sunday with a pleasant bike ride and took care of some housework, and just like that the weekend was over.

He and Jake carpooled on Monday, because Oliver wasn't a big fan of biking in the rain. They walked up to their workstations more or less in sync, which made Nina shudder. "That's all I need, the two of you mind melding or whatever. What's up with the two of you? You're not usually in at the same time."

Oliver just took his seat. It was Jake's story to tell. It wasn't Oliver's place to share it.

"I just signed a lease on a place in Oliver's building. Since it won't open up until July first, he's letting me crash with him until it does." Jake flashed one of his huge, charismatic grins at their boss. "So far, it's been great. Although I've got to say, he's got a lot of clean and healthy habits that are just a bad example for everyone."

Nina pursed her lips. "I'm not sure that it's a great idea to let you two spend more time around each other than you already do. I mean really, you're already starting to morph into one unit. What happens when your bodies merge and you become one mega-technician?"

"We get twice the pay and pay half the rent," Oliver told her with a straight face. "And twice the pension. It's kind of genius, if I do say so myself."

Nina threw her hands up and walked away, muttering to herself.

Oliver didn't have any current projects, since his other projects had been parceled out so he could focus on the Coucher case. Since he had the capacity, he worked on the rape kit backlog. Processing of a kit from start to the end of the report took about fifty hours, end to end. Then, another analyst had to conduct a technical review—three hours—and yet another analyst had to do an administrative review. He noticed that there was a stack of kits that had been processed and were awaiting reviews, so he grabbed a couple of those and sat down to work.

He hated the kits. They were part of the job, and he understood that they helped to put some pretty terrible people in jail. That part he liked. He hated the backlog. He hated how long some of these survivors had to wait. He hated the fact that it must feel like their trauma had been shunted off and declared not worth the time, or resources.

He hated the fact that more cases kept getting added to the backlog, like heads on a hydra.

He couldn't let that get to him, though. All that he could do was keep plugging away at it and do his job. Eventually the team would get the backlog back down to something manageable, if they continued to make it a priority, and as long as Nina was in charge it would continue to be a priority.

He got through one technical review and two administrative reviews before lunch, which he took at his desk while he continued to work. He was about to start on another technical review, just to try to move the bottleneck along, when Nicole called him and asked him to head out to supervise evidence collection in the Upton State Forest, where human remains had been discovered.

Oliver hid his squirming and complied. He didn't mind supervising, and he didn't mind collecting the evidence. He wasn't a huge fan of mud, but it was his job. He was going to have to go and do it.

He headed out with the pathologist from the ME's office in the same van, with a couple of other techs trailing behind in the crime scene unit van. The rangers that had been called to the scene had helpfully put a pop-up over the remains, and Oliver might have kissed them. That didn't change the fact that there was mud, but it kept the rain from getting down the back of his shirt, which would have to do.

It didn't take long to figure out that while a crime had almost certainly taken place, no one was likely to pay for the crime. The remains had only come to light when an old, dead tree had toppled over thanks to wind, rain, and soil loss on the side of a small hill. The tree's demise had left a small piece of bone exposed to the elements, which had excited a soggy dog walker's canine companion beyond reason. Once the woman had convinced her Golden that no, the bone really wasn't for him, she'd called the rangers.

Most of the clothes had rotted away, but the tree that had grown on top of the man had been at least a hundred years old. Most of the skeleton was still intact, and a bullet hole marred the perfect vault of his skull. Oliver took the pictures that he needed to take, and then Cissy from the ME's office carefully collected the bones.

Oliver took more pictures, and collected what evidence still existed in the grave. Then he let the detective on the scene tape it off. They would examine the bones, and the items found with the victim, but Oliver was fairly certain that the investigating detective would make a call to Boston University and their archaeology department.

He headed back into the office and got to work cataloging the evidence. There wasn't a lot. There was a pipe, rich with tooth marks. There was a tin tobacco box. There were a few rusty buttons. That was it. By four-thirty, Cissy brought him the bullet that had been in the man's head. It only cemented Oliver's assessment: the bullet could only have come from a gun from the nineteenth century.

Just as he and Cissy were discussing the Upton find, Nenci walked into Forensics. Oliver's mouth went dry. What could Nenci be doing here? Was he here for Oliver or for Jake? His skin looked paler than usual over his dark beard, and he couldn't keep his gray eyes in any one place. His unique scent—banana nut bread, as if Oliver needed any other reasons to adore him—was all over the place.

Nina walked right up to him. "Can I help you, Detective?"

Nenci cleared his throat and pressed his lips together. "Yeah. I—I'm here to apologize."

Oliver put down the evidence bag he'd been holding. He was afraid of dropping it; his hands had just gone slick with sweat.

Nina crossed her arms across her chest. "Apologize to whom?"

Nenci swallowed, hard. This couldn't be easy. Alphas didn't apologize, as a general rule. "I want to apologize to all of you, actually. The whole department, the whole lab. I was rude and out of line. But first and foremost, I need to apologize to Oliver Wesson. I was unsettled, and I lashed out because I was unsettled. I'm still iffy on treating a crime scene technician like a detective, but your work was damn good and it was absolutely right of you to take that initiative."

Nenci tugged at his collar. "And it was wrong of me to keep what I was doing from you. I'm used to doing things a certain way, and there are probably a lot of good reasons for that which don't reflect well on me. But this case is going to be solved by teamwork. It's not only going to be solved in the lab, and it's not going to be solved without a lot of detailed lab work either." He bowed his head. "I would greatly appreciate it if you would please come back onto the job."

Oliver gripped the back of his chair. He wasn't sure if he could come back to the case. He didn't know if he could face working with Nenci again. It was the only way that the case would get solved, though, and the sixty dead deserved some kind of closure.

Jake stood up and slipped between them. Oliver blushed. He hadn't realized that he was moving toward Nenci.

"What guarantee can you give us that you're going to treat him right, and not like some kind of pet lab tech that you've got on some kind of leash?" Jake met his father's eyes and set his jaw. He wasn't going to budge.

Nenci narrowed his eyes at his son. "I'm not entirely sure how to give you that guarantee, Son, other than just to give you my word. I can only promise you that I'm going to do my best. I know that Lt. Devlin is very anxious that we—that I—make this work, and that the lab be willing to accommodate Cold Case again. So he's going to be watching very carefully. And I can see that you're not exactly going to be slacking in that department either."

"None of us will." Nina stepped over and stood shoulder to shoulder with Jake. She craned her neck to meet Oliver's eyes. "What do you say, Oliver? You're the one who has to work with Captain Charm here."

Oliver ducked his head. There would only ever be one answer for him with Nenci. "Yes. Of course."

***

Sam meant everything that he said when he apologized to Oliver. He'd been wrong. He knew he'd been wrong. Oliver was damn smart, and Sam probably wouldn't be able to solve this case without him. None of that changed the fact that when he made plans to go up to Marblehead to talk to the current head of the Coucher family, Lt. Devlin insisted that he bring Oliver with him.

That meant not only bringing an omega into the field, but sitting in a car with Oliver, alone, for two and a half hours round trip. Never mind how much time he'd have to spend in Oliver's company, with that intoxicating myrrh scent, outside of the car.

Still, Sam knew that he was on thin ice right now. He needed to suck it up and be a professional. He made his way down to the lab, collected his temporary partner, and grabbed one of the unmarked cars that fooled no one.

They got coffee at the drive-thru before heading out, but that didn't make the first ten minutes any less awkward. Sam had no idea what he was supposed to say to the beautiful young man by his side. How was he supposed to contain himself with that scent filling his nose? At the same time, Oliver was literally the same age as his sons. He shouldn't even notice Oliver's scent, for crying out loud. "So," he said, as they watched the highway pass them by, "you got a new roommate this weekend. How's that going?"

Oliver chuckled. "It's going well. I mean, it's been a long time since I've lived with someone else, you know? Even in college, omegas don't usually live with other people after freshman or maybe sophomore year."

"Yeah, I'd guess not." Sam grimaced. He could see where that would get awkward pretty quickly. "But it's working out okay, he's not leaving his dirty laundry all over the kitchen or anything?"

Oliver laughed. God, but he had a beautiful smile. "No. He's fine. I mean, he pesters me about staying at work too late and stuff, but he did that before so I don't think it's got anything to do with him staying with me." He paused and gripped the passenger assistance bar. "So you're really okay with him living on his own?"

"Not really." A huge knot between Sam's shoulders released when he said it. He hadn't realized that it had been there, until it disappeared. He couldn't say that losing it was a good thing, of course. That knot might have reminded him that Oliver was untouchable. Still, Oliver had asked, and when Jake showed up on the poor guy's doorstep he'd involved Oliver in the family drama. "I'd rather have him at home with me until he finds an alpha to keep him safe, but I'm well aware that I'm being hopelessly paranoid and uptight about it. If I'm going to continue to have a relationship with at least one of my sons, I need to work on that."

Oliver raised an eyebrow, but he let that one slide. Sam gave him credit for that. Either Oliver was apathetic about the family's issues, or he was letting Sam have some dignity. "Well, like I told you, it's a pretty safe building. He's going to like it there." He shifted a little bit in his seat. "So, what did you find out last week? I know you were working hard."

Sam bit his lip. He knew that Oliver wasn't taking a dig at him about Friday's blowout. That wasn't his style. No, it was only Sam's own guilt making his skin crawl. "I did some digging into the history of that building. It turns out that the building was the subject of a bit of a bidding war. The Couchers won the fight, even though three other groups had higher bids."

"Huh. I wonder how that happened." Oliver looked out the window for a moment.

"Well, a property owner can sell to whoever they want, but it does seem curious that they wouldn't want to get top dollar for a property like that." Sam scratched his head.

"Almost as unusual as the fact that there've been that many attacks on Coucher properties and they haven't tried to convince anyone that it's happening." Oliver took a gulp of his coffee. "That never happens."

Sam grunted. "I did hear that you've done some arson work."

Oliver ducked his head and blushed. "That makes me sound like I work for the mob. But yeah, my thesis was about arson investigation. And I've never seen a case where one group was the target and didn't want anyone else to know about it. That makes no sense at all."

"So I guess the biggest question would have to be why wouldn't they say anything?" Sam risked a glance over at Oliver, only to find him adorably gnawing on his lip. That, of course, drew Sam's eyes directly to those lips, where he shouldn't have been looking at all.

"Maybe we'll get some ideas when we meet with Mr. Coucher today." Oliver fiddled with his seat belt.

Sam licked his lips. "Hey, Oliver, please don't take this the wrong way, but I'm just curious. Have you ever spoken with a witness before?"

Oliver snickered. "Yes. As a matter of fact, I have spoken to witnesses before. More than once, in fact. I promise not to ask if he did it for the insurance money. That's so early nineties anyway."

"Well the '92 attack certainly falls within that timeframe!" Sam waved a finger.

"True. But insurance burns don't usually involve tenants." Oliver leaned back with a smug little smile on his face. "At least not in Massachusetts."

"There was one case I did where the killer figured that would work in his favor." Sam told one of the stories from his earlier days as a detective, much to Oliver's apparent delight. It turned out that they'd discussed the case in one of his classes, but he hadn't gotten to see the more personal side of it. Seeing Oliver's face, rapt with attention and fascination, made something warm up inside Sam's chest.

They pulled up to Bill Coucher's place on Ocean Ave in Marblehead. The place was a little understated, but still left no doubt in anyone's mind that the owner was a person of means. It was out on the neck, a stately old gambrel-type of house with a lawn the size of Kansas that probably cost a fortune to keep watered out here. Sam parked in the circular drive and rang the doorbell.

A thirty-something man in khakis and a polo shirt answered the door. "You must be the detectives," he said with a smile. He held out his hand. "I'm Joel Coucher. My dad asked me to show you out to the pool; he's waiting for you out there."

Sam shook first. He couldn't help but keep his eyes on Joel Coucher as he shook Oliver's hand, just to make sure that he didn't make any sudden moves. That reaction gave him pause. He knew it was wrong, that he shouldn't be feeling all that protective toward Oliver, but maybe it was okay. Oliver was helping Jake out; it was okay to want to protect him too.

He hated himself almost as much for the blatant lie as he did for the fact that the lie was necessary.

Joel led them back to the pool, a pretty tiled thing deep enough to dive in and set into a stone patio. Bill Coucher sat on one of the big teak loungers, shielding his phone screen from the sun as he tried to read what was probably an email. He looked a little older than Sam was, maybe in his mid-fifties, with just enough of a tan to prove that he did a lot of work out here by the pool, and graying dark brown hair. He gestured to a pair of solid, comfortable-looking chairs that had been set up nearby. "Detectives," he said, rising from the lounger. "I'm pleased to meet you. Bill Coucher."

Sam introduced himself and Oliver, and they sat down in the chairs provided. "Thanks for meeting with us, Mr. Coucher. I'm sure that this is the last thing that you want to be thinking about."

Coucher's face wrinkled up as he sat back down. "To be honest, you're not exactly wrong. I was maybe five years old when that fire happened. I had a little measuring tape, and a little T-square. I didn't exactly understand anything that was going on around me, you know? I do remember that my dad and my grandfather made the whole family go to each and every one of those funerals, though." He bowed his head. "It wasn't until later that I understood what they even were."

Oliver put a hand to his mouth. "That must have been terrible for you."

Coucher flashed him a grateful smile. "Well, it wasn't fun. It was worse for the families who lived through it, you know? Us, we lived out here. I can tell you one thing. My dad made a promise. He said, 'Never again.' He did a ton of research. He put in the latest sprinkler systems, and once security systems became feasible he put those in too. I'm talking at all of our properties, you know. Not just the Cooper Block."

Sam nodded. "You sold that one."

"After the second fire, yeah." Coucher nodded. "Listen, I'm not going to complain about someone re-opening that case. I mean, over the past fifty years the place has killed sixty people or something like that. But I'm curious. Why now? Why not ten years ago, or twenty, when the person who did it might have been around to pay for it?"

Sam tilted his head to the side. "What makes you think that he isn't?"

Coucher snorted. "Aw, come on. Whoever was behind that, they'd have had to have been at least in their late teens, probably older to have pulled off something like that. I'm thinking older, because from what my dad told me, that mess took a lot of planning. Sure, you can prosecute a guy in his late seventies or eighties, but what are the chances that he's going to have all of his faculties long enough to understand what's happening at the trial?" He chuckled and leaned back. "That's assuming that he's even still with us. I mean, arsonist isn't exactly a career that drips with longevity."

"Valid." Oliver wrinkled his nose.

Sam grinned at him. "Mr. Wesson here has a master's degree in arson, as it happens. That's part of the reason that we went after this case. The Cold Case department isn't choosy about the length of time that a case has been cold, and this one had a pretty high body count. We have Mr. Wesson, who has a gift for this sort of thing. We decided to give it a shot before the window closed for good.

"Part of the reason we came out here today, Mr. Coucher, is that we noticed that there've been a number of other attacks on properties that belonged to the Coucher family." Sam met his host's eyes and held them. "We were wondering if you might be able to offer any insight into those issues."

Coucher frowned. "Attacks? No, you must be thinking of another case."

Sam grinned and pulled out Oliver and Jake's report. Coucher flipped through it, getting paler with every page. "My god," he whispered. "You're right. I hadn't noticed. How terrible is that to admit? I honestly hadn't noticed."

"It's okay, Mr. Coucher." Oliver leaned forward a little, resting his elbows on his knees. "The attackers were clever. They spread their attacks out over multiple towns and jurisdictions, and across time. It wasn't until the state police started looking at the case as a whole that the pattern emerged."

"This is almost unbelievable. Are you sure that this one is sabotage?" He pointed to the gas leak.

"Yes, sir. Those are cut marks, here and here." Oliver pointed them out on the photo.

"Do you have another copy of this? I'd love to take a look through it, if I may. I might want to reassess some recent business decisions based on this information." Coucher looked to both detectives.

Oliver looked to Sam. Sam shrugged. "Sure. We have it saved, so we can get access whenever we want it. Can you think of anyone who would bear you or your family this level of hate, Mr. Coucher?"

"No." Coucher rubbed at his chin. "Well, there's always the Marstens."

Oliver wrote that down but left it for Sam to speak. "The Marstens?"

Coucher waved his hand as though swatting at a fly. "Another real estate family. They've always been jealous. They wanted the Cooper Block, and they were furious when the sellers gave it to Grandpa and not to them."

Well, wasn't that interesting? "Thank you for your time." Sam rose, and Oliver followed him back out to the car.

They headed back toward headquarters, stopping once to get more coffee on the way. "That was productive," Sam told him. "He gave up the name of their most likely suspect like that." He snapped his fingers.

Oliver frowned. "Or at least he gave us the people he likes least right now. We don't know that there's any validity to that. We haven't looked into anything."

Sam laughed out loud and put an arm around Oliver's narrow shoulders. "That's right. You've got a good head for investigations, Oliver."

Oliver flushed pink at the praise, and his myrrh scent got a little bit more intense. "I don't know about that. But it is a good avenue to look toward." They stood in the parking lot, though, with Oliver making no move to get out from under Sam's arm.

Sam knew that he shouldn't do this. He was supposed to be better than this. He was supposed to be more in control of himself. None of that mattered when he could feel Oliver's body, right there and pressed into his arm. He leaned in and touched his lips to Oliver's.

Oliver tasted like coffee, of course. He tasted like coffee, and like the warm sun on a beautiful spring day. He tasted like grasses in a warm breeze or like clean and fresh air out at a park somewhere. He tasted like life, something that Sam hadn't let himself feel in a long time.

That was what brought Sam up short. He wanted more. He would probably get it, if he asked. Oliver looked up at him with shining silver eyes—and all of the trust in the world. What was

Sam even thinking? "We should get back to the office," Sam said. He looked down and stuffed his hands into his pockets, so he wouldn't give into temptation again.

"Of course." Oliver's cheeks glowed pink, and he kept his eyes downcast for the rest of the ride back to Framingham.

Chapter Four

Oliver sat at his workstation and stared at the words on the screen. He couldn't have said that he truly saw any of the words. He'd gone home after work last night just fine, but once the enormity of what had happened hit him he found himself numb. He could have been at work. He could have been at Stop and Shop. He could have been at a Resist concert, or on the moon.

The moon might have been a good place, actually. There wasn't any oxygen there; he'd soon pass out and not have to remember anything anymore.

Jake scooted his chair to the other side of the wall. "Hey, buddy, your eyes are going to dry right out. You might want to blink, convince people you're not a robot."

Oliver jumped. Then he curled up on himself. "Sorry. I'm just..."

Jake's face darkened, but Oliver knew his friend wasn't mad at him. "I swear to you, the next time that man shows his face around here I'm going to throttle him. What the hell was he thinking?"

"I don't know." Oliver rubbed at his face. "Obviously he wasn't. If he had been, he wouldn't have kissed me. I mean, he's about as interested in me as he is in dead trout."

Jake screwed up his face. "That's a lovely image. Just gorgeous. Truly. You should write greeting cards. But something made him do that. You're sure he made the first move?"

Oliver drew back. "I would never. Not in a million years. Not with anyone, but especially not with him!"

"I get it. Well, not really, but you know what I mean. It's not you." Jake sighed. "So what exactly are you going to do here? You just agreed to go back on the job. You can't avoid him forever."

"I can try." Oliver set his jaw. "I mean, it's just…" He clenched his fists and then released them. "It's just that I fantasized about that moment, you know? For years, I pictured that in my mind."

"And it was nothing like what you expected." Jake pursed his lips.

"Oh, no. It was everything I wanted it to be, at first." Oliver straightened his back. He wouldn't cry. "And then he pulled back, said 'We should get back to the office,' and stuffed his hands in his pockets. I mean I liked it, don't get me wrong, and I wanted it, but I still felt like I'd done something wrong. Does that make sense? I felt like I'd let him down somehow. Like I was a disappointment, or I was dirty, or I was just bad at it. I don't know." He took a deep breath to settle himself.

"More than sixty people are dead," he said, forcing himself to look at the screen. "The clock is running out on finding justice, or closure, or stopping whatever cycle is going on. It's up to us—him and me—to get to the bottom of it and stop the next attack. There's no room for stupid crap like kisses or flirtations in there, you know?"

Jake flicked Oliver's ear with his fingernail. "Are you kidding me? You know most people can manage to conduct healthy relationships while working. You get that, right?" He shook his head. "Parricide. That's the only solution. At least I know how to make it look natural. Anyway. Let's see what you've got going on here."

Oliver blinked at the screen. He'd been doing something for the past twenty-four hours. He'd be hard pressed to say what, but apparently his body had gone through enough motions while his brain was shutting down that he'd gone somewhere. "Vital records for the Marsten family, originally of Salem, Massachusetts." He bit the inside of his cheek. "I was looking into property records last night, apparently. I was having trouble sleeping."

"Oh." Jake tilted his head. "Do you always just do work when you're in a brain fog, without knowing what you're doing?"

"I don't think I touched anything in the lab." He picked his head up, panic rushing through his veins. "I didn't touch anything in the lab, did I?"

Jake patted his back. "You didn't touch anything in the lab, bro. You've been staring at the computer. That's all. You're not supposed to be in the lab right now. Remember?"

"Yeah. Sorry. I'd just hate to screw something up because I was mooning around over your dad."

Jake's whole face twisted in revulsion. "Ugh. Can you maybe not put it like that? I mean like ever? So you went to the vital statistics because you didn't find anything in the property records, I take it."

"Sounds about right. It was Sam who pointed out that this had all the hallmarks of half a vendetta." Oliver's heart fluttered, in spite of his heartbreak and disappointment. Nenci—Sam, for crying out loud they'd kissed—was so knowledgeable about these things. Oliver might be able to tell him a million little details about arson, but Sam could tell him why. "When the current head of the family brought up the Marstens, I figured I'd see what there was to see."

"And since the Couchers don't seem to be burning down apartment buildings, there had to be something to trigger the attacks. Good thinking. Have you shared it with Nenci yet?" Jake leaned back in his seat.

Oliver threw his hands up in the air. "I don't have a lot to show for it yet. I've got a death right before the Cooper Block fire, and one right before the gas explosion, but neither of those deaths were ever explored as anything other than accidental." He glanced at his own notes. "Car accident and overdose."

"Please." Jake scoffed. "How often have we seen car wrecks and overdoses that turned out to be something else entirely?"

"More often than I'd like to think about." Oliver looked down at his notes. "It shouldn't be too hard to get those autopsy records. And I'll dig deeper. I just don't want to go to him with nothing, especially after what happened."

Jake rolled his eyes, and then he sighed. "I'll go with you this time. Okay? You keep digging, and tomorrow you dress nice and professionally. We'll bring what you find down to him tomorrow morning. Have you let him know that's the angle you're taking?"

Oliver shrunk in on himself again. "I sent him a message, just a quick one. He didn't respond."

Jake snorted. "Typical. Okay, well, it's fine. Don't worry about that. We'll get you all nice and set up. Let me get some food into you and then we'll see where you go from there."

Oliver followed Jake down to the cafeteria, where they grabbed a quick bite to eat. Jake was right. Getting food into his belly helped Oliver focus and helped him to keep control of his emotions much better. When he returned to his workstation, he was able to tease out the deaths that he was looking for much more easily, and he had plenty of confidence in the conclusions he was drawing at this point.

No family was this unlucky.

The next morning, he dressed in his most professional attire. He wore his crispest white dress shirt, and his most demanding, I-am-an-expert tie. This was the one he wore on the witness stand, the one that made the jury sit up a little straighter. He wore dress pants with a crease so sharp that he could have sliced meat on it, if he'd been so inclined.

Then he grabbed a printout of his findings, put it into a file folder, and marched down to Cold Case with Jake in tow. He walked right into the Cold Case squad room and strode directly to Sam's desk. He didn't have to announce himself to his erstwhile partner. Sam looked up as he approached, probably alerted by Oliver's scent.

Their eyes met, and for a moment Oliver's knees went weak. He wasn't strong enough for this. He was too mild, too meek. He was just a little omega, just a lab tech. He needed to go back to his safe lab and probably never stick his nose out again. Then Jake elbowed him, and he remembered that he had a spine. He had every right to be here. He *was* right to be here. "I did some digging into the Cooper Block case."

Sam moistened his lips. "I—I heard that you were doing some digging."

"Yeah, I did a little digging." He slid his file across the desk. "You were right about there seeming to be a vendetta. All of the deaths in the Marsten family are labeled as accidental, but the pattern is too clear and there are too many *accidents* striking one family for it to be a coincidence."

Sam flipped through the report. "I get the feeling that modern forensics would probably give us more clues. But we've got enough of a pattern here to show that there's an issue, if nothing else." He tapped his pencil against his desk, eyes against the far wall. "I wonder, though. The Marstens were one of the families that the Couchers suckered when they bought the Cooper block. That's not enough to make someone kill fifty people, though. I mean, that was deliberate."

Oliver nodded. He couldn't look away from Sam's soft gray eyes or his perfect pink lips. "It was absolutely deliberate. But wouldn't the kind of guy who would kill fifty people, especially that way, probably not need a whole lot of prodding?"

Sam wrinkled his nose. "If he were just a firebug, maybe not. But this is part of a feud between families, see? Wealthy families, building their wealth. They're ruthless, but they're not unstable. Not the kind of unstable that kills fifty people without provocation unstable anyway; I don't know them personally." He gestured to his monitor, where he had tax records for the Marsten businesses displayed. "They wouldn't be able to grow their empire if they were."

"I see." Oliver pursed his lips and leaned a little closer, to get a better view. He thought he heard a little hitch in Sam's voice and backed away. "That makes sense."

Nenci's eyes narrowed, and he scratched at his chin. "How long did it take you to come up with all of this?"

Oliver shrugged. He wasn't about to admit that he'd spent the better part of a day staring at a computer screen without blinking because of their kiss and its aftermath. "A couple of hours, once I decided what I was looking for. Why?"

"Because I can't shake the feeling that there's something earlier. You don't just start out with that kind of carnage, not even if there was an 'accident' immediately before. What if we take it back another twenty-five years? There's not going to be anyone left to prosecute, I think. Not for anything that early. But we will be able to get back to the *why*, which will help when the case gets in front of a jury." Sam smiled up at him. "We can maybe get together at my place to compare notes and see what we come up with."

Oliver knew that he shouldn't go to Sam's place. It would smell too much like Sam. He wouldn't be able to concentrate on anything but his bearded, handsome alpha—the bearded, handsome alpha who didn't want him and hadn't enjoyed their kiss. Still, there was only one answer he could ever give, to a request that Sam made of him. "Yes. Yeah. That would be fine. I'll go get my car and meet you out there."

"Sounds good. It'll give me time to make sure there's food in the place." Sam grinned.

"Make sure it's takeout," Tessaro advised. "Your cooking sucks, Nenci."

Sam flipped his colleague off. "It's better than yours, Tessaro. Hey, when's the last time you had a haircut?"

Jake and Oliver made their escape while the two squabbled.

Once they were out in the hallway, and out of the alphas' earshot, Jake cackled. "Oh, man. I can't believe you're going to his place!"

Oliver elbowed his best friend in the chest. "Would you give it a rest? We're going to do work. On a case. With a body count that's probably over a hundred by now. That's not a recipe for sexy times, even if he didn't think I kissed like scrod."

"Dad only stammers when he's nervous. He'd only be nervous about inviting you over if he was, you know, nervous." Jake suddenly blushed bright red. "Oh, God, that's my dad. Stay out of my room!"

Oliver's cheeks burned even hotter than Jake's looked. "Dude. Nothing's going to happen, and even if it did it wouldn't happen in your room. That's creepy."

"So is the fact that I'm coaching my best friend about my dad, but here we are. Anyway, stay out of my room."

Oliver huffed out a little laugh and humored Jake. Then he returned to his workstation. He wanted to be so prepared for this meeting that Sam would praise him to anyone who would listen.

He had no illusions about how the meeting would go. He'd be a tongue-tied mess, sitting near Sam and going through the case like that. Preparation would be the key. At least then even if he did prove to be useless in the face of true love or true lust or whatever it was between them, he'd still have contributed.

Jake clearly had other ideas, but Oliver was fairly certain that his friend was just trying to wind him up. For his own part, Oliver wasn't sure if he hoped that his friend would be right or wrong. He decided that he couldn't afford the distraction of hope. If Sam was going to suddenly find him interesting, he'd have done something about it before now.

The memory of that kiss, before the devastation of the aftermath, sprang to his mind.

He banished it, immediately. He should find a way to kill that memory forever. It wasn't something he could have, and he knew it. He needed to focus.

He barreled through the research and wrote the report. At quitting time, he rode home and grabbed his car. He did not pause to change into something more comfortable and he did not pause to change into something sexier. Instead, he headed out to Hopkinton just as he was: professional. He had a job to do, damn it.

***

Sam looked around his living room. It had never bothered him before. He'd owned the house since 1990, for crying out loud. He and Chris had chosen those curtains, that couch, those chairs, that chandelier. Okay, maybe the couch and chairs had been replaced, but only by an exact copy of the original. He'd never thought of the place as dated. It was always just home to him.

He'd never had any serious dates, either. Not after Chris died.

This wasn't a date, either. This was just a work meeting. He couldn't let himself think of Oliver that way, no matter how much he wanted to. Sure, Oliver's lips had felt perfect against his. And Oliver's slim body had lined up perfectly against his own. Oliver was also Jake's best friend. There were so many levels of wrong layered into that that Sam couldn't begin to count them all.

Funny how they all went right out the window when Oliver was around.

He had enough time to get takeout, after a furtive and half panicked text to Jake to find out if Oliver had any food allergies. He could almost hear Jake's mocking laughter over text, but he ignored those echoes and concentrated on the fact that he'd gotten the information he wanted. By the time Oliver showed up, he'd gotten dinner set up on the coffee table and had notes and his laptop set up nearby. This was a work meeting. That was all.

"I hope you like Chinese food. Jake said you didn't have any food allergies, and this is one of the better take-out places in town." Sam gestured to the table. "Come on in. Grab a seat, make yourself comfortable."

"Thanks." A couple of spots of color appeared in his cheeks. "I can give you a couple of bucks for it." He reached for his wallet.

"Don't worry about it." Sam waved a hand. "My treat. We've got a lot of stuff to get through." He tore his eyes away from Oliver and shuffled toward the couch.

Oliver settled in as far away as he could while still reaching the table. He carefully avoided looking directly at Sam, and part of Sam felt bad about that. He wanted Oliver to look at him and see everything that he had to offer. That wouldn't be right, though. It wouldn't be right for the case, and it wouldn't be right for Oliver.

"Okay." Oliver cleared his throat a little and pulled another report out of his bag. "I went twenty-five years back. We've got some more fires and some more property damage on the Coucher side. We've got some more deaths on the Marsten side that I'd consider suspicious."

Sam took the file and looked at it. Oliver had organized the incidents into six groups—Coucher fatal, Coucher non-fatal, Marsten fatal, Marsten non-fatal, Other fatal, Other non-fatal. "What's with the *other*?" he asked.

Oliver reached for the takeout. "I wanted to make sure that we accounted for similar incidents that weren't related to the families. If areas with feud-related incidents happened to be going through an exceptionally violent or accident-prone period, it would show up in that column. Note that the numbers aren't really proportionate. That *other* column is for the entire North Shore. That's thousands of people. The average overdose rate should be higher than the average overdose rate for one family." He bowed his head. "Which dish is yours?"

Sam told him, and Oliver crouched down near the coffee table to dish the food onto a plate for Sam. He stayed in that position to pass the food over to Sam, and the sight made Sam's jaw drop. "What's wrong?" Oliver asked him, furrowing his brow with concern.

"Nothing." Sam knew that his voice sounded strangled. "Nothing. Just—that's good, the way you noticed the statistical rate there." He shuddered a little as his fingers brushed against Oliver's when he took the plate from him. "This might not have been the best idea."

Oliver turned his head away, shoulders rounded. "I'll take off. We can meet up tomorrow at work, with people around."

"It's just... I mean, look at you." Sam put his hand over his mouth.

Oliver turned his head even further away. "I get it, Sam. I'll head out." He rose to his feet, graceful even in dejection.

Sam put his plate down and rose. "You get that I have sons your age."

Oliver huffed out a little laugh. "It's not like they haven't both been in my apartment, Sam. It's not like I haven't been right here. To see Jake." He shook his head, sending his dark curls swinging. "It's okay."

"It's not okay." Sam blew out an explosive breath, too frustrated to be a sigh. "It's not okay for an old guy like me to sit here and make passes at my sons' friends like that. It's just not."

Oliver narrowed those beautiful silver eyes of his. "Okay, and if I were some young kid, your argument would have some validity. We're both adults, Sam. It's not like you knew me when I was a kid either. You don't have weird memories of me on the playground or something. You've only ever known me as a full adult."

Sam bit his lip and stifled a groan. "Don't remind me. I think about that a lot." He turned his head away. "I shouldn't have admitted that."

"Of course you should. It's a fact." Oliver paused, and then he stepped forward. "Look. I'm going to accept your decision, and

I'm not going to push. I guess I'm glad that it's not because you think I kiss like a dead fish —"

Sam stepped forward and grabbed Oliver's shoulder. It was a tactical error on his part, because now he was close enough to feel the heat radiating from the beautiful young omega. His scent was overwhelming, too. "You don't kiss like a dead fish," Sam hastened to tell him. "No. Your kiss is like, like holy water or something. I don't know."

Oliver grinned a little, his cheeks getting pink. "Holy water?"

"Sure, why not?" Sam let his hand down to rest on Oliver's hip. He should step away. He knew he wasn't going to. "I'm a cop, not a poet. I just don't want to be a dirty old man."

Oliver snorted. "You're hardly a dirty old man if you're with an adult who wants to be with you." He looked up into Sam's eyes, just for a moment. It was enough. All that Sam could see there was trust and love.

He bowed his head and touched his lips to Oliver's. This time the kiss was measured, controlled. He took the time to fully experience it, to let himself engage with his lover's mouth. Since Oliver was expecting it, the kiss should feel better for him, too.

Oliver let out a happy little moan, so soft and quiet that Sam almost missed it. Small, soft hands reached up to cradle Sam's face, and Sam let his other hand reach out to caress Oliver's hip.

He'd been fighting this for too long. He'd hate himself later. He was too old for Oliver; he was no good for Oliver. Still, Oliver wanted him. He'd said so, looking into his eyes with those shining silver orbs of his, and told him that he wanted to be with him. Sam could feel his heat under his skin, underneath those battle armor dress pants and that oh-so-crisp white shirt of his.

They sank back down to the couch. Oliver laced his hands behind Sam's and molded his body to Sam's. He just gave himself over to Sam, abandoned himself to the alpha just like that, and Sam could have sworn that someone was messing with the thermostat. The room had heated up by at least fifteen degrees. He ran his hands down Oliver's long, slim sides. "Can I?" he whispered into Oliver's ear, already untucking the dress shirt.

"Please." Oliver nodded. "I want your hands on me." He blushed after he said that, like he'd been bolder than expected, and Sam wasn't sure what to think about that. A man should be able to say what he wanted. After all, Oliver hadn't been hesitant to say anything earlier. Still Oliver watched as Sam carefully unbuttoned his shirt and helped him peel it off, and then he let Sam peel his undershirt off and toss it to the side.

Sam stared at Oliver's body for a long moment. The dress pants weren't doing much to hide his bulge. All of that dark skin, unlined and unblemished, just called out to Sam. He ran his fingertips lightly over Oliver's smooth skin and traced the lines of his lithe little muscles. Then, meeting Oliver's eyes, he very carefully reached out and rolled one of Oliver's pink nipples.

Oliver closed his eyes, tilted his head back and gave a loud groan. His hips rocked, and Sam could feel just how hard he was. "You like it when I do that?" he asked Oliver, a grin crossing his face.

"Yeah." Oliver's lashes fluttered as he opened his eyes. "I like it when you touch me."

Sam hesitated for just a moment. He should stop. He shouldn't be putting his hands or his mouth on this man, or tasting his bare skin like it was water in a desert. He shouldn't wrap himself up in Oliver's moans and sighs and little groans. Those sounds weren't some kind of defense against solitude or loneliness. They weren't a defense against his own surliness, proof that someone could see past it. They were proof that Sam was incapable of fighting his own urges.

But those sounds made such pure and perfect music for him, and that skin felt so right against his own. He could no more stop himself than he could stand against the tide. "Is this all right?" he asked, letting his fingers slide just under the waistband of Oliver's dress pants.

"Yes. Yes, Sam, please." Oliver lifted his hips.

Sam slowly stripped off Oliver's pants and underwear, like he was unwrapping a treasure. Then he yielded to the inevitable. "If we're going to do this, we should move into the bedroom." He stood up and offered his hand to Oliver.

Oliver stared at him in a daze for a moment, and then he allowed himself to be guided to his feet. Once upright, he followed close behind Sam, up the stairs and into the master bedroom. There, trembling, he started to drop to his knees.

Sam stopped him. "We have plenty of time for that," he told his lover, stroking Oliver's cheek. "Right now, if it's okay, I just want to be inside you."

Oliver's silver eyes shone bright in the reflected sunset for a moment, and he nodded. Sam threw off his own clothing, and then he guided Oliver to the bed. Oliver didn't seem to know exactly what to do with himself, but right now Sam wasn't worried about that. All he cared about was pleasing Oliver and bringing their bodies together.

He reached into his nightstand for lube, which he found after barely a moment. "I'm going to make this so good for you," he promised.

Oliver settled onto his back, and Sam started to prep him while continuing to cover that amazing skin of his with kisses. He couldn't believe how tight Oliver was. He seemed to be enjoying the process, but it took forever to loosen him up enough to take the second finger, and then the third. Even then, Sam couldn't be sure that he'd be able to take all of him. He stretched him as thoroughly as he could, until Oliver was rocking onto his hand and all but begging for more, and then he slicked himself up.

Good God. For a moment he thought he'd been right. He and Oliver might not be able to do this. Oliver was just so damn tight! He couldn't remember the last time he'd been with someone who was this tight. The last time must have been—

Oh. The last time had been Chris. And Chris had been a virgin.

At this point, it was a little late in the day to stop himself, even if Sam wanted to. He entered the rest of the way into Oliver with shallow, short thrusts and did his best to be patient. Oliver, for his part, wrapped himself around Sam in an attempt to make it easier for him. When Sam was fully seated, he gave Oliver a moment to get used to the intrusion. Even though he very clearly wanted it, this was a big adjustment. The last thing that Sam wanted to do was to hurt his lover.

When Oliver told him to move, he moved. Sam's instincts told him to drive a hard and fast pace, to claim every inch of Oliver inside and out. Sam wasn't about to do that to the guy, especially without talking to him about it. He aimed for a tender, loving pace instead and drew their lovemaking out as long as he could.

Oliver could only give away his virginity once, after all. He could have made a better choice about who to give it to, but it was too late now. The least that Sam could do was to make it good for him.

When he felt himself starting to lose the rhythm, he reached between them and touched Oliver's hard, heavy cock. It didn't take much to make Oliver come. He finished with a loud, wordless cry. His silver eyes rolled back, and his entire body clenched around Sam as his orgasm overtook him. That was enough to send Sam over the edge, and he spilled into Oliver's body.

After a moment, he got up and went to get a cloth to clean them both up. Sam didn't turn on the light. He couldn't stand to look at himself in the mirror. What had he just done?

When he came back, Oliver was in the same position he'd been in. His eyes were open and alert now, though, and a little smile graced his beautiful face. "Thanks," he said, as Sam wiped him clean. "That was incredible."

Sam huffed out a little laugh. "You could have warned me it was your first time." He sat down on the edge of the bed and tossed the washcloth over toward the laundry.

Oliver's face fell. "I didn't think it was something that merited an announcement." He pushed himself up into a sitting position. "I'm sorry if it wasn't very good for you."

Sam grabbed his hand. "Oliver, stop. It was fantastic for me. I'm just worried about you, okay? Your first time should have been special, you know? Important. You should've been with someone you could be with for the rest of your life, not some old fart you happen to be working with." He looked away. "I mean, you're not a virgin because no one wants you, okay? You were saving it for someone."

Oliver hung his head for a moment. Then he leaned over and kissed Sam's cheek. "Sam, I gave it to the alpha I wanted to have it. Okay? I'm happy." He let his hand run down Sam's bare shoulder as he got gingerly up from the bed. "I'd better get home. We've got a lot of work to do tomorrow."

"Yeah." Sam couldn't make himself look Oliver in the eye as he left.

Chapter Five

Oliver drove back to Framingham in silence. He didn't even have the radio on for company. He'd been building up this night, this moment, since he'd learned about sex and what it meant for an omega. On the one hand, he knew that nothing could possibly live up to the fantasy he'd built up in his head. On the other hand, he didn't think it had been bad. He'd liked it, even though there had been parts that were kind of uncomfortable at first.

At least, he'd liked it up until Sam got up from the bed. Everything that Oliver had ever seen, or read, or heard about, had implied that there was supposed to be more than just a roll in the hay and then out the door. Maybe if he'd been better at it, done more for Sam, he'd have let Oliver stay for a little while.

Then again, maybe not. *Your first time should have been special, you know? Important. You should've been with someone you could be with for the rest of your life, not some old fart you happen to be working with.* There was no relationship there, beyond what the state police forced on them. Sam didn't want Oliver, any more than he wanted any other omega.

He got back to the apartment, where Jake frowned at him. "I figured you'd stay the night." Jake took in Oliver's tousled look. "Oh God. It went badly."

Oliver held up a hand. He'd managed to hold off the despair as he drove home, but now that his mind wasn't occupied with keeping the car on the road it hit him. "I just really, really want a shower right now."

Jake wasn't the kind of friend to back off, especially when he could see that his friend was distressed. "Yeah. Yeah, I for one would rather have this talk after the shower. But Oliver? We're going to talk. Okay?"

"Sure." Oliver staggered into the bathroom and tossed his clothes to the side.

He carefully blanked out his mind as he turned the water up as high as his skin could tolerate. Only a short while ago, Sam had been touching him. That nipple was tender now because Sam had put his mouth on it and teased it, driven Oliver wild. If he thought too hard about it, he'd fall to pieces here in the shower. He couldn't allow that.

After he finished washing, he got into his pajamas and shuffled out to sit with Jake. Jake, being the friend that he was, had poured them both deep glasses of wine and set out cheese and crackers. "Let me guess. Dad got Chinese."

"That we didn't even eat." Oliver covered his face with his hands. "Sorry. You don't want to hear that right now."

"Not even a little bit." Jake picked up his glass. "I'm just going to sit here and pretend you're talking about some other guy."

Oliver squirmed. The last thing that he wanted to do was talk to Jake about his own father. He grabbed at his wine glass. "It's just… I mean…" He put his glass down. "It's like this. You know that I come from a pretty conservative background myself, right?"

"Yeah. I've met your mom." Jake swirled the wine in his glass. "So?"

"Well, I'd always wanted—planned—to hold off on sex until I was claimed. And I expected it to be something…" He shook his head. He'd gone into the explanation all wrong. He could see that from Jake's wide-eyed expression. "I didn't go over there expecting Sam to claim me or anything like that. I didn't go over there planning to have sex either. That just kind of happened. And it was good. Don't get me wrong. I just… it was just kind of like… in my head, and from everything I've heard, there's supposed to be more to it than finishing and then leaving. Especially for your first time, right?"

Jake's eyes bulged out of his head. "He kicked you out right after? I'm going back to Hopkinton, and I'm going to kill him. You'll be my alibi."

Oliver chuckled in spite of himself. "No, no. It wasn't quite that bad. He was upset that I hadn't warned him that it was my first time, for some reason. I was always told that giving your virginity to a guy was supposed to be special, but it turns out that it's the last thing they want. I should have gone out and gotten rid of it as early as I could."

"Aw, Oliver." Jake's face crumpled, and he took a deep gulp of his wine. "That's not… yeah, that's an awful way to feel. And I'm totally going to kick his ass, because whatever he was actually thinking he shouldn't have made you feel that way. But Oliver, I'm sure he didn't mean to treat your first time as a throwaway."

Oliver took a deep breath. His hands shook this time as he lifted his glass to his lips. "He told me that my first time should have been special, with someone I could be with for the rest of my life. Not with him. And then he watched me walk out the door. For him, it was nothing." Oliver gulped at his wine. "I guess I've been carrying a bunch of old-fashioned notions around, you know? I've been thinking of sex as some kind of big, special, wonderful thing. It's time for me to grow up. There's nothing special about it at all, is there? There's not even really any emotion attached, not for anyone over eighteen." He put his glass down and rubbed at his temples. "It's best if I just stick to the lab."

"You'll probably feel like that for a little while." Jake's voice was quiet. "Everyone does, when their heart gets broken." He sipped some more of his wine. "Don't tell my dad this, but my first time was with this alpha—captain of the lacrosse team, good friend of Joey's. I was sure it was forever. The guy had no idea what he was doing, and I didn't even care because I figured it was his first time too.

"Found out later that no, he had two or three other omegas on the hook too. He was just that bad at it." He gave a rueful laugh and leaned back in his chair. "I made sure that they knew about me and him before I dumped him, because you've got to do right by other omegas. Last I heard he was off in Florida somewhere."

Oliver chuckled. "Awesome." He finished his glass of wine. "I can't blame the guy for how he feels or what his intentions were. People feel a certain way, you know? And there's nothing you can really do about it. I'm just disappointed in myself, really." He washed his and Jake's glasses and headed to bed.

He couldn't quite bring himself to regret what he'd done. Maybe he couldn't give his virginity to his alpha anymore, and that would continue to give him a twinge of sadness for a while, but he'd wanted to give it to Sam for years and he'd been more than willing. Besides, he'd apparently been the only one to treasure his virginity.

He regretted his own foolishness, for expecting any more. He wasn't a kid, to make up fairy stories.

He went to work the next day and immediately went to the stored evidence from the original Cooper Block fire. He wanted to get through this case as soon as he could, if only to minimize his contact with Sam Nenci. Was it only two weeks ago that he'd been desperate for any opportunity just to be around the man?

Oliver was pretty sure that he'd done as much as he could, independently, with the Marsten properties. If someone decided that exhuming the bodies was worthwhile, then he'd have more to do with that side of the case, but that was a highly unlikely outcome and Oliver couldn't be happier. Exhumations, no matter how old, were disgusting.

He grabbed a notepad from his drawer and wrote down, OBJECTIVES, in huge letters at the top of the page. Underneath, he created bullet points. The first objective, of course, was to identify the arsonist responsible for the Cooper Block fire. Oliver created a sub-header under that objective, because simply saying *identify the arsonist responsible* was both too simplistic and too complicated a task to get it all done.

So underneath that first objective, he added space for *physical evidence* and *motive*. Sam had been right. People didn't often murder fifty other people out of the blue. There hadn't been any Couchers living at the Cooper Block, so the murders had simply been a way to strike out at the Coucher family's business interests. Oliver wasn't the kind of person who could really speak to the inner workings of the criminal mind—hell, he'd actually expected affection in a sexual encounter—but he knew that the person who would resort to such measures would usually be pretty careful about leaving things behind himself.

Criminals were always pretty careful about leaving things behind. They still usually managed to leave some trace of themselves. The thing with a fire like the one that had taken out the Cooper block was that it had moved fast, and the building had been open at least fifteen minutes before the building went up. The killer must have been able to move very quickly, sure, but someone moving in a hurry usually leaves something behind themselves. Detectives at the time of the fire had been more concerned about looking for the accelerant and possible weapons than they had for personal effects or scraps of clothing.

He brought the box over to a clean, hooded space and examined the contents. The soil samples he ignored for now.

Too much time had passed for him to learn anything new from analyzing those samples. He found plenty of items that were left at the scene and certainly by the killer, but none of them had any hint of fingerprints on them.

The area near the barred doors had been the location of most of the finds that couldn't be identified as building materials. That had been where most of the dead were found. Most of those personal items that survived the blaze in any kind of useful fashion had been identified by loved ones, and before an hour passed, Oliver decided that if he ever saw another child-sized cross on a little chain, in either gold or silver, streaked with greasy smoke, he might scream.

By the time that he sorted out all of the items that were found where he'd expected to find them, he was left with artifacts that were out of place for the time, place, and circumstances. These required special attention.

He returned the rest of the evidence to its box and spread the five items, in their plastic evidence bags, out on the workspace in front of him. He had the remains of an antique handgun, which had been noted in the evidence log but not treated as particularly unusual. Maybe one of the deceased was known to carry; Oliver would have to check.

He had a kitchen knife. According to the evidence log and the photographs, it had been found clutched in the hand of a deceased woman of nineteen years. That made two weapons among the dead; had they seen their killer? Had they made some attempt to fight their way out?

The third item that Oliver found, that was unexpected, was a clay bong, the type that people made in art class and convinced themselves that the teacher didn't recognize. It had been broken into pieces by the heat and by collapsing debris, but some kindly evidence tech had pieced it together again just in case.

The next item in the lineup was a silver pocket watch. It looked to have been an antique. Oliver was no expert, but the filigree on the case suggested something Victorian or maybe a little bit later. People were into that kind of thing back then. Notes indicated that the pocket watch was indeed an antique, dating back to 1904. It also indicated that the manufacturer was "Omega," which gave Oliver a little chuckle despite his foul mood.

The final item before him was a gold ring, sized for a man. The ring had three stones, two diamonds flanking a large emerald, and the detail on the ring made the metal look evenly twisted. It was a lovely ring; a person might give that to his omega after a claim.

He stepped on his own toe. People didn't do that anymore. They probably hadn't done that then.

He examined both of the jewelry pieces. Unlike the remaining outliers, these two items had no evidence of the fire on them. The silver watch bore some tarnish, but no ash or smoke. There were only two explanations. Either the crime scene technicians had cleaned these pieces of evidence, contrary to every protocol that had existed even back then, or the items hadn't been in the fire.

Someone had come back to the fire and put them there.

He exhausted every means at his disposal to get fingerprints from either find, but none showed up. He didn't expect them to. Fingerprints had about a forty-year shelf life, and these had been sitting in plastic for fifty. If the techs in 1967 hadn't been able to pull prints then, he wasn't going to be able to get them now. Still, there had to be some kind of clue there.

Well, he didn't have to find it today. He took several photos of the outliers, returned everything to storage, and returned to his desk to document his findings. By the time he'd finished, and cleaned up after himself, nine o'clock had come and gone. He yawned and stared at his monitor for a moment.

He had two options here. He could wait until morning and present the information to Sam in person, showing off his work and his knowledge. Or he could just send his report to Sam, and to Nina. That way he could leave a paper trail to show that he had indeed been working, that he hadn't just spent the entire day sulking.

He decided that sending the report electronically was probably the better option. He hit send and took his bike home. Jake was out by the time he'd gotten home, leaving a note on the bathroom mirror telling him not to wait up.

Oliver fixed himself some soup and headed to bed. If he'd had any illusions about Sam, or his intentions, or any future they might have had together, they were gone now. The only person to reach out to him on his phone had been Jake, inviting him to come out with him.

Oliver huddled alone in his bed, pressed against the red brick exterior wall. He'd acknowledged that he needed to grow up, but he hadn't realized how cold it would feel.

***

Sam's hand hovered over his phone a dozen times the day after he and Oliver made love. He pulled it away every time. What was he supposed to say to him? *Sorry I took your virginity; you shouldn't have done that? You gave me the best sex of my life, and I can't stop scrubbing myself because I feel like such a dirty old man? Thanks for the sex, let's never do it again?*

He needed to find someone he could talk to. Unfortunately, he had no confidants. His time with Internal Affairs had blown up every good relationship he'd had at the state police, and these guys in Cold Case were so incredibly young. Ideally, he'd find someone who could also talk to Oliver and explain the situation to him, but the thought of another alpha speaking to Oliver ever again made Sam want to punch things and maybe kick a few doors down. He didn't suggest it.

There wasn't anything to say, anyway. He'd been mooning around after Oliver for three years now. None of the things that had kept him back then had changed now that he knew what it felt like to hold Oliver in his arms. Oliver hadn't magically gotten older. Sam hadn't found the Fountain of Youth in the sweat on Oliver's smooth skin.

He needed to stay away.

When he got a text from Jake, just after quitting time, he cringed. *You're a dick*, his son told him.

Sam couldn't argue. He still wasn't about to take that attitude from his son, and his omega son at that. *I'm your father. You'll show me some respect. And stay out of my love life.*

I'm not in your "love" life, and you can't call what you did to Oliver love.

Sam called Jake after that, torn between terror and rage. "What the hell is he telling you?" he snarled into the phone.

"Nothing. He's certainly not disparaging you, anyway." Jake yawned. Sam wasn't fooled. "Let me share a quote with you though. 'I've been thinking of sex as some kind of big, special, wonderful thing. It's time for me to grow up. There's nothing special about it at all, is there? There's not even really any emotion attached, not for anyone over eighteen.' He's gone from feeling positive about saving himself for someone special, who would appreciate what Oliver was giving him, to thinking that only children think that there's any emotion attached to sex at all. In one night. Let me guess what changed in that one night? Oh, right. That would be you."

Sam sat down with a heavy sigh. "I'm so not talking about this with you."

"You called me." Jake's voice was colder than ice. "He's the sweetest guy I know. And he just about thought that you hung the moon. And you treated him like a throwaway. Just... ugh."

"I didn't mean to. I just—I don't have to justify myself to my son." Sam pinched the bridge of his nose and tried to think of some way to calm his racing pulse.

"Replace that *don't have to* with *can't* and you'll be a little bit closer to the truth. Got to go." Jake hung up.

Few things infuriated Sam as a parent more than being hung up on by his son, and at another time he might have called Jake back and lit into him. Right now, though, he couldn't deny that Jake was right. There wasn't likely to be much that he could do to justify his behavior in his son's eyes. He could barely justify it in his own.

He'd never hoped that Oliver felt the same way about him that he felt about Oliver. In the few moments when he'd allowed his fantasies to go there, he'd had to admit that no good could possibly come of it. When they'd been in the heat of the moment, he hadn't thought beyond the now or his need. Once the moment had passed, he'd thought only of his own remorse. He'd thought only of how wrong it was, to keep Oliver around for himself when Oliver should be with someone younger.

He'd suspected that Oliver would be hurt, mildly, when Sam let him go. Heartbreak like what Jake was describing hadn't been something he'd considered at all. He hated the thought of giving pain to Oliver, someone who had given him such perfect trust, but he couldn't see a way around it.

He lay awake a long time that night, staring at the ceiling.

He got to the office the next morning and found Oliver's message in his inbox. For a moment he bristled. He'd figured that Oliver would be too professional to go sending messages on work systems. Then he noticed the subject line—*Outlying Items Found at Cooper Block Fire*—and that Oliver's supervisor had been cc'ed on the message.

Sam needed to get his head out of his ass. Oliver knew his job better than anyone else. Sam needed to figure out a way to focus on his.

He read through the report. Oliver was almost obsessive about documenting his process, but that was par for the course for these crime scene guys. Jake had explained that to Sam once. If they didn't document even the tiniest part of the process, everything they'd done could be challenged and thrown out in court. Once Sam had mentally tuned out all of the parts where Oliver described how he'd cleaned the workspace and changed his gloves over and over, he could cut to the part that he needed.

Apparently someone had found, among other things, two pieces of men's jewelry among the ruins of the Cooper Block. Crime scene photos showed that the watch and ring hadn't been found on any of the human remains, or in a position to indicate that they'd been in a pocket. Instead, they'd been placed carefully on a brick, after the fact.

Sam's blood ran cold after he read those words. The watch and ring were expensive. No random wino had just stumbled over and tossed the jewelry onto the ruins just for giggles. Those pieces would have been placed there to send a message. The person sending the message would have had to slip in with all of the first responders, once the fire had been contained enough to keep the metal intact.

He sent both Oliver and Nina a meeting request to discuss the new information. Before he hit send, he added Ray Langer to the meeting request. He could use a good, steady presence to help him keep his behavior on the right side of the line between appropriate and offensive. He knew that he could be churlish at the best of times, and he was so twisted up right now he didn't think he could trust himself.

Nina and Oliver accepted the request without further comment. Langer accepted the request, but then he walked over to Sam's desk and sat on it.

"I sent a meeting request, not a request for a close encounter between your ass and my blotter." Sam glared up at his friend.

Langer gave him a cheesy grin. "Aren't you just a lucky little troll? I like to give a little something extra to all of my clients. Look, Sam, it's not like you to ask for a chaperone. Especially when your *objet d'amour*'s boss will be right there."

Sam grimaced and pushed his chair away from his desk. "Can you please never refer to him that way again? He's an omega, not a fleshlight."

"Oh ho! Sensitivity from the notorious Sam Nenci! Who would have thought?" Langer flipped his pen up into the air, but failed to catch it and let it clatter to the floor.

"It's complicated, okay?"

"It's probably not half as complicated as you think it is." Langer smirked. "And it's not worth giving yourself a permanent hunch. Relax. Unhunch those shoulders. There you go. Talk to Uncle Ray. Tell me all about it."

"I'm not here to give you a fresh source of gossip, Langer." Sam scowled, but he rolled his shoulders. He hadn't realized just how much he'd bunched them up.

"Of course not. It's not like you four didn't gossip amongst yourselves when I claimed Doug. And it's not like we haven't been gossiping about you and Oliver for three years." Langer waved his hand. "Talk to me. I realize that you're not a big fan of others' opinions, but it does help you to get some clarity."

Sam grumbled, but he could see Langer's point. He was too close to the situation. He explained what had happened the other night, and how Jake had told him how Oliver had responded. As Sam spoke, Langer's face grew grave, and then it darkened. "Okay, so you just basically kicked him out after you acknowledged that you were his first time."

"Why is everyone hung up on that?" Sam leaned his chair back and stared at the ceiling. "I mean, he was awfully eager. He can't have been that attached to it, or that committed to saving himself for his alpha."

Langer snorted. "Anyone who's spent five minutes in this place knows how he feels about you. He'd have done anything for you. Doug picked up on it in like half a second. And by the way, when Pretty Boy finds out about it, I think you might want to take to wearing your vest around the office full time. He's awfully protective of Oliver, and he uses a picture of you for target practice."

Sam snorted. "I can take Pretty Boy. And okay, I didn't handle that well. But better that I should let him be a little hurt now than let him be too attached later, right?" He picked his head up. "I mean there's no way I can claim him. He's younger than my sons."

"By a few months, Nenci." Langer shook his head. "That's not the important thing."

"Isn't it? I can't claim him. When I die, he'll die within a few weeks. He's so young! He's got his whole life ahead of him!" Sam stood up. "I can't do that to him. I can't do that to any kids we have between us, if we did have any. That's just cruel."

Langer snorted. "And any alpha cop takes that same risk when he goes out to work. Try again. You've been mooning around over that guy for years, literally. You finally get it together to do something about it and you blow it so spectacularly that you need two chaperones just to keep you from Nenci-ing yourself into a suspension."

Sam scratched his beard. "Am I really a verb?"

"You're a verb. Doug called me up last week to tell me that his client had just Nenci-ed himself into Solitary. You're not even a cop-specific verb." Langer shook his head. "Look. I love you, we all love you except maybe Robles, but you've got to admit that you've got a problem here. You *have* to get this case closed, and you haven't just shot yourself in the foot, you've shot yourself in the knee. You think maybe you should get some help?"

"I'm not crazy, I'm an asshole!" Nenci glowered at him. He knew he wasn't popular, and that his attitude wasn't the best sometimes, but what could he do? He was who he was, and at his age he wasn't likely to be able to change it.

"That you are, my friend. Didn't you tell me that you'd had a blowout with Jake that was so bad he's sleeping on Oliver's couch? And there's Joey. How long's it been since that son even spoke to you?" Langer put a hand on Sam's shoulder. "Look. I've got a buddy, a therapist, who specializes in helping alphas. I'm not here to out anyone, but you do know a few of her patients. I'll give you her number, okay? It's up to you if you think it's worth giving her a call."

Langer passed him the number and they went about their own business until the meeting with Forensics. Sam only gave it a couple of hours before he snuck off and called. He didn't know if the woman could help him, and he wasn't sure that there was anything wrong with him in the first place, but he knew that he should probably give it a try.

When the time for the meeting with Forensics came around, Sam collected Langer and they made their way to a neutral conference room. Sam was startled by the change in Oliver. For as long as he'd known Oliver, the slender omega had been there with a ready smile and a little blush every time Sam saw him. Now he greeted Langer cordially enough, but simply gave Sam a cold nod. "Detective Nenci." Then he sat down.

Nina looked between Oliver and Sam. She didn't seem to know what had happened between them, not that Sam could make out, but she narrowed her large gray eyes at Sam. "All right," she said, and sat down. "Interesting. We're here today to discuss two pieces of evidence that Oliver found collected from the Cooper Block fire."

Oliver produced the jewelry. It was still in evidence bags, where it would stay throughout the meeting. "There's still a great deal that we don't know about these pieces before we can draw any definitive conclusions, but they should be considered unique items. Similar items have netted substantial sums at auction."

Sam cleared his throat. "These were never in the fire. Someone snuck in with the first responders to place them at the scene. That's a cold act."

Nina glared at him. "We don't deal in emotion in the lab, Detective. We can't measure a person's motive for leaving these things behind, nor can we provide empirical evidence for their mindset at the time. We can say that the person who left them behind most likely would have had to prepare to do so, and seek an opportunity. The photographs show deliberate placement rather than haphazard deposits."

The scent of myrrh made Sam want to cry. Oliver was so close, close enough to touch, but Sam couldn't let himself do it. "What else would you need to know?" he made himself ask. He had to speak through the lump in his throat.

Oliver glanced coolly at his notes. "It would be most useful to know if anyone had ever filed an insurance claim for these pieces, obviously. Finding out if the items had ever been insured would be adequate. It's too late to get any biological information, or fingerprints, from them but the historical record may be most useful."

Langer cleared his throat. "I'm not overly familiar with the case, but from what it sounds like you have two feuding families. Maybe if we brought photos of the watch and the ring to people from those families to see if they had any recollection of them, any family stories about the day Uncle Ole's watch went missing or something like that, they could generate some leads for us."

"Sounds good." Sam could have kissed Langer for that, if he didn't think that Langer's omega would have sued him into the next galaxy.

"All right then. Excellent meeting." Nina rose, and Oliver rose with her. Neither of them looked back as they left the room.

Sam looked at Langer. "That was..."

Langer shook his head. "Oh yeah. You blew it, Alpha. He doesn't want to be anywhere near you now."

Chapter Six

Oliver could not have been happier when the workweek drew to a close. He was tired, profoundly tired, and he knew that the best thing for him would be to stay away from the office for a couple of days. Spring was finally giving way to summer, and Oliver had every intention of taking full advantage of everything that the MetroWest area had to offer for the next two days.

Jake approved of this plan, in theory. "You know," he said, "you don't have to spend the whole weekend on grueling hikes and dangerous bike rides. You can distract yourself with relaxing picnics and maybe a boat ride or something."

Oliver laughed at him. "What's wrong with pushing myself a little, Jake? I like to ride. I like to hike. Why not come hiking with me? It'll be fun. We'll go to Garden in the Woods. It's local, the 'hiking' is actually pretty easy and it should be stunning this time of year."

Jake wrinkled his nose. "It sounds like something that would be more fun with an alpha to hold hands with. But you know what? Why not? It's something different."

They headed out to Garden in the Woods and walked around the trails. The day was perfect for it, sunny and warm, and just as Oliver had suspected most of the flowers were in full bloom. Just being there put him into a better mood.

"So how are you holding up?" Jake asked him, as they took in a flowering meadow.

Oliver stuffed his hands into the pockets of his shorts. "I'm holding up. I mean, how am I supposed to hold up? I'm mostly mad at myself." He walked on down the trail.

Jake followed after him. "Why would you be mad at yourself? He's the one who's being a dick."

"Sure. Maybe. But I'm still the one who made the choices. I mean, it was important to me, saving myself for my alpha. Not just any alpha, but for the alpha I'd spend the rest of my life with. When push came to shove, though, that's not what I did. I just kind of went ahead and gave it up just like that. I gave up on one of my most important principles, and my most cherished dream, for a couple of minutes of pleasure." He turned his face away from the pretty shrub in front of him. "Who does that? I never thought of myself as being that weak."

Jake sighed. "Don't be too hard on yourself, man. Wanting it like that, it's in you. You can't fight it. You're an omega. It's part of your nature. You need that kind of affection and attention; it's built into your genes. It's important to you." He put a hand on Oliver's back.

"I know." Oliver closed his eyes. "I know. The science can't be ignored. I just… I've been able to get by just fine until now. I can't believe that I threw it all out the window without thinking about it. And it's like… you know, all these years, I've known that Sam was the kind of guy who would want his omega to be a virgin. He's old-fashioned like that.

"But now I'm looking back, and he never asked. He never picked up on the fact that I had no clue what I was doing. He was never thinking about me past that night. He never thought of me as someone he could consider being with. He never thought of me as someone he could respect, just as someone he could use. And that's on me." Oliver fought down a wave of anger.

"Look, Oliver, I'm sure it's more complicated than that. I know alphas tend to be kind of simple, in terms of motivation and needs and all that, but my dad's got some baggage and stuff. It doesn't excuse the way he's treated you, but I don't think it's as simple as all that." Jake nudged him with his shoulder. "I'm not saying you should forgive him. I'm just saying that there's probably more to the story."

Oliver faked a grin and kept walking. "Maybe. That's usually the case in what we do, right? Why would life be any different? That's not the point though. Why he did what he did, or didn't, is kind of secondary. I'm upset with myself, not him. I had an identity for myself, and it's gone now."

Jake bit down on the inside of his cheek as he contemplated that for a moment. "Okay. Fair enough. I'm going to be here while you forge your new identity, though."

Oliver's smile was genuine now. "Thanks, man."

"Okay, good. Now come on, there's some kind of butterfly bush over here. Let's see if there are any butterflies to be seen." Jake waved the map at Oliver and led him further down the trail, and Oliver followed gladly.

Oliver went for a solo bike ride the next day. He appreciated what Jake had told him, and to some extent he agreed, but none of that changed the deep sense of loss in his soul. He needed movement to find peace, movement and sweat. If he pushed himself enough, maybe he could forget the last time he'd worked up this much of a lather.

When he got home, he found Jake behind the stove and Joe setting the table. He froze with the door half open. "Um, hi?"

The twins waved at him with identical gestures, right down to identical timing. "Hey, Oliver." Joe grinned, but didn't advance toward Oliver. "Jake told me Dad's being an ass again. We figured it would be nice to have a *Welcome to the Family* party."

"All the folks he's let down." Jake chuckled. "Go on, there's still some finishing touches to put on. You've got time to shower."

Oliver scurried off to wash up. He really had worked up quite a sweat; his scent was incompatible with food at the moment. By the time he'd cleaned up and gotten dressed again, dinner was served and on the table. Oliver wasn't quite sure how he felt about the whole idea of joining a party for people let down by Sam Nenci, but he sat down at the table anyway.

Dinner turned out to be exactly what he needed to fortify him for the week ahead. They didn't talk about Sam, unless the twins were telling a particularly funny story from their childhood. The conversation was entirely relaxed and perfectly enjoyable, and by the time Joe headed off to his own place Oliver felt lighter than he had in weeks.

Sam cc'ed Oliver on correspondence with a high volume of insurers, but none of them recognized the ring or the pocket watch. On Tuesday, they headed back out to Marblehead to see if Bill Coucher recognized the jewelry. The ride took over an hour, and at no point during the ride was the silence broken by either man.

Part of Oliver felt badly about that. He certainly found it miserable to sit in stiff, unbreakable silence all of the way up to Marblehead. He couldn't think of any reason why Sam would feel any differently, even if he had no regrets about how their night together had ended.

Of course, Sam certainly didn't seem to still want Oliver. That, as much as the memory of his own behavior, was the source of Oliver's pain and shame. How could he still be affected by Sam's banana nut bread scent? Why would it still affect him? He should be ready to wash his hands of Sam and never think of him again.

Once they got to Coucher's residence, Sam took the lead. Oliver let him. He'd step in and correct the alpha if he said anything factually inaccurate, but Sam was the cop. He dealt with witnesses all of the time. Oliver hadn't gone into forensic science to make a habit of interacting with people.

Coucher seemed happy enough to see them. "Detectives! It's lovely to see you again." He shook their hands and led them through the magnificently appointed home and out to a stone patio overlooking the harbor. "It's a beautiful day, and we should enjoy it while we can."

Oliver frowned. "The weather report says that the good weather should stick around for another few days."

Coucher chuckled. "Meteorologists, right? It's the only job in the world where you can get it wrong eighty percent of the time and not wind up on the unemployment line." He gestured toward a damp-looking stone sticking up out of the patio. "That stone's been here since the eighteen hundreds. If it turns damp, a storm's coming. It's never wrong. I'll believe it over some guy sitting there with a computer, Detective. Now, Detective Nenci, you told me you had something to ask me."

Sam smirked. "Couldn't have said it better myself, Mr. Coucher. My sons are always giving me grief like that." He reached into his briefcase and pulled out glossy prints, both color and black and white, of the finds from the Cooper Block Fire. "Mr. Wesson here was going through the materials from the crime scene and he came across these jewelry items. Do they look at all familiar to you?"

Coucher ran his tongue over his lip as he stared at the picture. "As a matter of fact, they do. Come with me, gentlemen." He rose and led them back into the house and into a bar room with a huge picture window overlooking the harbor. "Have a seat." He gestured to the barstools and went over to a tall bookshelf.

Oliver watched as he went over the spines with a hooked finger until he came to the one he wanted. This book had a leather cover and seemed fragile even at a distance. When

Coucher placed it onto the bar counter and opened it, Oliver could see that it was a photo album. The pictures inside were ancient. Some of them were so old that they were printed on thin sheets of tin. Oliver watched, holding his breath, as their host turned the pages until he got what he wanted.

"Here we are. My great-grandfather, Walter Coucher. This portrait was taken in 1904, when Walter was seventeen. Of course omegas weren't open in those days, but records were kept within the family."

Oliver stared. "So the ring was a mark of his having been claimed."

Coucher beamed. "Precisely. He was born Walter Towne, but his name was quietly changed when he came into the family. You can see that the ring is very clearly on his hand there." His face darkened as he closed the book. "His family had initially promised him to the Marstens, but he wasn't willing to submit to Chester Marsten. He was only willing to submit to my great-grandfather, and made him a promise. They made several attacks on the family residence, looking to get him back and force a claim on him, but they were unsuccessful.

"The ring and the watch were stolen during one of the raids, this time during the 1920s. When Great-Grandpa Walter wouldn't give up his ring, they cut off his finger." Coucher shuddered. "I always thought that was more of a metaphor myself, but here we are."

Oliver gasped. "That's terrible! Why wasn't that prosecuted? I get that it was basically illegal to exist as an omega, but you'd think that someone would have pressed charges about someone else busting in and chopping off parts."

Coucher gave him a sad smile. "No one saw anything, of course. Not even Walter. In those days, people weren't willing to admit to having seen anything. Remember, the people who pulled of the St. Valentine's Day Massacre were pretending to be police officers. Walter survived well into his fifties." He straightened up. "I'm not going to pretend that everyone in my family was always on the law's good side. Some were, some were not. I can't account for my ancestors' decisions.

"What I can promise is that my grandfather made it his business to divest from anything that smacked of illegality all the way back in 1960, and my father carried his work on. We've been audited over and over again. We are clean, gentlemen. We're a squeaky clean business and we intend to remain that way."

Sam smiled at him. The record showed something different, but that didn't mean that the Couchers had been behind the *accidents*. "Of course. No one would suggest otherwise." He tapped his finger against his jawline for a long moment. "So this whole business of leaving the items at the crime scene, do you think that the killer might have been trying to send a message that it was in revenge for your family 'stealing' Walter away from them?"

Coucher's jaw dropped. It was only when Oliver's jaw started to ache that he realized that the expression mirrored his own. "That's horrific," Coucher said in a flat tone.

Oliver tilted his head to the side. "I have to admit that it's plausible. It's horrific, but so's the deliberate murder of fifty people."

Coucher shuddered. "You're not wrong." He turned around and grabbed a bottle of gin from a shelf. "You boys want some?"

"Desperately," Oliver told him. "Unfortunately, we can't while we're on the job. Thank you, though."

Coucher poured himself a gin and tonic. "Your loss. Anyway, I hope that helps you get to the bottom of all of this."

"It certainly helps us to narrow our focus." Sam shook Coucher's hand and excused them, and then he led them back out to the unmarked car.

At least the ride back wasn't going to be silent. "Well, that was interesting," Sam said as he pulled the Ford back out onto the road. "Unexpected anyway."

Oliver snorted. "It's not like there are more omegas being born now than there were before. It was just taboo to talk about it. You know, ever." He looked out the window. "Apparently it didn't bother the Couchers, though, because they recorded it."

Sam paused before he replied, and Oliver wondered if he'd gone too far again. Then Sam spoke. "I guess I'm surprised at the violence involved, over something that most people wouldn't have spoken about in public even thirty years ago. I mean, yeah, it was shady of the Couchers to steal the omega, but what was done was done. It wasn't worth killing over. And definitely not worth killing over sixty-three years later, when both the alpha and the omega in question were dead."

Oliver wrinkled his nose. "I'm dying to know what Walter himself thought about the whole thing."

"What do you mean?" Sam glanced over at Oliver. "I'm pretty sure that he objected to having his finger cut off."

"Most people would." Oliver leaned his head against the glass and watched the clouds roll in. "I mean, was it entirely voluntary for him to go off with the Coucher guy? Did he prefer the Marsten guy? Was there someone else entirely? All we know is that his father promised him to Marsten, and he was sixteen or seventeen when he was claimed by Coucher."

Sam sighed. "Does it matter? One alpha's pretty much the same as another, right?"

Huge drops of rain began to drop onto the windshield. "Apparently," Oliver said.

They didn't speak for the rest of the ride.

***

Sam looked at the screen and let out a long, low whistle. "This is huge. This is bigger than huge, this is… this is stupid."

"What's that, Nenci? Your love life?" Tessaro's head popped up from behind his own monitor, like a prairie dog sticking its head up out of a hole.

Sam flipped him off. "You've got some nerve. If I look up *messy* in the dictionary, my picture's not the one under definition number four."

"Okay, that's fair enough. Of course, my messy love life isn't getting every single Cold Case request sent to the back of the line down at the lab, now, is it?" Tessaro smiled sweetly at him and leaned back in his chair.

"Robles is getting things through." Nenci crossed his arms over his chest and glared at his colleague's empty desk.

"Robles' omega is a sergeant. In another department." Tessaro put his feet up on the desk. "How about this. You call Oliver down here, since he's supposed to be your partner in this, and I'll play referee. Sound good?"

Sam bristled. He didn't want to call Oliver down here to talk. They still weren't good together, and Sam still had to fight down his own reactions every time he caught so much as a hint of a myrrh scent. "Fine," he gritted out, clenching his teeth. This might be the last thing he wanted, but it would get the case solved more quickly. Once that was done, both Sam and Oliver could move on with their lives.

Sam sent Oliver a message asking him to join them, and then they sat back and waited. Oliver showed up ten minutes later, his expression cold but neutral. "Detective Nenci." He nodded. "Detective Tessaro. How can I help you?"

The formality of it hit Sam like a knife to the heart, but he pushed through it. "Thanks for coming by, Oliver. I pulled up a list of crimes related to Coucher properties, and to members of the Marsten family, going back to 1904. It's starting to look like the Hatfields and the McCoys here. That's not something you usually think of when you think about Massachusetts, you know?" He looked up at Oliver.

He wasn't sure what he expected to see. Oliver had always been a curious guy, with an interest in every case that crossed his desk. Now he just stared impassively. "And this has what to do with the lab?"

Sam choked on his own breath. He looked at Tessaro to double check; had he heard what Sam had just heard?

He had. "Well it doesn't sound like it's got much to do with the lab, not on the surface," Tessaro said. He got up and crossed the room, hands stuffed into his pockets. "You're supposed to be Nenci's partner here in this, Oliver. He's supposed to be talking about the case with you."

Oliver huffed out a little laugh. "Yeah, sure, but that was only while we were working on cases that had a strong forensic component. The case has changed. This case—these cases, really—the whole nature of the project has changed. There's not much of a forensic component anymore, is there? I mean this stuff, the human motivations and the patterns to what they do, that's all your area of expertise. It's not something that I work on, and it's not something that I've studied. I'm not much good to you out here. When you come to me with something that I can analyze, run through a GC-MassSpec, or look at under a microscope, I'm a hundred percent on board with it. Until then, I've got a bunch of other cases that need attention, and honestly I'm more comfortable in my lab." He nodded once at Tessaro, turned on his heel, and walked back toward the door.

Tessaro raced to catch up with him. "Hey, Oliver, buddy, I get that folks are pissed at Nenci, everyone's always pissed at Nenci, but how come the rest of us are blackballed?"

Oliver snorted. "Detective Tessaro, I hate to be the one to break it to you, but a department full of alphas isn't anyone's idea of a dream team. Not when you're on the downhill side." He smiled, just a little, and kept walking.

Tessaro and Sam looked at one another. "At least I'm not the only one," Sam said finally.

"I think we're a garden of joy and chivalry, frankly." Tessaro glowered at the door. "So that was really weird, and not in a call-Mulder-and-Scully way. Can he really just take himself off the case like that?"

Sam snapped his fingers. "I'll have to check with Devlin, but I don't think that he can."

Tessaro pinched the bridge of his nose. "I'm not sure that's the best way to win him back."

Sam turned on him. "I'm not trying to *win him back*, Tessaro. It's a matter of trying to solve the case. I don't expect him to come back. I don't want—I can't have him back."

Tessaro's lip curled. "Are you kidding me right now? Everyone knows how much the two of you want each other, we sit there and we watch you moon over each other for three years, we practically gift wrap the guy for you, and you're balking?"

"I'm doing what's right for him!" Sam snapped. "Sure it all seems like fun and games now. *Oh, let's stick some sweet, innocent kid with the nasty old troll that lives under our bridge!*

But if he stays with me, forever, then what happens to him?" He turned away.

Tessaro cleared his throat. "Don't you kind of think that's his choice to make?"

"Not really." Sam sat back down behind his desk and got back to work.

He had his appointment with the therapist that Langer had recommended the next day. Lucia Trujillo was a neat and trim woman, maybe forty years of age, who had an office in a huge old house in Arlington. She had a digital recorder, "So that I'm not focused on writing things down, but on actually talking to you while we're together. Is that okay?"

"I guess." It wasn't okay. Sam knew that those recordings were going to come back to bite him in the ass someday. Still, what choice did he have?

"I need you to be honest with me, Sam." She looked at him over the horn rims of her glasses. "Otherwise we're not going to get anywhere."

Sam rubbed his hands together. "Okay, then. I'm not comfortable with it. I know that those recordings are going to come back on me someday, because I've had similar recordings used against people I was investigating. That said, you're the expert. You know what works for you, with this fixing people's heads stuff. I don't. I'd be pissed as hell if you came in and told me how to investigate a cold case. So I'm going to sit back and let you do your job."

Trujillo nodded. "Okay. That's actually pretty good, Sam."

He laughed and put his hands on his thighs. "I've never had a problem being honest. You could say that it's always been kind of the opposite for me."

Trujillo sat up a little bit straighter. Someone else might have missed it, but Sam had been trained to look for little cues like that. "Is that why you're here today?"

"Yeah. Actually it is." Sam bit his lip. "I'm kind of an asshole, doc. I mean, kind of a lot."

One corner of her mouth twitched up. "We try to avoid making value judgments like that, especially about ourselves. This is your story, though. We can work on editing some of the descriptions later. Go on."

Sam huffed out a little laugh. "Even the other guys in my unit refer to me as their troll. They say I hate everything, and I probably don't do a lot to correct that impression. I have a long history of being kind of nasty to everyone around me. I chased one of my sons away years ago—chased him right out of town, in fact. We haven't spoken in years. His twin just moved out in a rage, and let me tell you it's hard to get Jake to walk away." He took a deep breath and let it out, overcome by the bleakness of his empty house.

"I get the sense that there's more."

He licked his lips. "There's this omega. I'm into him, and I'm pretty sure that for some reason he's into me. He's Jake's best friend."

Trujillo frowned. "Your son."

"Yeah. They both work in the lab. I mean, I know he's an adult, he's twenty-four, but it's still wrong on so many levels, you know? I'm old enough to be his father." He closed his eyes. "Anyway, we were assigned to work together as partners for a kind of a weird case, and it went about as well as you could expect." He folded in on himself.

"You claimed him and you're afraid you won't live up to the promise of your honeymoon period?" Trujillo blinked owlishly at him.

"Er, no." Sam scratched at his head. "I mean, we did sleep together once, but that was dumb of us. But through this whole thing, I've been pretty rude to him and the folks at the lab have taken it personally. They're putting everything from my department on the back burner. Everything. It's my fault—I don't try to be an asshole, but I just can't help it and now it's affecting more than just me."

"Okay. I see a lot of law enforcement officers coming through here. That concern for the rest of your team is admirable, and it's very normal for men like you. I see it in a lot of soldiers, too, and firefighters. In order to help you to curb the behavior that you want to change, though, I think we're going to have to explore what's causing it. I can already see some potential suspects, but we're going to have to talk about some of the things that've been going on with you. Some of that discussion will probably be uncomfortable."

"Lady, I'm already uncomfortable."

"Excellent. Let's move on. You mentioned your team first and last, but most of your words were spent talking about your more intimate relationships—your relationships with your sons and with the omega. Let's talk about those. You're free to claim an omega now, correct?"

Sam understood what she was suggesting. "My prior omega died." He swallowed. He could feel the sweat dripping down his back. "He was murdered."

Trujillo bowed her head. "I'm very sorry."

"Me too." Sam turned his head. "I mean, I should've been there, but I wasn't. It was a long time ago. There was supposed to be someone else watching him, it's not like we

didn't know there might be retaliation, but he got distracted."
His foot bounced up and down, more or less independently of
him. "So is that it? Am I cured?"

Trujillo hid her laugh behind a hand. "No. But you're making a
good start. Does this new omega remind you of your late
partner in some way?"

"No." Sam shook his head, and then he tilted it to the side. "I
mean, me and Chris had an arranged thing. It was good, and I
loved him, but it wasn't like this. It wasn't this, this need." He
squirmed in his seat and looked out the window. "He can't
come into a room, or even walk by an open door, without me
wanting him."

"So working with him must be difficult." She leaned forward,
just a bit.

Sam blushed. "You could say that." How was it possible that
he was just blurting all of this stuff out to a stranger? He
guessed that was what he was paying for, after all. "I mean,
maybe it was inevitable that we slept together, but he'd been
saving himself for *his* alpha, you know? Next thing—bam.
There we are. He said he didn't regret it, but he sure seems
to."

"Do you?" Trujillo met Sam's eyes.

"Oh hell yeah." He looked down. "I mean, he's all sitting there
waiting for The One, and then along comes me. I'm supposed
to be stronger than that. I'm supposed to know better. I'm his
best friend's dad. And we're working together, for crying out
loud. I shouldn't be touching him." He shrunk in on himself, as
though his shame could consume him.

Trujillo cleared her throat. "And your sons. How would you
characterize your relationships with them?"

"Well I don't have a relationship with Joey anymore, so that answers that question for you." Sam let his head fall back until it rested on the back of the chair. "Jake and I have always butted heads, but at the end of the day he always stayed by me. I mean, he was an omega; he couldn't live on his own. Or so I thought."

Trujillo raised one eyebrow. "I see."

"He took exception to the way I was treating the omega. His friend."

Trujillo nodded. "Is there any part of your life that isn't bound up in the rest of it?"

"Um… no." Sam had to admit that after careful consideration. "I don't think that there is."

"My first piece of advice is that you get a hobby. Something that no one from your other connections is involved with. That way you have some way of disconnecting for a little while. I honestly don't care what it is, as long as it doesn't involve cops or your family in any way. Knitting. Quilting. Fly fishing. Just go do something. Now. Let's talk about some of these other potential issues."

Trujillo steered the conversation toward his work on the force, but Sam knew that wasn't the real issue here. Sure, his time on the force had made him bitter. It did that to a lot of cops. The fact was, they could turn it off when they left the office. They could live as full, functional human beings after work.

Sam needed to get to that point too. He couldn't see a clear path for himself, but maybe Trujillo could help him to blaze one.

Chapter Seven

Oliver yawned and retrieved the results from the DNA sequencer. Okay, so he was using work to block Sam from his mind. So what? It was a perfectly healthy mechanism to keep him going until time numbed the hurt, and it helped to bring justice to some of the victims whose cases were brought to the Crime Lab too.

Sometimes it even helped to clear the names of the mistakenly accused. That helped a different kind of victim. Oliver was just as proud to help that type of victim as he was to help the first. Justice wasn't justice if just any old person got sent up for the crime, after all.

He could see from the printout that the DNA from the sample was a match to the DNA in the other cases. His eyes weren't foolproof, of course; he'd use the computer to verify the match. And, of course, they didn't have a suspect against whom they could compare the samples. Still, it was just a little bit more information that would help to nail the guy when they did catch up to him.

He picked up his desk phone when he got back to his cubicle. He knew that Sergeant Tran would still be at his desk. "Hi, Sgt. Tran. It's Oliver, in the lab. I'll send you the full report once I get it written, but it's like you suspected. The Academy Street case was the same suspect as the other three. You've got a serial rapist on your hands."

Tran let out a long, low sigh. "That's just awesome. Love those serials."

Oliver cleared his throat. He liked Tran. He liked Tran on a personal level, and he liked the fact that Tran wouldn't let his omega status stand in the way of doing what he wanted. He hated to hear him sound so sad. "Okay. So I can tell you that you're looking for a white guy, most likely with brown, wavy hair and hazel eyes. The hair color and eye color are a little unreliable, though, so take those with a grain of salt. I can tell you that he's likely to be lactose intolerant and that his skin will be light in tone. Also, he's had a vasectomy."

Tran sounded a lot more awake when he finally responded. "You can tell all of that just from a stain on a kid's skirt?"

Oliver grinned. "So the stuff about his appearance, is just what's more likely than not. I know a woman who's got blonde hair and gray eyes, whose genes tell me she should have black hair and brown eyes. I wouldn't go arresting every guy with brown hair just yet. The lactose intolerance has a higher probability of being right. The vasectomy is a hundred percent right, because that's something I could see with my own two eyes when I looked at the sample."

"You're a god among men, Oliver. I'm going to reach out to the locals and see if they have anyone on the list of potential suspects that matches that description." Tran hung up, and Oliver sat back and smiled. He'd done well.

He cleaned up after himself before heading out to write up the report. Suspected serial rapists always got bumped to the top of the line. Part of Oliver cringed from that. If he were a victim whose case risked going over the statute of limitations thanks to the backlog, he'd be livid. To go through all of the misery of reporting, and the shame and degradation of submitting to police questioning and the rape kit itself, only to lose any possibility of justice because of a higher profile case would be infuriating. At the same time, a serial rapist could be stopped. Furthermore, the risk of a serial rapist escalating was too great.

He sat down to work on his report when his phone buzzed. He had an incoming message from Jake. *I can't help but notice that you haven't come home yet. I don't know if I should be worried that you're still at work, or worried that you're not still at work.*

Oliver took a selfie over by the DNA sequencer. *Fun times.*

Dude, you know you don't have to be there. Go home. Watch some Netflix. Check out some of those terrible movies you like. You'll have the house to yourself tonight; I'm going out.

Oliver leaned back in his chair. *You don't have to go out just so I'll come home.*

He could almost see Jake's leer, which just proved that they spent too much time together. *Ah-ah. The agreement was no hookups in the house. Anyway, I'll see you tomorrow. Dinesh is outside.*

Oliver frowned. *Isn't Dinesh the guy from that medical device maker?*

Yup. Gotta go.

Oliver didn't reply, but he grinned. Jake had been out with Dinesh three times. Oliver had met him once, when he'd stopped by to see Jake at the office. He seemed nice, and he was clearly besotted with Jake. If Jake was staying with him the whole night, maybe he was thinking about getting serious. Good for Jake. He deserved good people in his life.

Oliver finished writing up his report and sent it on for review, with a flag that marked it as high priority. Then he looked around. He could probably go ahead and start work on another case. There were drug cases to test and three new murders to work. Even if those failed, there was always the backlog.

Jake was right, though. Those would still be there on Monday. It was nine-thirty on a Friday night, and here he was being a pathetic loser working himself half to death just because of an alpha. He locked his workstation down, got onto his bike, and headed home.

Once home, he fixed himself some ramen and sat down to eat it. He hadn't realized how hungry he was until he walked in the door. He couldn't wait long enough to actually cook; he needed food and he needed it quickly. That was why he had the ramen on hand, he guessed. Just as he lifted the first forkful of noodles to his lips, though, someone buzzed his apartment.

He checked the security camera. He expected to see one of his neighbors had forgotten their keys. Instead, he saw Sam Nenci.

"What is it?" he asked.

Sam looked around and found the camera. He looked up into it, right into Oliver's eyes, before he replied. "I'd like to come up and talk to you, if you don't mind. I'd like to explain a few things, you know, out of the office."

Oliver pursed his lips and glared at the screen. He was hungry, he was tired, and he was still hurting. The last thing he wanted to do was talk to the one who had hurt him. Still, he doubted that Sam would go away. He wasn't sure he wanted him to, either. "Fine." He buzzed Sam in.

Sam was dressed casually when he got upstairs, so he'd gone home and changed before coming over. Oliver could have wished he hadn't done that. At least in the suit he usually wore at work, Oliver could pretend that he didn't remember the solid, well-developed muscles of Sam's body. "Hope you don't mind, but I'm going to eat in front of you. I just got home and I'm starving."

Sam scowled. "Quitting time was hours ago. And where's Jake? He should be taking care of you."

Oliver rolled his eyes and sat back down to eat his dinner. "That's not Jake's job. And he had a date."

"That Dinesh guy?"

"Yeah." Oliver finally got to eat a little bit of his food.

"Oh. Good. He's not too bad. I mean, I'd rather see him with a cop who can protect him, but other than that I like Dinesh." Sam pulled out a chair.

Oliver didn't look at Sam. He wouldn't. Sam's scent was bad enough. "So did you have something you wanted to share about the case?"

"No. No, I wanted to talk to you about us." Sam cleared his throat a little. "About me, really. It's been brought to my attention that you might have gotten the wrong impression from some of my behavior after that night."

Oliver pushed his food away. Damn it, he'd gotten a whole two bites. "I'm pretty sure I got the right impression, Sam. I was wrong for hoping that I could be more to you than a one-night stand."

"Oliver, no." Sam reached out and put a hand over Oliver's. "I mean no, we can't be together, but it's not because of you. It's entirely because of me. You shouldn't waste your time on me. I'm old enough to be your father. If I claimed you, you'd die a good twenty-five years before your time."

Oliver snorted. "You do realize that I could get hit by a bus tomorrow, right? So could you. You're in a risky profession and it's something anyone knows when they get involved with a cop."

"Okay, but the risk is higher. Like, a hundred percent certain. I'm going to die before you." Sam shook his head. "I can't do that to you."

"So you'll just go ahead and make my decisions for me." Oliver pulled his hand away. "You won't actually be my alpha—which by the way, we never discussed—but you'll go ahead and make decisions for me, regarding my life."

"I'm the alpha. And the older one in this situation." Sam licked his lips. "It's probably not great of me to phrase it like that. I'm trying to do better, Oliver. But some things are just ingrained, and you can't unlearn them in one therapy session."

Oliver blinked. He hadn't expected that at all. "You're in therapy?"

"I said I'm trying, okay? I mean look, it's not like I want to hurt you. I don't want to hurt Jake and I never wanted to hurt Joey, either. I've only ever wanted to keep the people I love safe. I only seem to hurt them when I try, though." He hung his head. "Some days I just want to retire, stick to my place in Hopkinton, and not come out again."

Oliver huffed out a little laugh. "You'd never be able to pull it off." He tried to tuck a lock of his hair behind one ear, but it wasn't long enough. "You're too driven." He paused and after a moment of silence he said, "I'm not your son, Sam."

"Well no, that would be pretty gross." Sam grimaced and pulled away. "What I'm trying to say here is that I'm not pulling away because I don't want you. I'm fighting myself here, because I do want you. I want you in so many ways, Oliver. I just shouldn't."

Oliver stood up. "Sam, no one can help who he loves. Alphas and omegas are even less able to help it than other people. Is it a little weird that we have this age difference between us, sure. That doesn't mean that it's not something that we could have worked with." He walked toward the closed door of the bedroom.

He didn't mean to suggest anything by it. He'd just gotten used to the living room being Jake's space. Still, when Sam got up and followed him, Oliver froze. "What are you doing?"

"Oliver, I'm sorry." Sam put his hands on Oliver's shoulders. "I feel like I'm... I feel like I've dropped the ball here somehow, even though I know I'm doing the right thing."

Oliver turned to face him. "You're not doing the right thing here. You can convince yourself that you are, but if you can't trust an omega to know what's right for himself, then you're not doing the right thing by writing him off."

Sam leaned in and kissed Oliver then, not soft or gentle but rough and demanding. Oliver cradled Sam's face and let it happen. His mind reeled from the whiplash of it. "You make it so hard to keep control," Sam growled into his ear, edging him into the bedroom door. "All I can think about is you, do you understand that?" He pinned Oliver against the door, and Oliver didn't resist.

Oliver lifted his head and turned it to the side. "I'm right here," he said, baring his neck as Sam mouthed along his jaw. "Right where I've always been. I've always given you what you wanted."

Sam just made a wordless sound and unbuttoned Oliver's shirt. Oliver let him. He would have loved to say that he didn't want this. He'd have been thrilled to say that he'd convinced himself to get over Sam Nenci so much that he was able to push him away and tell him no. The truth was that he'd never been able to tell the big alpha no, and he didn't want to.

He treasured the feel of Sam's rough hands as they slipped under his undershirt, seeking out the most sensitive parts of his skin. He moaned as Sam's lips teased the flesh of his neck and his collarbone. When Sam pulled the undershirt over his head, he offered no resistance but opened the bedroom door.

Sam blinked, and some of the haze cleared from his eyes for a moment. "Lube," he said. "We need lube."

Oliver didn't have any lube. He'd never needed it before. "I think Jake has some." He winced, only remembering after the words were out of his mouth that Sam was Jake's father.

Sam just tightened his mouth. "Be naked when I get back."

A shiver of delight ran up Oliver's spine, and he rushed to finish disrobing. Rustling sounds reached him from the living room as he tossed his dress pants into a corner; he'd deal with them later. He turned the covers back and sat on the edge of the bed as he heard his alpha returning, his dick standing up from the thatch of hair between his legs.

Was he really this needy? Was he really going to sleep with Sam again, when he knew that there was no future?

Sam came back. The lustful haze returned as soon as he crossed the threshold of the bedroom. Oliver's more scientific mind could tell him the exact chemical reaction that caused it, the precise hormones triggered and in which amounts by Oliver's scent. The rest of Oliver just glowed with pleasure. He had caused that reaction. "Hands and knees," Sam ordered, after pausing to drink in the sight.

Oliver complied. He'd rather be able to see Sam, but if Sam wanted to do it this way, he'd give him what he wanted. He got into position and listened to the rustle of cloth as Sam undressed. The bed dipped as Sam got into bed behind him, and Sam's hand ran along the lines of his body again. "Oliver, you have no idea how beautiful you are like this, do you?" He peppered Oliver's back with kisses and love bites just as Oliver heard the cap on the lube bottle pop off.

One cool, lube-slick finger slid into him, and then two. Now that Oliver had a better idea of what to expect he was less tense, and it felt better. It felt amazing, and he moaned out in his pleasure. By the time Sam added the third finger, Oliver was rocking back onto his fingers with abandon.

Of course, Sam's cock was different than a few fingers. Sam entered him slowly. Oliver panted through it and relished the stretch of it. He tried not to focus on the fact that it was *Sam*, who he loved in spite of everything. Instead he concentrated on the incredible feeling of fullness. When Sam started to move, Oliver was able to move with him.

It was just as well that Jake wasn't here tonight. Oliver was learning something new about himself tonight: he was loud. Sam didn't seem to mind. As he thrust into Oliver, harder and faster than he had during their first time, he added a few loud moans of his own. Oliver could do this all day, and he kind of wanted to.

After a while, Oliver felt Sam's rhythm falter. Sam hauled Oliver upright and grabbed hold of his cock, jerking him to completion just as he finished inside of him. Oliver cried out as he came, all over himself and Sam's hand. Sam held him up for a long moment, before lowering him carefully to the bed.

They lay there for a long moment, still joined, before Sam pulled out. He held Oliver for a long while, and then he sighed. "We shouldn't have done that." He kissed Oliver's shoulder.

Oliver sighed. "I'm sorry you feel that way."

"I know." Sam got out of the bed and left.

Tomorrow, Oliver would cry or something. For tonight, he decided that he would pretend. His bed smelled like his alpha. He would sleep in that illusion for the night and wash the sheets in the morning.

***

Sam drove back to his house alone. He slumped so low in the driver's seat of his Ford Taurus that he almost couldn't see over the dash. He hadn't felt so low since Chris died.

It would have been so easy not to feel this. He could have been back in that apartment, back in that big and comfortable bed. He could have had those arms wrapped around him, all night long, and then maybe a little bit of something in the morning. Or not; Jake would have come home eventually and made them do a whole lot of uncomfortable explaining.

A father shouldn't have to explain that sort of thing to his son.

It had been physically painful to leave that bed, but it was the right thing to do. He shouldn't have been so weak. He hadn't planned to touch Oliver. He hadn't even planned to stay long. He'd just wanted to make things right, to make sure that Oliver understood where he was coming from.

All of that had gone out the window when he'd gotten close enough to pick up on Oliver's scent. The only thing that had kept him strong after that had been his own willpower, and that faded once he put his hand on Oliver's.

He'd been wrong to give in to his desires, even if it was what Oliver wanted. At least he could leave before things went further, before it got to be harder to leave. That didn't make him feel any better when he crawled into his cold bed, but he'd told his sons that right didn't always feel great at the time. It was time to take his own advice.

On Saturday, he got a phone call from Jake. Jake's voice was quiet, as though he was trying not to be heard. "Hey, dad. I don't know what happened last night, and for the record if you try to tell me I'll burn out your vocal cords and make it look like a coffee burn."

Sam chuckled in spite of his pain. Jake had more of his old man in him than anyone could have expected from an omega. "Son, it's not a big deal, I promise."

"It's a big deal because he hasn't said a word all day. He did take his sheets out to the dumpster, though. Look. Just... stay away, okay? You can work this case with him, to the extent that you have to communicate at all, electronically."

"Jake, this is between me and Oliver. Don't interfere." Sam sat down in his favorite chair.

"Wrong. Oliver is my friend, and you're screwing with his head and his heart. I'd love to be able to say, *You know what? You're grown adults. You do your thing, I'm not going to get in the way.* But the thing is, Dad, this is all new to him and you've already convinced him that love is a myth, okay? That it's something alphas just don't feel for omegas. He deserves better. He deserves to be cherished."

Sam's stomach sank. "Look, Jake, you know I'm not trying to hurt him."

"I know, Dad. I know. In a very real way, that makes it worse." Jake sighed. "Dad, look. I know you're trying not to hurt him, but every time you do this stuff you're basically just twisting the knife. Just stop. Just stop. If you can't behave like a real alpha, and treat him with respect, then avoid him. I'm going to ask Nina to have a talk with your boss and keep you away from the lab." He coughed. "Anyway, Joey, I'll give you a call later when I know what's going on. Talk to you later, bro." The line went dead.

Sam stared at his silent phone for a few minutes. Jake had clearly called him behind Oliver's back; he'd pretended to be talking to Joey when Oliver had come back into the room. Could Oliver be that devastated? Oliver had seemed to understand last night.

Or maybe his need, or his desire, had just been so great that he hadn't been able to stop himself any better than Sam had.

Damn it. Why couldn't Oliver understand that this was right for them?

Sam tried to distract himself with housework for the rest of the weekend. He'd never thought of this place as being all that large. Neither he nor Chris had wanted an enormous house. They'd been happy to get the water view. After Chris died, Sam had been too caught up in taking care of the kids and working to think about moving.

Now the kids were gone. Chris was gone, the kids were gone, and Sam was alone in the house. Fourteen hundred square feet had never seemed so vast as it did that weekend. For the first time, Sam wondered if he should sell.

Even though his footsteps echoed on the floors, Sam dreaded going into work on Monday. He knew that the lab tended to start earlier than Cold Case. Jake would have made sure he got there early, which would have meant that he spoke to Nina. Still, there was no getting around it. He had to go to work, or else he'd probably explode.

Much to his surprise, there was nothing waiting for him when he walked in. He headed for his desk and pulled up a chair. Sure, he was apparently flying solo on this case now, but that didn't mean that the clock wasn't ticking. He had work to do.

The guy currently running the Marsten family was a guy by the name of Isaiah Marsten. Sam made an appointment with him to meet up the next day, and then he cajoled Langer into heading out with him for the meeting. Sam wanted to have as much information as possible before he headed up to Manchester-by-the-Sea, so he started digging as soon as he made the appointment.

The Marsten family story looked a lot like the Coucher family story, at least on the surface. Both families had been some of the first settlers to come to Salem, and they'd risen to prominence relatively quickly as the town gained in stature as a shipbuilding and mercantile center. As their fortunes grew, both families invested heavily in real estate. After the Revolution, both families invested outside of Salem, although both families continued to reside in the city until 1904 for the Couchers and 1929 for the Marstens.

A suspicious man might think that the 1904 date might be a little too coincidental, given the overlap with the claiming of young Walter Coucher, né Towne. Sam had been a professional suspicious bastard for a very long time.

He wouldn't have bothered digging this far back into a family's history under normal circumstances, but the Cooper Block case wasn't a normal case. It was bound up in the history between the families. He knew that he didn't need to spend a lot of time on a duel between Frederick Coucher and Alfred Marsten back in 1807, but it certainly played a role in building up to the fatal fires in Cooper Block.

He compiled as much information as he could, working late into the night. The work was absorbing, and it kept his mind off of Oliver and his beautiful eyes. He managed not to think about Oliver until he went home and faced that oversized house again.

The next day, Sam drove Langer up to Manchester-by-the-Sea. The town was pretty, although Sam figured he had enough angst to make up for the difference between reality and the film version of the town. Langer seemed to be a little uncomfortable with some aspects of the case, but he was willing to come along anyway. "So we're just going along to mess his day up because some other guy said so?" Langer scratched his head. "I'm no lawyer, but I'm pretty sure that's not probable cause."

"I told you, sleeping with the enemy." Sam shook his head. "That defense lawyer of yours is getting to your head. Seriously, though, it doesn't have to be probable cause if the guy agrees to talk to us. A guy who's made it this far, and who's got such varied business interests? You'd better believe that he's got lawyers out the wazoo. And I mean really, just because this Coucher fellow seems like a nice enough guy doesn't make it so, right?"

"Oh, so you're going there just to see what his side of the story is?" Langer smirked and cracked his knuckles. "I think my defense lawyer might be getting to you too."

"Ugh, now I feel dirty," Sam complained. He grinned, though, so that Langer would know he was only teasing.

Marsten lived in a veritable palace overlooking the harbor. One thing about this case that Sam would not miss was wealthy, old money semi-criminal families with family compounds that overlooked harbors. A maid, dressed in black with a white cap and apron, let them in and guided them through the elegantly decorated house to a gray back porch that overlooked some kind of small marina or dock. Their host waited for them there.

Isaiah Marsten rose to meet them. His deeply lined face was tanned, and a silver-tipped walking stick was balanced on the edge of the table, but he had no visible difficulties rising to his feet. "Gentlemen," he greeted, shaking their hands. "I'm pleased to meet you."

"We're pleased to meet you, Mr. Marsten. I'm Detective Sam Nenci, this is Detective Ray Langer. Thanks for being so willing to meet with us. I appreciate you taking the time." Sam sat down in the wicker chair indicated by their host. Langer did the same.

Marsten gave a thin smile. "I'm always willing to help the police. A man in my position almost has to be, don't you think?" He chuckled quietly to himself. "How can I help you today?"

Sam and Langer exchanged glances. They got a lot of different types of responses from people in the course of their interactions, but it was safe to say that Marsten's behavior was just a little bit off. There was nothing that they could point to and say, *This is suspicious*, but Sam could feel comfortable with his own judgment that Marsten didn't come off as a typical real estate mogul.

Not that Sam came into contact with all that many real estate moguls in his line of work. It happened, but not very often. He chose not to contemplate the reasons for that.

"Mr. Marsten, Detective Langer and I work on the Cold Case squad. All that we do is investigate cases that have gone cold. Now that arson investigation techniques have advanced, the State has decided to take another look at the Cooper Block fire in 1967."

Sam kept careful watch of Marsten as he spoke. Marsten crossed his arms over his chest, but otherwise showed little reaction. "My God, that was a horrible business. So many people, killed so horribly!" He twisted his face in disgust. "You know, I was just a young man when that happened, in my mid-twenties. I had this long hair—you'd laugh at me now! I remember the bidding for that block. I remember that my father was livid, just livid, when we lost out." His eyes narrowed, and one of his hands clenched into a fist. "The Couchers bid less than we did, and by a lot of money too. They should never have gotten the place, but they did." Then, Marsten's whole body relaxed. "But of course the whole thing worked out for us in the end. If we'd won out, it would have been our tenants that died. It would have been us living with that on our consciences, and I'm not sure that we could have handled it."

Sam had to exercise all of his self-control to keep his opinion to himself. After all, these people weren't like him, or like anyone else that he knew. Their minds were always attuned to profit first. The fact that Coucher had accused them didn't make them guilty.

Langer stepped in. "You think that it was just some random arsonist, someone who decided to escalate?"

Marsten knit his eyebrows together. "What other explanation could there be, Detective?"

Sam cleared his throat and reached into his briefcase. "One of our crime scene technicians found these while he was going through the old evidence." He found the page with the images of the jewelry and passed it over to Marsten. "That's actually how we found your name. The person who identified the jewelry mentioned that someone in your family might know something about it."

Marsten laughed, deep and rich. "Ah. Coucher. I see. Still trying to start trouble, is he? As it happens, I do recognize these. They belonged to my grandfather." He picked up the printout and studied it. "I remember seeing them in his study when I was a boy." He looked up at Sam and moistened his lips, just a little bit. "Of course they were stolen sometime in the fifties. It could only have been the Couchers."

Langer frowned and leaned forward. "Did you file a police report or an insurance claim?"

"My dear detective, I was still in grade school when they disappeared. I don't believe that my grandfather would have filed a police report, though. He was always mistrustful of the police." He smirked again. "He said that they reminded him of the omega that he should have had."

"Your grandfather was an alpha." Sam scratched at his beard.

"He was. It wasn't something that people tended to advertise in those days, of course, but there you are. He was supposed to have had an omega from Salem, but the Couchers intervened and kidnapped the poor thing. I don't know how that all played out, but I know Grandpa never quite stopped carrying a torch for him. My uncle, who was an omega himself, was named for him."

"Was he?" Sam lifted his eyebrows. He wasn't feigning his surprise. Maybe Oliver had been onto something. Sam had been very sympathetic to the Coucher ancestor, believing in the alpha's love for his omega, but Marsten made it sound like his own grandfather had loved Walter to an equal degree.

Neither side seemed to have considered Walter's feelings on the matter at all, at least not well enough to record them. Of course, the Couchers hadn't mutilated Walter and stolen his ring, but there was no proof that the Marstens had been the ones to do that either.

"Tell me," Marsten said, leaning back and crossing one arm over his body, "how did these things come to be at the site of such a devastating murder?"

"They were left there, after the fire was put out." Sam met Marsten's eyes.

Marsten didn't have any physical reaction to the news. "Good Lord," he said, in an entirely appropriate tone of shock. "And you think that they'll lead you to your killer?"

"That's the hope, Mr. Marsten." Sam rose. "Thank you again for your time."

He and Langer left the same way that they had come out. Sam couldn't get far enough away from Isaiah Marsten.

Chapter Eight

Oliver sat down and woke his laptop up from its slumber. The answer to the case was in here. More to the point it was in *there*, in the vast amounts of data stored in the agency's data warehouse. It was all well and good to get at the motivation behind the crimes. That probably counted for a lot, when it came time to get up in court and prove things to a jury. If they wanted to have a face to stick behind that defense table, though, they needed science.

Oliver knew that solving this case wasn't going to win Sam for him. Sam might say that he was doing this for Oliver's own good or whatever, but if he wanted Oliver enough he'd push through that. Oliver was going to solve this case because fifty people had died. He was going to solve this case because ten people had died after that. He was going to solve this case because a dispute between two families had spilled out to affect unrelated people.

He was going to solve this case because it was the right thing to do. He was going to solve this case because he was the best, or one of the best, and people who were good at their jobs didn't just let things lie.

He found the accelerant analysis report for the Cooper Block fire and stared at it for a few minutes. There wasn't a lot there that he didn't already know. Kerosene had been liberally distributed throughout the building, with larger pools near the doors. That was consistent with the high casualty count; people couldn't escape.

A chill ran down his spine. Oliver had known that this wasn't just destruction of property gone awry. He understood that this had been deliberate; he'd seen the evidence that some of the doors had been barred. Knowing how thoroughly the killer had erased any chance of the victims' escape turned his stomach.

Oliver had seen a lot of terrible things in the course of his work with the folks from Cold Case. He'd examined the remains of a teen-aged girl battered to death and left to rot. He'd handled the remains of organized crime victims. He'd processed the remains of victims of a serial killer, right down to an actual harvest of heads from the killer's home. He'd never felt this level of nausea before. Was this normal, or was he starting to lose his stomach for the work?

He pushed it aside and focused on the job. He needed to be here, and present, for those people who couldn't tell their own story anymore. Technology in 1967 wouldn't allow analysts to recreate the crime scene electronically, but Oliver could do it from their notes and crime scene sketches now.

He built an animated reconstruction of the crime based on investigators' notes and known variables, such as weather that night and the properties of kerosene as an accelerant. Then he tested it a few times, both to check his work and because arson was his favorite type of crime to investigate.

Next, he repeated the process for the second Cooper Block fire. His jaw dropped as he watched the crime scene take shape on the screen in front of him. It looked like the same crime, with the exception of the additional sprinklers and the less flammable materials.

The electronic records had a video attached this time. Some enterprising soul in the archives had converted the VHS security tapes to digital recordings at some point in the past few years. Oliver suspected that it was a project they'd given to an intern to keep them busy; it was useful, but not immediate, and it kept them from screwing up anything that would be called into court. Whoever had done it, the video had given them an invaluable resource that didn't exist with the 1967 fire. They had an image of the suspect on camera.

The 1992 arsonist was tall, about six-foot-two. The security footage on the film didn't offer close-ups, but the image analysts' notes said that he had a narrow build and had been wearing big suede gloves. There was no doubt that he was the culprit; Oliver watched as the man barred the door shut.

He was watching a man commit cold, calculated, deliberate murder.

He turned his head and vomited into his wastebasket. He couldn't go on like this, could he? If he was going to keep throwing up every time he saw someone do something bad, how could he keep doing crime scene work? Of course, his job rarely involved watching someone commit a crime. He might shudder away from the things that people did to one another, but he only got to the cases after the fact. By the time Oliver was involved, he could only process the aftermath. He didn't have to watch it happen.

He stopped watching the video and checked the image analyst's notes. They'd managed to get more from the video than he had. They got the fact that he had darkly tanned skin, with deep lines, and a long and pointed nose.

He made a note on his notepad and moved on. There were a few other fires at other Coucher properties, none with the level of carnage found at the Cooper Block fire. All of them, however, showed the same patterns. All of them used kerosene as an accelerant. All of them involved accelerant being poured into the doorways, forcing residents to escape by the windows.

Only one or two had any security camera footage. Oliver declined to watch the video himself and turned to the analysts' notes. Every one of the arsonists apparently looked the same—dark and lined skin, six-foot-two, big suede gloves.

Oliver wrote up his findings and sent them to Nina and to Sam. He'd already heard about how he wasn't supposed to be interacting with Sam anymore, not privately. He tried to swallow his resentment about that. He'd done everything right, damn it. He'd stayed away from him, treated him with professional distance. It had been Sam who'd showed up at his house. Why should Oliver be the one to get censured?

It wouldn't do him any good to get upset. All he could do was send his report and get rid of the shameful evidence of his illness. Only then did he notice that Jake was walking into the office.

In different clothes.

Crap.

Jake was too observant not to notice that Oliver hadn't left. In fact, Jake narrowed his eyes and changed his stride, making a beeline for Oliver right away. Oliver couldn't avoid it. "Were you seriously here all night?"

Oliver hunched over. "Maybe?"

Jake sighed and pinched the bridge of his nose. "Let me guess. Cooper Block?"

"Okay, yeah, but not because I'm trying to impress anyone. I got really into what I was doing. I honestly didn't realize that I'd been here all night until I saw you walking in." He looked into Jake's eyes and saw only suspicion. "Oh come on, Jake, you know how I get with arson."

Jake pressed his lips together and grabbed his arm. "Come on, we're going to go talk to Nina."

Nina took a similarly dim view of things until she opened his message. "I see. Hey, Jake, get a load of what he was actually doing all night."

Jake circled around her desk to watch Oliver's animations while Oliver stood on the other side, holding his wastebasket liner and feeling like a recalcitrant little kid. "That's kind of

awesome. And I can see where it would be pretty absorbing."
Jake glanced up at Oliver. "Okay, I'll believe you this time."

"Thanks ever so much." Oliver waved his arms. "Can I go throw this out now?"

Nina bit her lip. "Take the rest of the day off, Oliver. It's okay. You've been here all night, the hours are fine. Don't make a habit of it, but this is really extraordinary."

Oliver frowned. "I'm being dismissed?"

Nina held her head in her hands. "Oliver, you need to take care of yourself. There are times when we have to pull all-nighters. I get that. But this wasn't one of those times, okay? I'm grateful for the work. And this isn't a punishment. But we can't have you making yourself sick so you're out when we really get slammed."

"Yes, ma'am." Oliver hung his head and slunk out of the office. He tossed his bin liner into the dumpster on his way to get his bike and headed home.

Just to make the morning complete, the skies opened up when he was halfway home.

He took a long, hot shower when he got inside. Why not? He had the place to himself for now, and nothing felt better after an accidental drenching than a long, hot shower. Okay, maybe he didn't know what would feel better. He knew what he thought would feel better. A nice nap in his alpha's arms, skin pressed into skin, would probably feel amazing, but he had no context for it. All that he had were fantasies born of romantic novels and urges he'd spent his entire life suppressing.

Alphas didn't do that. They didn't do comfort. What Oliver was going to get was a long hot shower, by himself, so he might as well enjoy it.

Once he'd warmed himself up, he did go and take a nap, on the brand new bedding that he'd found for himself the morning after Sam left. He liked this new bedding. It didn't smell like anything or anyone. He could never go back to pretending that he'd never turned away from his values, but at least here in the privacy of his own room he could re-dedicate himself to science.

After his nap, he felt a little bit better, and he got up to do some housework. He'd just finished decontaminating the bathroom when Jake came home.

Oliver checked the time. "Hey. Isn't it a little bit early for you?"

Jake shrugged. "I've got some time. You're not the only one who banks hours, you know." He grinned, and then he sobered. "I figured we should talk."

Oliver groaned. "What did I do this time?"

Jake huffed out a laugh. "It probably does seem like everything's coming down on you, doesn't it?"

"You think?" Oliver washed his hands and went to sit down at the table. Jake followed him, pouring him a glass of wine. "I did everything right that last time, with the exception of letting him into my house in the first place. But I'm the one who gets in trouble."

"You're not in trouble, Oliver." Jake poured himself a glass of wine, too, and sat down. "I know that Nina probably made it seem like you were. And, uh, I might know why."

Oliver held himself very still. "Why is that?"

"I was kind of worried about you this weekend. Because, you know, you'd kind of lost the power of speech and stuff." Jake grimaced and took a sip from his wine. "So I called up my dad, and he made some noises. So after I told him to stay the hell away from you I talked to Nina about making sure my dad stayed the hell away. I might have threatened my dad once or twice."

"Oh." Oliver sipped from his wine glass and put it down. He felt completely disconnected from his body, somehow. "I'm not sure how to respond to that. I mean, I should be pissed, you know? Blah blah, shouldn't have interfered, blah blah. And I think I am a little pissed on some level. But it's like… you also care enough to step in when you think someone's not treating me right. No one else does."

Jake nodded and looked down. "Look, I know it's wrong to interfere. I do. Dad doesn't listen to anyone, not really, and I had to find a way to get through to him that he's hurting you." He sighed. "So, what I wanted to talk to you about was what's going on. Yeah, your expertise with arson is crucial to the investigation. But you could have done that from the lab, the whole time."

"What's your point?" Oliver gripped his glass.

"Nina went to Devlin to light into him about Dad. And Devlin apologized. Apparently he'd requested the arrangement, putting you in the field with my dad, to bring you two *closer together*." Jake's face twisted into an expression of unfathomable disgust. "It was a ploy, a prank. He was trying to manipulate you and my dad. He admits that it backfired."

The room went out of focus. Oliver couldn't think. He couldn't breathe. His stomach turned and his body clenched. Nothing made any sense. "Why would he do that?" he asked, once he found his voice again.

"I don't know." Jake put a hand on his shoulder. "But to say that Nina was pissed would be an understatement. You're not the one being punished here. Even telling you to have no contact with Dad, that wasn't her being mad at you. That was for your protection. She lost her mind at Devlin, and then she went and told Ryan Tran *everything*."

Oliver's face burned with shame. "Why would Sgt. Tran be interested in what happens with me?"

"Because he's the most senior omega officer on the entire force, and because he has a very special hate-on for my dad. He's going to make sure that none of them gets to hurt you, or any of us, again." Jake squeezed Oliver's shoulder. "He's pissed."

Oliver hunched in on himself even further. "But... I mean... I said yes. I let myself... I let him use me."

"I know. You were manipulated. That whole mess was manipulated."

Tears sprang to Oliver's eyes. "Does it matter? I'd always have said yes to him. It doesn't matter what Devlin instigated or pushed."

Jake wrapped Oliver up in his arms. "I know, bro. I know. And I don't know if this helps or not, but Dad would never have made a move on you, because he didn't feel that he could offer you what you needed. He would never have made a move if he hadn't been manipulated into it." He sighed and rested his chin on Oliver's shoulder. "I think that Devlin was probably hoping that he'd get over himself and do right by you, but this is why he shouldn't have interfered."

Oliver let the tears flow. He didn't know if it was helpful to have that information or not, but it didn't matter. The fact was that Devlin's interference had cost him, and dearly. Before, Oliver had the fantasy. Maybe he would have found another alpha that he wanted someday, but in the meantime he had a dream of an alpha whose mere scent made him weak at the knees. In his dreams he had someone who would care for him, and hold him through the night.

Reality came with a hard lesson. He mourned his innocence, more than his literal virginity. He regretted the loss of those dreams and knowing that waiting had done nothing but set him up for disappointment. The fact that it had entirely been done to amuse a third party was just salt on the wound.

***

Sam sat down at his desk on Wednesday morning to find a message from Oliver waiting for him. Part of him cringed away from it. What if Oliver was taking him to task for cutting and running on Friday night? What if Oliver was taking him to task for not reaching out between then and now? Okay, so Nina had almost certainly told him not to, but surely he'd be angry about how Sam had left things.

He had every right to be.

As it turned out, Sam needn't have been concerned. Oliver hadn't reached out to chastise Sam for being more of an asshole than he'd ever been before. Oliver hadn't reached out to declare his undying love for Sam, either. No, he'd sent a report about the Cooper Block fires as well as about several smaller fires that had taken place over the past few years. He cc'ed Nina on the message, too.

Sam's hand shook as he clicked on the attachment. He shouldn't be surprised. This was what he wanted, wasn't it? He wanted separation. He wanted a professional relationship. He wanted Oliver to move on and find someone better suited for him, even if it was a little painful for both of them. It was the right thing to do.

Maybe Oliver and Joey would hit it off.

He watched the animations that Oliver had made of the fire. His first instinct was to dismiss them. After all, anyone could say that the fire had done such-and-such. Backing it up in court would be a different story. Then he remembered that Oliver's master's thesis had been on exactly this sort of thing, and he'd always focused on arson investigation.

He made himself go back and read the technical details about the background information that made up the animations. As near as he could tell, they were impressive. He couldn't pretend to understand everything, but he was willing to accept that Oliver did. And each and every fire turned out to be the same, right down to the clockwise direction that the fire spread.

There was no possible way that the fires had been the work of more than one person.

Well, that wasn't necessarily true. It was possible, even likely, that the Cooper Block fires had required accomplices. The way that the accelerant had been distributed through the entire building without being detected suggested the work of more than one individual, but someone had coordinated that. And, of course, someone had struck the match. That was one thing that was incontrovertible. The ignition point had been the same at each fire—one of the pools of accelerant in the doorway, which led to ignition of the rest of it.

Oliver must have worked his fingers to the bone on this.

Sam shook his head. A guy like Oliver was one in a million. All of their lab guys were hard workers. All of their lab guys were brilliant. Even the ones who'd been caught up in the drug scandal had been brilliant and hard-working, in their way. They'd just been dirty.

The good ones were all still brilliant and hard-working, but Oliver was head and shoulders above them. He was the kind of guy that could look at a problem and say, "Oh, I wonder if we look at the science this way, if it will show us the answer." And it just would. Sam had known that for three years; it was part of the reason that the guys in Cold Case loved working with Oliver. He didn't wait to get a request for DNA, and then wait for an analysis on a hammer, but threw everything he could at the evidence to come up with answers to questions the detectives hadn't asked yet.

Oliver was brilliant. He was sweet, too, and so loving that he could make Sam feel like he had something to offer again. Sam had never felt so right, such a sense of home, as he did when he was buried inside Oliver. What might it feel like to hold him all night long? What might it be like to watch Oliver's face as the sun rose over the lake, casting its first rays over his bronze skin?

He couldn't afford to let himself think like that. Oliver was out of reach and off limits. He was young and reckless. It was up to Sam, older and wiser, to make the right decision for both of them.

Instead of calling Oliver and thanking him for his work, he read it in greater depth. Apparently some image analyst had taken the grainy security videos from the 1992 fire, refined the images, made notes in the file, and then put everything away in a box. Of course he did; why would he do something else like tell someone to re-open the damn case? It wasn't like people were dead or anything.

He took the description that analyst had left and tried to be grateful that they at least had that much. Then he called up an old buddy who worked in Arson Investigations now, Kayode Samuel. Kayode had risen through the ranks to become the lieutenant in charge of that division. Sam wasn't even that resentful of him for it. Kayode was a good guy and a damn good cop who knew his fires.

"Kayode, it's Sam Nenci over in Cold Case, how are you?" He tapped his pencil against his desktop.

"I'm doing pretty well, Sam, all things considered. We're about to start on wildfire season, so I'm a little on edge. What's going on with you all? I hear you guys have made some pretty big collars lately. Nice one with that serial down in Lakeville."

"Thanks." Sam rubbed the back of his neck. "I won't lie; it was a while before any of us could sleep normally. That one was mostly Langer's case, but we all worked on that."

"You'd kind of have to. What's going on, Sam? You don't usually call in the middle of the day unless you've got a burning question." Kayode chuckled at his own pun.

Sam groaned. Kayode didn't have many flaws. Bad fire puns was one of them. "Well, as it happens, I'm working on a cold murder and arson. Two of them in the same place, actually. Twenty-five years apart. The second fire had security footage, so we've got a description of a possible suspect. I was wondering if you had some kind of a list or database or whatever of known arsonists who were active on the North Shore in the late eighties or early nineties who might match this guy's description."

Kayode hummed. "As a matter of fact, I could probably come up with something. Why don't you send me the description and I'll see what I can do? It could take a couple of days, just to warn you."

"Not a problem. Time is our friend over here in Cold Case." Sam cut and pasted the description and emailed it to his old buddy. "Thanks for your help, Kayode. I appreciate it."

"Hey, if you're working on an arson case, you need to get Oliver Wesson in the lab to help you out. I'm telling you, there isn't anything that boy can't do."

Sam slid down in his chair. "Yeah. Oliver's been helping on the case. He's the one who found the footage. He built this whole animation, to prove that the same person did both crimes."

"Did he now? Well, I'll have to talk to him about sharing with the class. Thanks for the tip, Sam. I'll get back to you as soon as I hear anything."

"Thanks, Kayode."

After he hung up, Sam stared at his screen for a long time. He didn't need Kayode to sit there and tell him how amazing Oliver was. Maybe they had an alpha down in Arson Investigations who was looking for an omega. That would be just perfect for Oliver.

Sam broke a pencil. It was one thing to say that Oliver would be better off with someone else. It was something else to plan for it.

He had a therapy appointment that day. He took off from work a little bit early and headed into Arlington, to Trujillo's office. She gave him a cool, professional smile when he got there, and then she looked at his hands. "You've been biting your nails, Detective."

"Have I?" Sam looked down at his nails. "Oh my Lord, I have. I've never done that before."

She nodded. "You're under a lot of stress. Anyone can see that. Why don't we have a chat about that?"

Sam squirmed on the edge of his seat. "I don't know, it's kind of embarrassing."

"If it's embarrassing, then it's probably something we should talk about. Maybe we can address the reasons you feel embarrassed and help you to accept yourself." Her lips curved, just a little bit. "Why don't you start at the beginning?"

Sam pressed his lips together, but then he forced himself to relax. This was supposed to be a safe space and he was paying to talk about this crap here.

He took a deep breath and told Trujillo about his week, starting with his brilliant decision to go and confront Oliver on Friday night. Trujillo listened to Sam's explanations. She listened to him pour his heart out. She made little notes here and there, even though she typically didn't write things down. He ended with his reaction to his own suggestion of fixing Oliver up with an alpha from Arson Investigations, and hung his head. "It's all so embarrassing. I dug a hole for myself that I can't get out of."

Trujillo just pursed her lips. "Okay. I don't know Oliver. Let's try the story again. This time, I'm going to stop you every time you say something negative, and we're going to find a way to re-frame that thought. It's going to feel incredibly cumbersome and ridiculous at first, but believe me it's going to be helpful in the long run."

Sam glowered, but he yielded. He did want to get better, and Trujillo was the expert. "Okay. So Friday night I made the brilliant decision to go over to Oliver's place and explain why I couldn't be with him."

"Sarcasm and self-directed anger. Reframe that."

Sam gaped. How the hell was he supposed to reframe it? "On Friday night I made a... I chose to go to Oliver's place to explain myself, even though I knew that this might not be the best course of action."

The corners of Trujillo's mouth twitched. "Better. We'll work on that. Go on."

Sam's story took more than twice as long to tell with all of the interruptions, and Sam got frustrated enough to shout more than once. That didn't bother Trujillo, who just sat through his ranting and kept going. "What the hell was the point in all of that anyway?" he asked her.

"A lot of our issues—such as the issues you've described—ultimately stem from what are called *errors of thought*. I don't really like that name for it, but that's the technical term. What they really are is destructive thought patterns, usually about ourselves. If we want to change the way that we behave, we have to change the way that we think. Instead of thinking, *I'm weak because I slept with this man that I truly care about*, we need to change that to, *I did something that I didn't intend to do, but it doesn't reflect on me as a person.* Does that make sense?"

Nenci crossed his arms across his chest. "But I am weak for sleeping with him. I'm supposed to know better."

Trujillo sighed and put her pad aside. "Sam, I'm not here to tell you what's right or wrong in terms of this omega. That's not something I'm allowed to do. I can tell you that your behavior is hurtful toward him, but you know that. That's why you came in to see me, or at least part of the reason. You want to stop hurting him. That's fine. We can work on that.

"Let's talk about what it is about Oliver that you love." She picked up her pen again.

Sam closed his eyes. He forced himself to relax. "I love his mind," he said after a long moment. "I love how agile it is. I love his scent. It makes me feel good. Safe. Protected. Protective." He opened his eyes again. "I love his trust in me, which is probably long gone."

She held up her hand. "Mind reading, Sam."

"Sorry. I love his trust in me." He bit his tongue against the rest of the sentence.

"Good. What is it that Oliver loves in you?"

"I have no clue."

Trujillo hid a laugh behind her hand. "Come on, Sam. Work with me here."

Sam bit down on the inside of his cheeks. How the hell was he supposed to know what Oliver loved about him? "Well, he trusts me. So I must make him feel safe." He opened his mouth to say that he couldn't see how, but he closed it again. It wasn't constructive, and Trujillo would yell at him for mind reading again.

"Very good." She rewarded him with a full smile. "What else?"

"My scent probably has something to do with it." Sam's cheeks warmed up. "That's just an alpha and omega thing, I mean, I can't explain that, but it's mutual."

Trujillo held up a hand. "Don't worry too much about it. I work with a lot of alphas." She put the hand down. "What else?"

Sam took a deep breath. What else made Oliver want him, as opposed to any of the more appropriate alphas? "I'm good at my job," he decided after a long moment. "I try to be empathetic toward the victims, and I try my damnedest to get justice for them. That seems to be important to him."

"Good." She made a note. "Now just think about each of those things. Hold onto them and focus on them, okay?"

Sam closed his eyes. He was damn good at his job. He was good at his job because he cared about it. He hadn't just learned to care about it after Chris died, either. He'd always cared about crime victims. He'd always wanted to help people.

"Now. All of those negative things that you talked about earlier. Do you think that Oliver sees those when he thinks about you, or talks about you?"

Sam swallowed. "I don't know. I haven't been treating him well."

"But he still keeps letting you in. He still sees you as someone he can love. It's hard to remember that, when you're in the heat of the moment or when you're in a bad mental place and down on yourself. But there is someone who can see those good sides of you, even though you're trying hard not to let him.

"That means that you do have something to offer, Sam. Now, I'm not going to tell you to pursue Oliver or not. What I am going to tell you is that if you choose not to, it's because of a choice you made, because of you, not because of any lack of something to offer. You're a good man. Don't forget that."

Sam hung his head. The ball was in his court. Why did it still feel like he couldn't touch it?

Chapter Nine

Now that Oliver knew what had really been going on with the case, and with Sam, he felt sicker than ever. He thought he'd been foolish before. Now he knew just how foolish. He hadn't just been used by the man he loved; he'd been used by that man's boss for his own entertainment.

Who else from back there in Cold Case had been in on it? He didn't want to believe that Sam had known, but he'd have put almost anything by the other alphas in that department. None of them gave Sam the respect he deserved.

He couldn't let himself dwell on it. The merest thought of what had happened left him running for the bathroom or a wastepaper basket. As the immediate misery faded, he decided that he would exonerate Sam from complicity. He didn't have any evidence, but he'd been just as much a victim as the others. The fact that he'd continued to hurt Oliver after the fact was a separate issue.

Nothing was really changed. Oliver would never trust an alpha again. Who knew what was really going on behind the scenes, or what their friends had put them up to? No, Oliver would consider himself mated to science from now on. Sure, sharing his body with another human being for the first time had torn down all of the barriers he'd built up between himself and his desires, but that was okay. He would just build them up again.

He'd done it before, after all.

The nausea was a problem, but that would fade once he distanced himself from his brief affair. How fragile was he, anyway, that he was left throwing up after a one-sided affair that had lasted for all of two nights? Honestly, the thought was ridiculous. He'd have snickered at anyone who admitted to such a thing, behind his back of course.

The dizziness and lightheadedness were another problem. Good God, Oliver was a mess. He was turning into an official Victorian Lurid Potboiler Heroine. Pretty soon he was going to faint at the sight of blood, and given that he worked with blood all day long, that was a problem.

He knew that all of these wretched side effects would pass. He might be a pathetic example of a man, and more fragile than antique porcelain, but he would ride it out until time passed. The parts of his soul that had been rubbed raw by Sam's defection would scab over, and then they would scar. He would survive, and he would be stronger for it. Eventually, he'd be grateful.

Today was not that day, but it would come. In the meantime, he would stiffen his upper lip and do his best to hide his weakness from those around him.

He finished out the workweek and helped Jake pick out furniture for his new apartment. That turned out to be a lot of fun, and he managed to forget about his own problems for a little while. They moved him in on Sunday, July 2nd, and christened it with homemade pizza and a bottle of wine. Joe came by to celebrate too, as did Dinesh. It felt downright pleasant.

He started the next week at work with a message from Lt. Samuel in Arson Investigations. He was moderately irked—miffed might have been a better term—that Oliver had developed a system to animate a fire scene for Sam but not for him. Oliver just laughed. "It's hardly favoritism, Lt. Samuel. I came up with it on the fly when I was trying to find a way to prove that a series of fires were linked, across time and jurisdictions. I'm more than happy to come down there and show you the program. I'm sure someone down there can improve on it."

He did go down to Arson Investigations, with his laptop, and demonstrate the animation program he'd created. It took him about an hour to explain how the program worked with the different variables, and then the detectives all wanted to play with it. Oliver didn't mind. He liked sitting down there in Arson, and he could have watched the animations run all day.

He'd been fine when he'd been down in Arson, but by the time he got back to his desk his nausea had come back full force. He struggled to keep it contained, but resorted to technical reviews and a lot of ginger ale for the rest of the day.

The next day brought him new samples from a fresh arson investigation to work on. This was a current case, so time was of the essence. Oliver was able to block the nausea for long enough to get his work done. He felt Jake's eyes on him, but he didn't say anything. Jake was his best friend; of course he was going to notice if Oliver was running off to the bathroom every couple of hours.

The rest of the workweek stretched on and on. Oliver's phone didn't ring, other than for work-related questions. Oliver had friends other than Jake, of course, but they mostly connected by social media and they'd scattered after college.

Sometimes he checked out their social media pages when he needed a breather. Richie Heijmans was working out in Seattle. He was strictly a toxicologist; sometimes Oliver called him to consult. For the most part, though, Richie's posts were about why you should only buy drugs from someone you could trust and about coffee. Richie had become a coffee connoisseur.

Tom Alemagna was working down in Florida. He worked for the Florida state crime lab, and his work-related stories were always great, but his social media posts were always from parties and nightclubs. Oliver had never been the nightclub or party type, but right now he couldn't help but wonder if he hadn't wasted his youth. He was lonely. He was always going to be lonely.

Jim Yamada had a steady alpha, down in Austin. They looked happy together. Oliver had to turn his head and click away.

He tried to exercise through his issues that weekend. The dizziness made it a little difficult at first, and he figured that mountain biking might not be in his best interest but regular cycling might not be bad. He took some nice long country rides and enjoyed the scenery. He didn't fall off the bike at all, and he only had to get off and throw up in the bushes once. He considered that a win.

He wondered what Sam was doing.

He shouldn't let himself think about it. He knew damn well that Sam wasn't thinking about him. Still, he couldn't help it. Had he found a new omega to toy with? Was he alone in that house of his that overlooked the lake, or was he entertaining someone else? Someone older? Someone younger? What was it that Oliver didn't have, that he couldn't give Sam?

Oliver shook his head. He couldn't let himself think like that. That way lay madness. Sam had been manipulated just like he had.

He looked up potential causes for nausea. Maybe he had a stomach flu, but it was more likely that the nausea was just a response to his own emotional distress. Just as he'd thought, he was a delicate emotional little flower and needed to toughen up.

He got a message from Sam during the next week. His pulse rose, and he turned his head to puke as soon as it entered his inbox. Jake poked his head over the wall between their workstations, but he didn't say anything. He just shook his head and went back to whatever it was he was doing.

Oliver's hand shook when he opened the message, but it wasn't anything personal. Oliver needn't have worried, or hoped. It was just a request for him to look through the evidence from the 1992 fire for evidence of any trophies such as were found at the 1967 fire. Nina and Devlin had both been cc'ed.

Oliver snarled at the screen, unable to express much beyond wordless rage. He was too good, the lab was too good, to be reduced to the role of servants, getting told to snap to at any request that might come up.

Then he took a deep and calming breath, letting it out slowly. Losing his temper wouldn't get him anywhere. Instead, he considered how long it would take him to process another rape kit, do a technical review on another, and handle one other issue that came through. Then he hit the reply all button. *Estimated 72 hours until delivery.* He didn't bother to sign it. The message was clear enough.

Nina came out from her office ten minutes later. "I'm proud of you," she said, putting a hand on his back. "Devlin is unhappy, but I'll deal with him. He needs to learn not to meddle. Good for you, for standing up for yourself."

Oliver beamed. It was the nicest thing he'd heard in a while.

He worked on the Cooper Block evidence when he was in between tasks on other jobs over the next three days. A lot of the time spent on processing a rape kit was spent waiting; samples could spend eight hours at a stretch in the machine. He went through the evidence, still in its bags, while the machine did its work.

Much like the first Cooper Block fire, there were a handful of artifacts that didn't make sense for the context in which they were found. He found a knife, which had been buried under rubble. No one in the building had identified it as theirs. He found a Saint Barbara medallion. And he found a painted rock, with blood on the underside.

He dutifully waited until he was done with the DNA extraction he was already working on before he cleaned that up, documented his efforts, and moved on to the next step in the DNA process for the kit. He asked Jake to prep the samples from the old items, because he was in the middle of working on the rape kit and didn't want to have to take the time to change before working on the blood samples. Jake was on board, and got those samples ready to be processed.

Once Oliver had gotten the kit samples ready for the PCR, he got them onto the machine and let them run. Then he sent the message to Sam, to Nina, and to Devlin. He cc'ed Jake as well, since Jake had done the physical handling of the samples. The next day they would switch it up, by mutual agreement, because the Cooper Block case was Oliver's case.

Sam didn't reply to the message. When Oliver got to work the next morning, Devlin wanted to know why the samples had been handed off to Jake Nenci. Nina had Oliver's back, though, explaining proper procedures against cross-contamination in such minute detail that Oliver couldn't help but grin.

Oliver ignored them and got back to work on the blood sample. The knife, as it turned out, had a blood sample too. He worked to extract DNA from that sample, although he had minimal hope of finding anything. Fire wasn't kind to biological samples.

The process for getting any potential DNA out of the blood was consuming, and it was fifty-four hours before they could claim that they were finished. That was before the final report was submitted for review, but that was out of Oliver's hands. Under other circumstances he might have called to tell the detective in question that the report had been submitted and to give a preliminary heads-up about his findings, but that wouldn't be appropriate here.

That hurt. Oliver did that sort of thing for other departments. He'd done it for Ryan Tran, whose hatred for Sam was legendary. Oliver's feelings about Sam might be complicated now, but he still loved Sam. He should be able to reach out and give him information related to a case that they were both on, for crying out loud.

It would be a terrible idea, though, and Oliver knew it. Sure, Sam had been manipulated, but he'd also known about Oliver's feelings for him. He'd know that Oliver would never tell him no. And Devlin thought of Sam as some kind of chess piece, or maybe a reward. Something that he could use, at any rate, because Oliver's obvious feelings had made him a target.

Oliver bore responsibility for that. It was up to Oliver to contain himself. He would never show that kind of partiality again. He couldn't afford to. If the results had him vomiting into a trashcan on a daily basis, he needed to learn to keep his thoughts to himself.

As he sat alone in his silent apartment, though, he couldn't help but get resentful. Everyone else in the world seemed to be able to have a normal, romantic relationship. What was it about him that made him the butt of everyone's joke? Was it because of his choice in alphas? Surely everyone involved knew that it was no more of a choice than anyone else with a pull toward someone. Was it his own nerdiness? *Oh, we can use him for his brain to solve our cases, let's use him for our own entertainment too?*

That couldn't be it. No one treated Jake like the town fool. Jake wasn't a joke. So why was Oliver?

Bitterness wasn't going to get him what he wanted, but neither was anything else. Oliver needed to accept reality. He wasn't going to change the alphas in Cold Case. He didn't have control over them. All he could do was change himself. That was the only factor that he controlled.

Someone out there somewhere had to have a book or a webpage or something for omegas, a self-help resource on calming one's own desires without suppressants. Most of them were probably quacks, but Oliver couldn't go on like this. He had to find a way to toughen himself up.

Once he'd wanted to have it all. He'd wanted an alpha, a house, children, a yard. He was ready to moderate his wants. This apartment would be his home for the rest of his life. It was a good apartment. It was safe, and it was near the work that gave his life meaning. All that he needed to do was find a way to heal the ache inside when he thought about Sam.

He grabbed his laptop and started searching. He expected to find a certain number of crackpots. Some swore by drinking eight glasses of cucumber juice every day. That made Oliver's scientific mind skeptical. Cucumber juice might be very hydrating, but it had no known effect on mental health or on libido. Some swore by a combination of essential oils.

And then there were the naysayers. Plenty of essayists had written about why it would be wrong for an omega to even try such a thing. One in particular struck Oliver as exceptionally offensive. "Omegas are naturally built for desire," the author wrote. "To attempt to kill that desire is to kill off a part of ourselves. If you've been through a trauma, seek counseling or find an alpha who will heal you. If you're older than a typical unclaimed omega, find an alpha who will love you in spite of that. Don't shut out half of your soul."

The author's name was Chris Nenci. The article had been published in *Modern Omega*, back in 1990.

***

Sam stared at his screen. He put his elbows on the desk, ran his fingers along his scalp, and tugged at his hair. "This is ridiculous," he groaned, to no one in particular.

Morris looked up. "What's ridiculous? The fact that the entire squad's been blackballed by the lab because you couldn't keep it in your pants?"

'You're hilarious." Sam couldn't manage more than that weak reply. He knew that Morris was right. "This Masshole Hatfields and McCoys nonsense. I can't untangle it. I can barely make heads or tails of the older records."

Morris didn't scoot his chair like other guys did. The others all pushed like normal people. Morris treated the wheeled chairs like his personal playground. He scooted past Langer and over to Sam's desk. "Okay. Why are you looking at Salem trial court records from 1691? I mean, that's before the witch trials, buddy. You're not going to find anything interesting in there."

"On the contrary. I've found two cases of 'unnatural men bearing forth children' — so, omegas—one case of a drunken man who 'became befuddled by strong drink, sold to him by Amos Cloud the Frenchman near ye Docks,' and lay down next to his neighbor's wife to go to sleep. The neighbor happened to be already in bed with his wife. It turned into a delightful threesome until the neighbor stopped by."

"Why did the neighbor stop by in the middle of the night?" Morris scratched his head.

"The records don't say. It was a charming week in the stocks for everyone involved, plus a flogging for the wife because that's how things rolled back then." Sam shuddered. "Next time I hear someone talking about how they were born in the wrong time, I'm going to make them read this stuff. If they can read the handwriting."

Morris nodded. "Sounds like a plan. But seriously. Why are you reading this when you've got an arsonist to chase down?"

Sam resisted the urge to mimic Morris, because he was learning to be a better person. "Because. We've got those things that... that he found in the evidence locker, right?"

Morris held his hands up. "It's your case, Nenci. I've been staying out of it, as much as I can."

"Okay. Well... he found a couple of things in the evidence locker that were on the scene that were out of place. And those things had blood on them." Sam looked back at the screen.

"Right. Because blood at a fire in 1992 has a lot to do with records from the trial court in Salem from three hundred and one years before that. With you so far." Morris gave him the thumbs up with a big, cheesy grin.

"So let's pretend that the blood he found belongs to our suspect, and not to someone else who was on the scene. I mean, there's plenty of other reasons that the blood could have gotten onto the underside of a painted rock in a building that collapsed, right? It could have fallen onto someone's head." Sam sighed. "Or someone could have seen the killer and attacked him. We don't know. Even if... he gets the DNA from those cooked bits, we're not going to know unless the guy's been in the system or unless we find something to compare it to."

"In 1691." Morris nodded. "Gotcha."

"No, dumbass. If I'm going to go in front of a judge, even a friendly judge, and get a warrant to make some guy let me stick a q-tip in his mouth, I'm going to need to have a damn good reason and *he just looks shifty* isn't it. I need a motive. The only people with motive to lash out against the Couchers this way are the Marstens."

Morris grimaced and tilted his head to the side. "They're going to kill fifty outsiders, plus the ten from the 1992 fire, over a business dispute?"

Sam tapped the screen. "See, here's the thing. It's not a business dispute. I thought the same thing at first, but no. At the '67 fire the killer left a calling card—jewelry belonging to an omega who had been claimed by the Coucher head of household at the time, but had been promised to the Marsten head of household. That fight went all the way back to 1904. The ring? That had been cut off of the poor guy's finger in the 1920s.

"That's not all though. If you go back through the historical record, all you see is these two families fighting. For hundreds of years. They've been butting heads, whether in the courts or in the streets, since Salem was still a dusty little outpost. Listen to this." Sam cleared his throat. "Third ye May 1674. Benjamin Coucher brought suit against Perseverance Marsten for ye slaying of three Indentured Servants ye Thursday last. Marsten insisted that he did but seek recompense for the theft of thirty head of cattle."

Morris' eyes went flat. "Human lives aren't cattle."

"It was a different time. We're better than that now. This was the same village that thought it was an awesome idea to hang nineteen women because someone else got high off moldy bread." Sam shook his head. "Anyway, it's not done. Both Coucher and Marsten got down to it right there in the middle of the courtroom, 'with Coucher delivering so great a blow to Marsten that he did not rise for three days and three nights, and when he did he did walk with a limp.' The court decided that God favored Coucher since he delivered such a mighty victory."

"All righty then. I guess that's better than deciding that humans and cattle are the same." Morris ran his hand through his hair. "But why did Coucher steal the cattle in the first place?"

"Who knows? Who knows if he even did?" Sam threw his hands in the air. "It's not relevant to the case. You can see, though, why I kept wanting to go back further."

"It's like you know it's got to have an origin point but you don't want to find the origin point." Morris rubbed his face. "For all we know the feud started back in England. I mean, talk to Langer's mate, he's the lawyer, but I think you should be good if you just document that the feud is long-standing." He gestured at the screen. "This is pretty long-standing." Morris scooted back to his desk.

Sam did call Langer's omega. Doug Morrison was one of the best defense attorneys in Massachusetts, if not the country, and he was in high demand. He was also absolutely besotted with Langer, for reasons that Sam couldn't quite understand. He guessed he didn't have to. Morrison listened to Sam explain the situation, and then he hummed for a second. "Well, here's the thing. I'm a defense lawyer. I know what the evidentiary standard should be in order to get a warrant, and I know how I'd fight it after the fact, but I haven't seen the rest of your evidence. I'm going to give you another number. That number goes to my buddy Chris, he's a prosecutor for the Superior Court down in Plymouth County. He'll be able to go into greater detail about whether or not this would pass a judge's smell test." Doug chuckled. "I've got to say, I've never seen a warrant that included information from the seventeenth century, unless it was for art theft."

Sam thanked him, and then he called Chris. Chris was a lot more helpful, for obvious reasons. "I think that Doug might have played prosecutor in Mock Trial once or twice, but he's more interested in being a pain in my ass than in doing my job." He chuckled. "I think it's definitely helpful for you to establish that the feud is of long-standing. I'm a little weirded out by just how long-standing it is. Why is this the only time that anyone's been brought to justice for it?"

"A lot of things were kept quiet. What can I say? Nobody sees nothin'. You know how it is." Sam grinned for what felt like the first time in weeks.

"Yeah, I hear that one a lot. Go in prepared to show reams of history, but make your request very succinct. If you want to be most successful, have a suspect or two in mind. They'll never give you a warrant to just type everyone in the family."

"Thanks, Chris."

"Anytime."

Sam's next task was to sit down and go through a list of everyone in the Marsten family who might have committed the murders, and eliminate them based on their physical description. There weren't many people left in the family who were old enough to have set a fire in 1967 and in 1992. At least, there weren't many who were still alive today.

He had a list of ten who fit the bill. He eliminated three because they were women. The person on that surveillance tape had a distinctly masculine appearance. He wrote off another four because of height issues. That left him with three, all brothers. Charles Marsten would have been eighteen in 1967 and forty-three in 1992. He certainly could have done the deed. Dale Marsten would have been twenty-one in 1967, and already had a record for various kinds of aggressive behavior. He'd have been forty-six in 1992. Finally, Isaiah Marsten had been twenty-five in 1967, and fifty in 1992. It certainly wasn't beyond reason that he might have been able to set the fire.

Sam smacked himself in the face. This was ridiculous. These were men of privilege, wealthy people who ran a real estate empire all across the North Shore. They wouldn't get their hands dirty with something like arson. They wouldn't risk losing everything, and going to prison, just to perpetuate a feud. They'd hire someone. They'd parcel it out to a cousin.

Of course, Sam himself always said that they never met the smart criminals.

He left the office that night and went home to his empty house. Once he got inside, though, he realized that he wasn't alone. He picked up on the scent of sandalwood and omega as soon as he crossed the threshold. "Pretty Boy," he growled. "Does your alpha know where you are?"

"Pretty sure he does, yeah." Ryan Tran stepped out of the shadows and into the light. He was a beautiful man. He'd always been beautiful, despite the fact that his picture was in the dictionary under the word *hostile*. "The more important question is, do *you* know why I'm here, Nenci?"

"Robles isn't enough man for you?" Nenci kept his head up and his back straight, but his palms were damp with sweat.

"Wrong answer. I've already had a little chat with Lt. Devlin." Tran rubbed his knuckles. "It was illuminating, I have to say. I'd planned to talk about your behavior toward omegas, or more to the point toward one omega."

Sam punched a wall. He didn't have to take this crap. He didn't have to take it from an omega or from anyone else. "It's after hours and on my own property. Property you broke into. No one's going to care if I break your goddamn nose, Pretty Boy."

"You can try, Nenci. I kind of want you to, so I can put you in your place once and for all." Tran smirked. "Why do you think I came here when I did? Let's face it, you and me? We hate each other almost as much as your two feuding families do. In fact, I hate you enough to tell you the truth."

"Oh, and what's that?" Sam crossed his arms over his chest. "Oliver's already found himself a new alpha? Good. He should."

"Oliver, from what I've heard, has sworn off of alphas. Never wants to see another one again, and you have yourself to thank for that. You ruined his future. That was you." Tran poked Sam in the chest, just hard enough to make his point. "But you didn't do it alone."

Sam swallowed. "Oliver will get over it eventually. He'll have to. He's an omega. He's got needs, for crying out loud."

"Get over yourself, Nenci. No alpha's good enough to overcome that kind of humiliation." Tran snorted. "No. But Nenci, haven't you wondered why it was so damn important that you have a damn lab tech out in the field with you? I mean Oliver's amazing at his job, don't get me wrong, but he's not trained to be out in the field and he's not even trained with firearms. Why in the hell would Devlin insist on sending you out there with someone who couldn't actually be of any help to you?"

"Because the job needed a high level of technical knowledge." Sam frowned. "That's obvious."

"Oliver could have provided that from the lab. He's good at that. No, Nenci, Devlin deliberately sent you out there, with him, because he was hoping something would happen."

Sam lost his voice for a long minute. "You're lying."

"Nah. The truth hurts you more, Nenci. And while I do loathe you, and everything you stand for, what I'm actually pissed off about is the way that Oliver's being treated. You were both used and manipulated for Devlin's reasons." Tran rolled his shoulders. "The difference is, he did it because he wanted to see *you* happy with *Oliver*. He didn't give a crap about Oliver. He was just an omega." He turned on his heel and walked toward the door.

"Wait!" Nenci raised his arm. "Where are you going?"

Tran gave a nasty grin. "Me? I'm going home to my alpha, and my kid. I'm going to go home to enjoy the life Oliver Wesson never will. Devlin manipulated you, but you still made your own choices. You toyed with that man. You knew he was vulnerable and you toyed with him. You should be ashamed of yourself."

"It wasn't like that." Sam raced to catch up to Tran.

"Really?" Tran sneered as he put his hand on the door. "You couldn't prove it by me. I'm going to talk to Oliver tomorrow. Hopefully it's going to be okay." He shook his head and then he sighed. "This goes beyond sexual harassment, Nenci. I mean, you get that right?"

"I love him!" Sam balled his hands into fists and slammed them into his thighs. "Why won't anyone listen? I love him! I'm doing this for him!"

"If you loved him, you'd treat him better than this." Tran shook his head. "I mean, you've had a mate. Did you screw him and then leave the house?"

"He told you about that?" Sam covered his mouth with one hand.

"No, Nenci, I figured it out from other things that he's said. Because I'm damn good at my job, which contrary to what you believe is not 'looking good and filling out a diversity requirement.'"

Sam blushed. "Look, about that —"

Tran held up a hand. "Save it. All I wanted to do was to make you aware of what was going on. That's it. Now you know, leave me the hell out of it."

Sam frowned. "You broke into my house."

"Door was unlocked."

"The hell it was!"

"It was when I was done with it." Tran winked at him and left.

Sam watched him go, tears running down his face.

Chapter Ten

Oliver tapped his pencil against the desk and tried not to think about everything going on outside the lab. The lab was his safe space. Everything that didn't relate to a crime, a specific crime, had to be left outside the door. There was no room for alphas. There was no room for heartache. There was no room for manipulative superiors, or well-meaning colleagues, or sneaking suspicions in the back of one's mind.

There were only facts.

Right now the fact was that he had DNA that he'd pulled from two blood samples. The blood came from the same person, a male. There was no way to know for certain how that blood had gotten onto the knife, but none of the bodies found in the wreckage from the 1992 Cooper Block fire had come with stab wounds or pre-mortem blunt trauma. All of them had died from smoke inhalation. Someone, it seemed, had tried to fight someone else off.

It hadn't worked.

He hadn't heard back from Sam about the report, but he didn't expect to. Sam would have gotten the report from Nina, so he would have replied to her. Everything was over. Oliver would probably never see Sam again. If they found someone who fit their suspect profile, who was still alive and able to give a DNA sample, Oliver might be asked to process the sample or it might be given to someone else. He might not even be told.

He found it funny that he hadn't wanted that level of involvement, but now he missed it. If he thought about it properly—scientifically, based on facts, as befitted someone sitting in the lab—he didn't miss being directly involved with the case. He missed access to Sam. He'd been waiting for years to have an excuse to speak with him and spend time with him. Then he had it.

Now he didn't.

Those were the facts. Anything else, any other direction that his brain might take, would be fantasy. Fantasy was supposed to be banned from the lab.

He was about to start work on the eternal backlog when his computer pinged, alerting him to the presence of a new message. He had a new case to add to his load. That was good. It meant that the Cooper Block case was truly over for him. It shouldn't feel like a nail in a coffin.

This one was another arson case. This time someone in the Blue Hills had decided to torch an old car and the fire had spread. A good chunk of that particular section of the Reservation had gone up with it, broken only by the wide roads that limited the size of the section near St. Moritz Pond. Oliver caught a ride with Lou Horvat from Arson Investigations, the lead detective on the case.

Firefighters from five towns had come to get control of this blaze. According to one of the Braintree firefighters, the smoke was clearly visible for miles around. They'd gotten the call from a resident near Braintree Fire Headquarters, three miles away, because she could smell the smoke inside her home and see it out her window.

By the time Oliver and Horvat arrived on the scene, firefighters had gotten the blaze contained to a small section over near the cemetery. Oliver, the crime scene crew, and the detective could feel free to approach the burned-out shell of the car.

There was pretty much nothing left of the car. The tires had melted, creating a foul stench that lingered long after the tires themselves had soaked into the baked-hard ground. There was another smell though, something a little bit different. Oliver paused. He could pick up burned hair. He thought he caught the scent of overdone barbecue, along with something that was a little bit like beef frying in a pan. Riding high, just on top of it all, was something that almost smelled like a musky and sweet perfume, but just a little bit off.

Oliver knew what it was. He covered his mouth and nose. "Check the trunk," he ordered, and stepped back.

Horvat turned to look at him. "What are you talking about? Are you okay? You look a little green."

"Just check the trunk." Oliver staggered away, toward the pond. At least all he'd have to smell there was acrid smoke and stagnant water.

One of the crime scene guys found a crowbar. They managed to open the trunk. Oliver didn't need to look, and he didn't need the confirmation when he heard Horvat curse. "Call the ME's office!"

Horvat approached. "So you just knew the body was there?"

Oliver wrinkled his nose. "You didn't? It reeked."

Horvat frowned. "I mean look, I know you're an omega. If you want to tell me something, I know we don't know each other well, but I'm here for you."

Oliver lost his breath for a moment. The whole world disappeared as his vision narrowed down to a small point, a singed blade of grass on the ground near his feet. He heard nothing. He saw nothing else. He felt nothing, until he felt Horvat rubbing circles into his back. "You with me there, Oliver?"

Oliver gasped, sucking in as much of the stagnant air as he could. "Yeah. Sorry about that."

Horvat gave him a gentle smile. "Maybe now's not the time."

Oliver waited for the medical examiner to arrive. They couldn't touch the body until he got there. Once he did, and removed the body, they could begin to process the scene. Oliver directed the crime scene guys to work in an inside-out pattern. Ordinarily he'd have them work from the outside in, like a spiral, but in this case they knew exactly where the primary scene was. They needed to work out what else had happened, and where the killer had gone.

They worked until dark processing the scene and collecting evidence. Afterward, Oliver gave orders to have certain items processed by the night shift in the lab. He'd be in early the next morning to start work, notwithstanding the fact that it was Saturday. Something like this, an arson and murder, needed a quick resolution.

He showered as soon as he walked in the door. He felt like he had the stink of the crime scene on him. If he didn't wash now, he'd never get the scent of a cooking body out of his skin. He got out of the shower and put on sweats, because he was officially in for the night.

That was when someone knocked on his door.

Oliver was on friendly enough terms with his neighbors. They weren't best friends. They'd help each other out in a jam, but they weren't on the kind of terms where they'd just drop in and borrow a cup of sugar and exchange building gossip. The visitor had knocked, not buzzed, so he knew that they were residents. Probably residents, anyway.

He walked to the door to check through the peephole, but he didn't need to go so far. He recognized Jake's scent through the door. He was less familiar with Joe's scent, but he figured that was the alpha with him. It was familiar enough to him.

He considered walking away and pretending to be asleep. It had been a long day, and Horvat had put ideas into his head that had no business being there. All he wanted to do was to curl up in his bed and block out the world, until he could go to work and block out the world a little bit more. Jake was his best friend, though, and Joe was his friend too. If they wanted to visit, he had to let them in.

He opened the door. "Hey," he said. He didn't bother to pretend to be energetic. "How's it going?"

The twins exchanged glances. "It's going," Joe said. "You know how it is."

"You mind if we come in?" Jake stepped into the apartment. "It's been a while, man."

"It's been a week." Oliver grinned. "Not that long. Although the place does feel a lot quieter without you."

"You mean empty and lonely." Jake waved a finger at him. "I'm a perfect roommate."

Oliver sat down on the couch and grabbed a pillow. He held it in front of him, like a soft shield. "Actually you were," he admitted with a soft smile. "You were a great roommate, and you've always been a good friend. I'm really lucky to have you here in the building."

"Damn straight you are." Jake preened for a moment. Then he sobered. "Look. Me and Joey, we wanted to talk to you. About some, ah, family stuff."

Oliver closed his eyes for a moment. "Guys, I like you a lot, but I probably don't need to be read in to your family stuff. I'm pretty sure that we've established that as close as we are, I'm not going to be part of your family. And that's okay." He forced himself to put on a content face. He couldn't quite manage happy, but he could do content.

Jake and Joe exchanged glances again. "About that," Joe said and looked away. He tugged on his collar, and two bright spots of color blossomed on his cheeks.

Jake reached out and took Oliver's hand. "I've noticed that you've been feeling kind of, um, unwell lately."

Oliver shook his head. "That's just because I'm having trouble coping." He withdrew his hand and curled in on himself. "That's all. I looked it up. It's not that unusual for someone to get sick from emotional fragility."

"Oh for crying out loud, Oliver, you're about the least emotionally fragile person I've met. You've taken everything that those jackasses have dished out and you've shined, do you hear me?" Jake shook his head and turned to his brother. "Do you see what they've done to him?"

Joe held up his hands in a placatory gesture. "I know. I know. It pisses me off too. Tell me, Oliver, have you been having dizzy spells?"

Jake's eyes bulged as he wheeled on Oliver. "Dizzy spells? While you're on your bike? Are you nuts?"

Oliver curled in on himself further. "Look, I just need to get out of the lab more, get fresh air. It's not like… it's not like that."

Jake covered his face with his hand. "Tell me you at least used a condom with my father."

Oliver's gorge rose, but he had nothing to bring up. "I don't own any."

Joe covered his face with both hands and peered out from between his fingers. "You don't own any."

"I was a virgin. I expected to stay a virgin until I was claimed. There was no point when I said, 'Hey, I might choose to have sex, I'll go out and buy condoms just in case.' It happened out of the blue, both times." Oliver stood up and walked over to the window. "I'm an idiot."

"Yeah." Jake got up and followed him. "You're an idiot. But only a little bit of an idiot, because you should have made him wait until he found condoms. He, on the other hand, is certainly not a virgin."

"Oh my God, Jake, must you?" Joe buried his face under a pillow. "That's our dad! I think I'm going to be sick!"

"You're going to be sicker when you're changing diapers for your little brother or sister!" Jake snapped.

The world grayed out for a second. Jake caught Oliver before he could fall. "No. I can't be. There has to be some kind of mistake." Oliver couldn't get enough air into his lungs.

"Sorry, sunshine." Jake helped him back over to the couch. "I know you want to be in denial about it and everything. I would too, all things considered. But it's real. It's happening."

"No. No!" Oliver got up again and ran to the kitchen. He wasn't sure why he was going there, he just had to get away.

"Are you feeling strangely sensitive to smells? More so than usual?" Joe asked him.

Oliver clutched at his middle. "Oh my God."

"Oliver, I'm so sorry." Jake approached and put an arm around his shoulders. "I know that this is the last thing you'd want. But this is happening. You are pregnant. You can take a test if you want. We brought you one. But I think, deep down in your heart, you know what's going on. You're going to have a baby."

Oliver bit down on his lip, hard enough to draw blood. This was a disaster. What was he supposed to do now? "I can't do this," he whispered. He sat down on the floor with his back against the refrigerator. "I just can't do this."

"You can." Jake sat down beside him. "You can, and you will. You've made it this far. And whatever else happens, I'm going to make damn sure that you get the support you need. You're not going to be on the hook for this yourself, okay?"

Oliver nodded, but he knew the truth. There was no way that Sam was going to pay a dime toward this baby. There was no way that Oliver would ask him to, and even if he did, Sam didn't care enough about Oliver to actually do it.

There were more forms of support that Oliver would need than simply financial, anyway. His apartment was fine for one person. It was far too small to raise a child, at least once the child was old enough to go to school. He had no family in the area, no one who could step in to provide childcare during the odd hours Oliver worked. There was no one who could even take Oliver to the hospital when the time came for the baby to put in an appearance. No, Oliver's solitary life precluded any children.

Everyone else that he knew who had children brought them into the world in love and joy. That was the life that he'd always envisioned for his own children. He would have an alpha that loved him, and together they would love their children. Instead, he was going to bring his child into the world alone, just them against the world. Jake and Joe would help out where they could, but they'd have families of their own someday soon. Oliver shouldn't let himself get dependent on their help.

This was an unmitigated disaster, and it was one of his own making. Forget condoms—sure, he should have insisted that they use them. Better yet, he should never have said yes to Sam. He should never have been alone with Sam. He should have conquered his own desires and ignored Sam. Then none of this would be a problem.

Oliver deserved his fate.

***

Sam waited on pins and needles for word. First he waited for word to come from the lab. He was disappointed when the word came from Nina instead of from Oliver, but he reminded himself that this had been his own choice, undertaken for Oliver's own good, and he needed to stop complaining about it.

Of course, there had been a time when Oliver would still have called. Oliver would have given him a kind of early heads-up and let him know what to expect. That would have been too much, though. He used to do that for everyone in the department. It would be too much to expect Oliver to continue to give him that kind of treatment when he had to take a step back from everyone, because of Sam's behavior.

Well, Sam's and Devlin's. He held his temper about that, until the time was right. He wasn't going to get into it with Devlin about it until he'd dealt with the case.

Once he had that report, he waited for the warrant. Then he had to wait to serve the warrant. Fortunately the warrant came through quickly. It only felt like an eternity, since Sam had lost so much on this case already. Should he go to Human Resources? Or should he simply go to Devlin and see what he had to say?

Did Oliver know?

He brought Langer with him again, so that it would be a familiar face. He decided to go in with a soft approach and give the brothers an opportunity to voluntarily donate their DNA for the cause. All three showed up at the family compound for the meeting, just as asked. Sam had no illusions about who was really calling the shots. If Isaiah hadn't ordered Charles and Dale to be there, Sam and Langer would have had to go hunting.

Sam decided to go with a slightly modified version of the truth in his pitch to the Marstens. After all, they were far from stupid men. They could read the warrant for themselves, if things got that far. "Gentlemen, thanks for coming out today. Listen, I'm going to be honest with you. We're looking at another fire on the same scene, and we found some blood on the scene. Now, the property owner, he's screaming the name Marsten. That's not proof of anything. Frankly, I'd like for him to stop, you know?"

"Can't you just shoot him?" asked Dale, with a nasty little chuckle that made Sam's blood chill.

"Not legally," Langer told him with a shrug. "It's the little things. Anyway, we were able to pull a little bit of DNA from those samples. If you guys would give us a voluntary sample, it would go a long way toward shutting him up, you know? He'd have to stop screaming *Marstens!* every time he stubs his toe, and we wouldn't have to bother you about it anymore."

Isaiah Marsten caught and held Sam's eye for a long minute. Then, the paterfamilias stood up. He limped over to the two detectives. "I don't see what harm it could do," he said with a jovial grin. "I mean seriously. I know none of us has been there since we put a bid on the place, and no blood samples could have survived a fire anyway. He opened his mouth and let a technician swab the inside.

The process was repeated for the two brothers, and then Langer and Sam headed home. The technician had his own vehicle and rode alone; he'd get the samples right to the lab and make sure that they got top priority.

"Do you think that they'll actually get top priority?" Langer asked, watching the cars pass by out the passenger side window.

Sam grunted. "I don't know. I mean, they're just as eager to put this mess to bed as we are, so maybe." He paused. "Did you know that Devlin did it on purpose, Langer?"

"Did what?" Langer stared at him with guileless green eyes.

"Put me and him together. To try to move things along, like some kind of romantic laxative."

Langer clutched at his stomach. "Please don't ever combine those two words again. And I think you're being paranoid."

"He admitted it to the head of the lab. And to Pretty Boy." Sam tightened his grip on the wheel.

"That's…" Langer blew out a long whistle. "That's hugely unprofessional. Why would he do that?"

"I have no idea. But I mean to find out."

"I hope so." Langer shook his head. "I'm so sorry. I mean, I know we've had our differences but that's beyond the pale. Whatever happens, I've got your back."

"Thanks." Sam hated how choked up his voice sounded. "I appreciate that."

Langer let a moment go. Then he spoke again. "So what are you going to do, though? About Oliver, I mean? Now you know where he stands, and all that."

"He's better off looking for an alpha who'll still be with him fifty years down the road." Sam sighed. "I wish it were me, but it can't be. Maybe my Joey could do it, if he likes our family so much, but I'm just too old."

Langer frowned. "Does he want Joey?"

"I have no idea. But he's got to get over the idea of me." He shifted. "And anyway, he can't be too attached. I haven't heard from him in weeks."

Langer frowned. "Probably for the best, then."

Sam nodded. It was absolutely for the best, even though he woke up with the memory of Oliver's lips on his. Oliver needed more, even if he didn't know it.

Once the samples were brought back to the lab, there was more waiting. Sam had hoped to get results back immediately, but he knew that real life wasn't like TV. He wouldn't see anything until Monday at the earliest, and that assumed that there would be someone working on those samples over the weekend. He headed home and prepared to watch a lot of baseball.

The next day, the sound of a key in the lock startled him in the middle of the second inning. He pulled his service weapon and spun around. Had Tran come back to take him to task again? But no. The person standing there, with a perfectly legitimate key in his hand, was Joey.

Sam hadn't seen Joey in years. He'd pushed Joey away. Joey hadn't wanted to be a cop. Sam had demanded that his alpha son follow in his footsteps, even though it would never be acceptable from the omega son. When Joey continued to refuse, Sam had demanded that he leave the house, and that had been the last that Sam had heard of him.

For a moment, he thought that Joey might be a ghost. Then he snapped himself out of it. "How the hell do you still have a key?"

Joey snorted and walked in. He sprawled out on the couch and turned off the television. "Still the same old Sam Nenci. Some things never change, I guess."

"What the hell do you think you're doing? I was watching that!" Sam didn't want to yell at his son. He wanted to throw his arms around him. He wanted to ask where he'd been, what he'd been doing. Had he claimed someone? Did he have children yet? Was he happy doing whatever it was that he was doing other than being a cop?

Instead, his controlling side came out. Maybe it was the attitude, smug and a little bit angry. Maybe it was the way that he'd just waltzed back into Sam's life, as though he'd never left. Maybe it was Sam's own issues, demanding that he build up a good defense now.

Maybe it was just the fact that Sam was the parent, and he would always need to establish his authority with his children.

"Some things are more important, old man. And anyway, there's still plenty of baseball left to play this year. Don't worry; the Sox will continue to break your heart. Assuming, of course, that yours wasn't surgically removed sometime between the last time that I saw you and now. From what I'm hearing, I'm not too sure."

Sam saw red for a moment. "Why is it that everyone in the MetroWest area thinks that they're qualified to comment on my love life?"

"Well, probably because we're all friends of Oliver. Well, except that boss of yours. He can go to hell." Joey gave him a bright, cheery, and utterly false smile.

Sam rolled his eyes. "Oh, poor Oliver. Okay. I could have handled that better, but it's not like he's some fifteen-year-old kid. That would be gross. He's an adult, for crying out loud. He agreed to everything that we did. I never lied to him or pretended that anything was going to happen that wasn't."

"You took a guy who was a virgin, and you treated him like a throwaway. You made him a throwaway." Joey shook his head in disgust. "I'm kind of shocked at you. I mean, you always raised me to be respectful of the omegas I was with. Take care of them, treat them well, make them feel like a million bucks. Oh, and always use a condom. But hey, do as I say and not as I do, huh, Dad?"

Sam froze. "I didn't think that Oliver would be the type to kiss and tell." Joey couldn't be suggesting what he thought he was suggesting.

"He didn't have to be. You can smell him. Also he's been throwing up and miserable for weeks, but hey—that's what omegas are for, right Dad? I mean, he was dumb enough to sleep with you without a claim, why would you have any concern for him now?"

"You watch your tone," Sam growled. He clutched at his head. This couldn't be happening. "You're making this up. You're making this up to try to guilt trip me about him or something."

"No. That guy, he used to have dreams. He had a job he loved, and he was saving himself for an alpha who would appreciate him. Instead, he got you. He dreamed of having a family, you know? He dreamed of raising up a nice little family with a loving alpha, maybe two or three kids. He wanted kids, Dad. Now he's pregnant and we can't leave him alone. We're afraid."

"So claim him yourself." Sam looked at the floor. His heart was in his throat, but he couldn't show that to Joey. "You're the right age, you can take care of him."

"Are you honestly suggesting that your child be raised as your grandchild?" Joey shook his head and moved away from his father. "What is wrong with you? You have no interest in your own child?" He stood up. "Were you interested in us?"

Sam stepped into Joey's physical space. "I told you to watch your tone."

"It's a legitimate question. This child is our brother or sister. It's no different from us." Jake met his eyes. "Look. You do what you're going to do. But don't pretend that you're being noble by abandoning that man, or your child." He walked out the door.

Sam sat down on the couch and buried his head in his hands. Joey couldn't be serious. He couldn't become a father, not at his age. Whoever heard of such a thing?

Of course, the alternative was Oliver alone. Maybe Oliver could have moved on and found an alpha who would have been better for him, in time, but he'd never find someone with a kid attached to his hip. Not if the kid was conceived outside of a claim. Maybe Oliver should have been firmer in his resolve to wait, but it had been on Sam to make sure that this didn't happen. He was the alpha. He was the one with experience, for crying out loud.

It didn't make sense for someone who never had sex, and never intended to, to carry condoms around. Sam, on the other hand, was no monk. He had condoms, for crying out loud. He just hadn't used them, hadn't suggested them, and now it was too late.

He took out his phone and flipped through it until he found Oliver's number. Once he'd pulled that contact up on his screen, though, all he could do was stare. What was he supposed to do now?

Oliver was with Jake. Jake would help him get through the initial shock. The last person that Oliver would want to hear from right now would be Sam, who had single-handedly ruined his life. What comfort could Sam offer, anyway? Now instead of an alpha who was too old to claim him, he had an alpha who was too old to claim him and a baby on the way whose father would be seventy on his twenty-first birthday. Awesome.

He hid his face in his hands. He'd already screwed things up with his sons anyway. He'd chased them both off. What the hell good could he possibly be to a new baby?

A new baby, one that he and Oliver had made together. It would have Oliver's dark skin and his silver eyes, but it would have Sam's nose and chin because Sam's nose and chin were awesome and they tended to breed true. It would have Oliver's brains. It would have Sam's courage. It would have a heart as big as the sky itself.

Sam stared out the window at the lake for a long while. Maybe Oliver would let him see the baby sometimes. He'd explain himself away as an old uncle. If he could convince Joey and Oliver to get together, maybe he could be the little angel's grandpa. It would hurt. As he stared out over the shimmering water, he had to admit that he wanted that baby. He didn't want to see another man raising it, even his own son.

What choice did he have, though? He couldn't have Oliver. Oliver probably wouldn't let Sam anywhere near him anymore, and even if he did that didn't change the age difference between them.

He couldn't stand to hear Oliver's voice right now, but they did have to talk. They were adults. They were about to become parents. They couldn't just not speak for the rest of time.

He decided to send a text. *We need to talk.*

Oliver texted back ten minutes later. *Not sure if that's a good idea, Dad.*

Jake? Sam covered his eyes with his hand. The whole scenario had a kind of comic quality to it, with his sons getting so involved with his sex life.

Yeah. He's real shaken up.

Okay. Sam sighed. *Look. He and I need to talk about this. You can be there with him if you want.* Of course Jake would want to play chaperone. Nothing good ever came of leaving Sam and Oliver alone together.

Jake went silent for a moment. *Fine. Yeah. Tomorrow at the Natick Mall. California Pizza Kitchen, 1:30.*

Fine. Sam ended the conversation. His hands shook. Tomorrow he'd face the consequences of his own idiocy.

Chapter Eleven

Oliver rolled his shoulders, shook himself out, and tried to find his center as he got out of the car. Jake glanced over at him. "You okay?"

Oliver moistened his lips. "Yeah. Yeah, I think I am. I'm as okay as I'm going to be." He took stock of himself. "I mean, I'm not thrilled about this meet up, but he was right. It needs to happen, I guess. Might as well get it over with."

"You're coping awfully well, all things considered." Jake stuck his hands into his pockets and started off through the parking lot.

Oliver followed. "I mean, I'm still reeling, if that's what you mean. I'm always going to be reeling. It's not going to kill me, you know? Breaking down isn't going to solve the problem. I've got a lot to do before March, and it's not going to get done if I'm cowering on the floor."

"That's disgustingly healthy." Jake led the way into the restaurant.

Sam was there. Oliver's breath caught in his chest, but he managed to hide it from Jake. At least Sam had the good grace to look upset. That was something. It wasn't much, but it was something.

He kept his pace up as he made his way over to the table. Jake sat across from his father, and Oliver sat beside Jake. This was not some kind of reunion. It was just a meeting, no more. Sam's warm, enticing scent was just an illusion, one Oliver would do well to learn to ignore. He picked up the ice water that had been left out for him and sipped from it to cover his distress.

Sam nodded. "Jake. Oliver. Thanks for coming out."

Oliver swallowed and let Jake answer for him. "We figured it was important to talk this out and figure out what the way forward is, where you two stand." Jake pressed his lips together, and Oliver hunched in on himself. "Like it or not, it's not all about the two of you anymore."

The waitress approached, and they agreed to table the discussion until the food arrived. That didn't take long, and once she returned Jake cleared his throat. "So. Like I was saying. Before, it was just an issue between the two of you. And I was pissed, Dad, because Oliver deserved better. Now, though, there's someone else. And you can argue with me about how maybe Oliver should have said no, or how he should have made you use protection, or whatever. I mean, it would make you a bigger dick than normal, but you have that right. That baby, on the other hand, isn't at fault for anything. And it's my sibling."

"I'm sorry." Oliver looked over at Jake. "I should have said no, you're right. Everything that I believed in went right out the window, and it's my fault."

Jake glowered at him. "That's not what I meant. You going to let him off the hook?"

Oliver snorted. "Show me the alpha who gives a crap about what comes after he finishes." He hadn't meant to say that. He hadn't meant to be quite so bitter. He'd still spoken from the heart.

Sam's jaw dropped. His son's face mirrored his expression. "Oliver, I never said that. I've been telling you from the beginning that I love you, that I can't be with you because of the age difference. When have I ever told you that I didn't care what happened after the sex act?"

Oliver's lip curled. "Oh yeah. You were just so loving. You couldn't wait to get rid of me after that first time. And then you all but burned a hole in the carpet trying to get out the door the second." He pushed his food away. "You make these big speeches about how it's 'for my own good,' but that's just because you don't trust an omega to know what's best for himself. I should have known better. I should have stayed away from you."

Sam looked away for a moment. All of the color had drained from his face. His eyes shone wetly when he looked back, but his jaw was clenched. "Look, you've said yourself that you have no experience with alphas."

"No. I said that I was a virgin. It's not because I didn't have opportunities, Sam. It's not because I didn't have plenty of alphas sniffing around and looking for a roll in the hay. I wasn't waiting for some jerk to come along and show me what I'd been missing, I made a conscious choice. And when I gave that up, I wound up losing everything." Oliver closed his eyes.

"Oh come on, Oliver." Sam shook his head. "You haven't lost everything. You've got a roof over your head. You're going to have a baby. That's what all omegas want."

Jake cringed and put his fork down. "You didn't seriously just say that."

"I wanted kids—with an alpha, as part of a loving family. I have a small one-bedroom apartment. I have no family support and no child care options. When this child asks me who its father is, I'm going to have to tell it that its father so despised me that he threw me away after two nights, and sat here and looked me in the eyes and said it wasn't so bad because I still had a roof over my head." Oliver clenched his hands into fists.

"I don't despise you, Oliver. I love you!"

"I don't think you can spell love, Sam."

Sam fell back against the back of the booth. He looked like Oliver had slapped him. Oliver couldn't find it in his heart to feel bad about that.

Oliver wasn't done. "I used to dream about being with an alpha and raising a family together. Even before I knew I was pregnant, after you threw me away, all that I could think about was staying away from alphas. I knew that most of them were the same. I thought you were different. You're just as bad as any of them. I'm angry, and I'm resentful, and I'm hurt.

"And I wonder what the point of any of this is, because you don't care. You're going to give me some speech about how it's all for my own good, because you don't hear my words. They bounce off some kind of helmet. Nenci knows best, after all, and us dumb little omegas should just do as we're told and accept that it's better than some alternative that involves our own agency." Oliver took a deep breath and gripped the edge of the table.

Sam looked up and into Oliver's eyes. "I'm real sorry you feel that way, Oliver. I was never going to approach you. You have to understand that."

"Oh I know. Devlin thought it would be hilarious. I'm still weighing a lawsuit. You can participate or not, I don't give a crap." Oliver leaned back in his seat and crossed his arms over his chest.

Sam was quiet for a long moment. "You've been pretty good about maintaining radio silence," he said finally.

"Why would I want to talk to you?" Oliver lifted his eyebrows. "We have nothing to say to each other that hasn't been said already. It's painful. It's painful to be in your presence."

Jake turned to face him. "I don't think I've ever seen you speak so angrily to someone in your life."

"I guess I'm due, then." Oliver rubbed at his jaw. It hadn't been all that long since Sam had kissed along that jawline. Even through all of his pain and his grief and his misery, Oliver wanted that again. He hardened himself against it.

Sam sighed. "I know you don't see it right now, Oliver, but it's still for the best that we're not together. Even if we want to be."

"Spare me, Sam." Oliver hung his head. "You've said it all before, and you saying it over and over again doesn't make it right. Maybe it's the right decision for you. I'm sure it is. You get off free and clear. I'm the one who has to figure out what to do about a baby."

Sam shuddered. "My baby."

"Biologically, anyway." Oliver rubbed at her temples. "I don't expect you to be a father. It's not like you were ever going to be a lover."

Sam's eyes blazed. "That's not fair!"

"Oh, so you were planning to stick around that night?" Oliver rubbed at his face. This was all getting out of control so fast. He didn't want to be this. He didn't want to be so raw and so angry. He liked being the nice guy from the lab. "You were planning to make me feel good instead of used? You just forgot?"

Sam pounded a fist on the table. "What went on between us has nothing to do with the baby."

Jake snickered. "Do I have to explain to you how pregnancy works?"

All of the energy ran out of Oliver then. "Just go away, Sam."

"Excuse me?" Sam's eyes widened.

"Just go away. You're not going to be a father to this kid. You're not going to be a partner to me in this whole mess, not even platonically. You're going to avoid any kind of responsibility here and you're going to pretend that you're being noble about it and tell me it's for my own good." He held up his hand. "That's making me angry and turning me into someone I don't want to be. So just go away." He huffed out a little laugh. "You're good at that."

"Ouch." Jake cringed.

"Were you even going to tell me?" Sam leaned in. "Or were you just going to write me off, like you just did?"

"You wrote yourself off, Sam." Oliver looked up at his former lover. "If a guy can't reach out after taking a guy's virginity and check on him, or hold him for an hour after sex, he's probably not father material. I mean, you were once. You raised two great sons, but sometime between then and now that part of you just withered and died."

"Everything that I've done, I've done for you, Oliver. Why won't you see that?" Sam shook his head.

Oliver pursed his lips. "Tell me, Sam. What's the outcome you want here?"

Sam opened his mouth. He closed it again. "What do you mean?"

"Do you want to be part of my life? Do you want to be part of this child's life? Do you want to be this child's father? Because you've said none of those things. All that you've done, through this entire conversation, is try to justify the way you've treated me."

"Well you've been pretty goddamn accusatory," Sam shot back. "I have the right to defend myself."

"And yet, you've never said, *Look, I want to be part of my child's life.* I've given you the opportunity. I've asked, for crying out loud. You still haven't said it. When the subject of the baby has come up, you've avoided it or told me I should he happy I'm having one."

Sam looked down. "You still haven't answered my question either."

Oliver rolled his eyes. Sam was never going to admit that he didn't want the baby. "No," he said. "I wasn't going to tell you. You're out of my life, by your own insistence."

Sam looked up and met his eyes. "One of the things that I always loved about you was how much you trusted me."

"You took that." Oliver didn't have to think about his words.

Sam rolled his shoulders. "I destroy everything I touch, Oliver. I'm sure you can see that it's for the best that I stay away from the kid. Joey and I haven't spoken in years, except yesterday when he came over to light into me about you. I chased Jake right out of the house too. I destroyed you. Now you want me to have another kid?"

"I don't want you to have another kid." Oliver narrowed his eyes. "I want you to take responsibility for yourself and your actions. I shouldn't expect something so difficult from an alpha." He stood up and threw some cash onto the table. "That's for the food." He walked out of the restaurant.

Jake followed him. "Wow. That was some harsh stuff to hear, but I think he needed to hear it. What do you want to do now?"

Oliver considered. "Let's head home. I'll head into the lab. I've got some work to do on that murder/arson in the Blue Hills."

Jake nudged his shoulder. "It's the weekend. You should relax. Take care of yourself. Do you want to go look at some baby stuff? This place has a bunch of cute baby-stuff stores."

Oliver bit his lip. There was a lot to be said for cute baby stuff, but who was he kidding? He couldn't let himself get excited for the baby yet. He didn't want to get excited about the baby. He just wanted to get back to work. "I still haven't decided what to do about the baby yet," he admitted. "I don't want to buy a bunch of stuff if I'm going to give it up or just not have it."

Jake paled. "Would you really get rid of it?"

Oliver shrugged. "I don't know. I have to consider all of my options here." He blinked back tears. "I don't necessarily like the idea, but, I mean, it's not like I should be having a kid."

Jake put his hands on Oliver's shoulder. "Oliver, forget about the fact that the baby would be part of my family for a minute. A termination in men is surgical. This early, it would have a forty percent chance of leaving you sterile."

Oliver rolled his eyes. "And this is a problem why? I should look into that anyway, even if I carry the baby to term." He shook his head. "There's still time, I need to think about this carefully, but let's face it, Jake. I'm an idiot. I make bad choices. I shouldn't be out there having kids."

Jake gave him a little shake and then threw his arms around Oliver. "C'mon, bro. Don't let him do this to you. You're a fantastic guy. Don't let my dad change you into himself."

Oliver ducked his head. "I don't want to. Lord knows, I don't want to. I'm trying. I'm just really, really lost here."

Jake kept an arm around his shoulder and guided him out toward the parking lot. "We'll go home and watch some B movies, you love those. Come on."

Oliver let his friend drive him home. They did curl up on the couch and watch some truly awful movies. Jake brought some popcorn and yogurt, urging one or the other on Oliver since he hadn't eaten his lunch. By the time bedtime rolled around, Oliver had started to feel a little bit more human.

He still hadn't come to a decision about the baby. His mind hadn't changed about his own fitness as a parent, but it was less clouded with despair. He would figure out what to do with clear eyes and a calm heart, and he would make a decision based on reason.

***

Sam needed someone to talk to, and he needed it badly. He'd gone home after the disastrous meeting with Oliver and Jake, and he'd tried to puzzle through everything that had gone wrong. He couldn't figure it out. There was no point at which he could say *yes, here's where things unraveled, here's where I lost control.*

Maybe he'd never been in control to begin with.

He called in to work and made an emergency appointment with Dr. Trujillo. It did bother him, on some level, that there wasn't anyone in his life with whom he was close enough that he could call and talk things out, but there wasn't anything he could do about it now. He needed to get his crap together.

Trujillo had an opening at ten, so Sam drove into Arlington and sat himself down in her office. "You look like you're in a bit of a crisis, Sam." She pulled out her recorder. "What's going on?"

"The omega's pregnant." The words had been echoing through his brain all night. Hearing them finally find their way out of his mouth still made him jump. "He's pregnant."

Trujillo pursed his lips. "Use his name, Sam."

Sam opened his mouth. He closed it again. Oliver's name was on his lips, but he couldn't get the word out. "If I say it, that makes it real."

"Why do you think that I want you to say it?" Trujillo smiled, just a little bit. "You can't come up with a plan, or even confront the situation properly, until it's real."

Sam closed his eye. He grabbed one of the throw pillows on the couch and hugged it to himself. "Oliver is pregnant." He opened his eyes and found them wet. "Oliver's pregnant, with my baby, and he told me to go away."

Trujillo's eyes widened. "That's a little extreme, even for someone in a hormonally charged situation. Why don't you go ahead and tell me what happened. From the beginning."

Sam swallowed. He told her about Ryan Tran's visit, and his revelation about Devlin's manipulations. He told her about Joey's visit and his announcement. He told her about the disastrous meeting with Oliver and Jake, and about how he'd spent the whole of last night rocking on the floor and looking at baby pictures of the twins.

She spoke only to ask questions until he was finished. Then she sat in silence for two full minutes as a cold sweat ran down Sam's back. "Your boss' behavior troubles me," she said finally. "We'll get to that in a minute. But first, it sounds like Oliver is very angry. Why do you think he's angry?"

Sam cradled his head in his hands. "I don't understand it. Not really. I've explained that we can't be together because of my age and everything, and he doesn't really have the right to expect that I'll just roll over and claim him in spite of what I've told him. But the things that he said, that I treated him like trash?"

"From what you've said, you were out the door or urged him to be out the door within minutes of intercourse. This isn't normal sexual behavior, but he's been led to believe that it is. And, given his sexual history, for Oliver it now *is* normal sexual behavior." Sam felt his face getting red with anger, but Trujillo held up a hand. "I'm not passing judgment here, Sam. I'm trying to help you to see things through his eyes, because you already know how things look through your own eyes. That's one of the things we're working on, remember?"

Sam forced himself to unclench his fists. "Yeah. Sorry. I'm just—he knows I love him. I've told him."

"He told you that your actions don't line up with your words. I think that one of your issues, something we've talked about, is control, Sam." She took off her glasses. "You are a good man. I know that you are. Unfortunately for you, the loss of your first omega exacerbated normal alpha tendencies toward control. You've developed a need to be in control of a great many things, because when you weren't in control something bad happened. This is an understandable outcome.

"The problem is, that this tendency has had negative consequences for you and your family. You've lost your sons because of your attempts to control their careers, as you've discussed. Your attempts to control the entirety of your relationship with Oliver have exacerbated the rift with Jake.

"And now you have the situation with Oliver."

Sam shook his head. "That's completely separate from my issues with my family." He hugged the pillow tighter.

"Well, it isn't. Your sons are backing Oliver, for one thing. They know what you're like, and they're demanding better treatment for their friend. Which, I want to point out, means that they know that you're capable of behaving better toward Oliver. Furthermore, Oliver is carrying your child. That makes this a family issue for you as well as a romantic one."

"He told me to go away. He said he didn't expect me to be a father." Sam slid down on the couch. "He doesn't think I can be better."

"That should trouble you." Trujillo rested her elbows on her knees. "You're trying very hard to get better but you're going to lose him."

"I'm not trying to get him!" Sam picked at the corner of his pillow. "I told Joey to claim him."

"Does Oliver not get a say?" She raised an eyebrow.

"It's for his own good." Sam shook his head. "It's a better provision for him, and the baby, than I could offer. I mean, look at me. There's not a single person in my life that I haven't pushed away yet. Except you, and that's because I'm paying and because you like the challenge."

Trujillo chuckled. "Valid. Have you ever tried to get any of them back?"

Sam scowled. He was going to have to talk to this pillow's parents if he held it any closer. "Why would I do that? They're right about me. When Joey came over, I wanted to hug him and talk to him about himself. I hadn't spoken to him in *years*. For all I know I'm already a grandfather. Instead, I was nasty with him, because he started mouthing off about Oliver and I got mad. I couldn't make myself tell Oliver that I wanted to be in the baby's life, even though I'd just been thinking about it. I just couldn't do it."

"You have a hard time showing that kind of vulnerability." Trujillo nodded. "You've been burned before. And, to be honest, it's probably difficult for you to put aside your parental side when dealing with your sons. You haven't had a co-parent since they were five. It's going to be difficult, to say the least, for you to learn to let go and accept that they're adults."

"I want to." Sam spoke into the pillow. "I just don't know how."

"Write letters."

"Excuse me?"

Trujillo grabbed a notepad and a pen and handed them to him. "Write letters. I'm not saying that you should only employ non-verbal communication for the rest of your life, but if you start out by writing letters, it will be easier for you to sort out your thoughts and feelings in your own time. You can do it when you're calmer, and you can do it when you don't have that emotional stimulus right in your face. Also, it's something that they can refer back to if they're having doubts." She grinned. "You can tell them your therapist made you do it if you want."

"Okay." It sounded like a lot of half-assed science to Sam, but he'd give it a try.

"Now, about your boss. Why would he do something like that to you? Does he seem like a deliberately cruel man?"

"No." Sam didn't have to think about that one. "He's always been a good guy. He's stood up for me a bunch of times, when my mouth has gotten me into trouble." He hung his head. "I honestly should just let him get away with it and not say anything. He's done so much for me."

Trujillo bobbed her head from side to side. "So he's done a lot for you. And you say that you've been interested in Oliver for a long time."

"Yeah. For years. I thought that I'd kept it well hidden, but apparently not." Sam looked over at her. "You think that he did it to help."

"You do have people around you that care for you, Sam. You had a colleague who noticed that you were unhappy about some things in your life, and recommended that you get some help for it. That's how you got here." She gestured around the office. "Your boss seems to have wanted you to be happy as well. It was misguided, and it was wrong of him. It hurt Oliver, but he was trying to help you."

"It was wrong of him to hurt Oliver." Sam clenched his hands into fists.

She gave his fists a pointed stare but said nothing. "It was. Alphas are supposed to protect omegas." Then she sighed. "I'm not going to pretend to know what you should do about the baby, Sam. That's not something you can decide on in an hour, and it's an intensely personal decision for the couple. Or for the person carrying the baby." She met his eyes. "It's entirely possible that it's too late. I won't lie. But it will definitely be too late if you don't make the attempt to share your feelings with Oliver."

Sam nodded. She was right. "I'll do it. The letters, I mean. Everything I said in person just pissed him off more." He looked up at her again. "Why wouldn't he be happier about having a baby? I mean, Jake even got pissed at me for saying that."

She bowed her head for a second. "He'd be raising a child alone, with no support. He might face discrimination for being a single omega parent and he might be censured at work for having sex with a colleague."

"Oh. I hadn't thought about that." He hung his head. "I raised my kids alone, but I had their grandparents and stuff."

"And you were a widower. It's different for someone who got pregnant when they shouldn't have. Especially since I'm guessing he comes from some sort of religious background, considering that he was saving himself as you mentioned." The timer pinged. "Give some thought to what I've said, and I'll see you for your regular appointment on Thursday."

Sam shook her hand and headed home. Once he got there, he headed out onto the deck and stared at the lake for a moment. Then he took out his pen and started to write.

He wrote to Joey first. He apologized for his behavior on Saturday. *I'll probably always have an issue with falling into that "parent" mindset. That's what the therapist said, anyway, but I'll do better if I know about it and try to fight it. I don't know if it makes you feel any better, but my plan was to ask you how you were and talk about what you were up to. I disappointed myself by fighting with you.*

I miss you.

You're a good man, and a good alpha. I'm proud of you. I still think that what we talked about would be the best solution for Oliver, but I have to say that I'm proud of you for thinking of Oliver's wants and needs first. That's what makes you the better choice, honestly. A good alpha protects omegas. I've failed in every possible way.

But that's not here or there. My point is that you're amazing, and I love you, and I'm proud of you. Even over the past few years when we weren't speaking, I've been proud of you. Please come home.

His next letter was to Jake. *I wanted to thank you for taking care of Oliver. I know I've dropped the ball, and you're right to be disappointed in me. You're a good son, an incredible man, and an amazing omega. I'm proud of you.*

I know that you're not doing what you wanted to do your whole life. I'm sorry that I blocked that. I hope you've learned to love the lab. I know that your work is considered top-notch. I have my biases, and I couldn't overcome what happened to your dad. Not even for you. I'm sorry. That's not on you, that's on me. I'm so sorry that it's taken me this long to get my head out of my ass.

And then there's the whole thing where putting my omega son in harm's way made my blood run cold. It shouldn't be different for omegas, but it is. I'm working to get better.

Finally, I'm glad you're standing up to me. I don't always act like it, but I am. I think I need that. It means that you haven't given up on me. If you're still willing to stand up and get in my face, you still think there's someone in there worth saving. I love you, son. Thank you.

The last letter was to Oliver. He had to sit there for a long time before he could figure out what to say to Oliver. Finally, he put pen to paper. *Oliver, I know I've put you in pain. I'm still putting you in pain, and I'll probably never even know all of the ways. I'm an alpha. I can't understand everything.*

I do want to have some presence in our child's life. I don't know in what capacity yet. I'm too old to become a father. I'll be on my way out when the baby's just starting out in life. What kind of a legacy is that to give? I'm a mess, and I know it. Rather, I'm just learning how much of a mess I am. You've seen how much damage I've done with my sons, who hate me.

I could play the part of an old great uncle, though. And I'll do the child support thing. You won't be on your own in that way.

I'm so sorry I made you feel the way I did. I have this thing where I just shoot my mouth off, I push people away. Losing your respect and affection is the biggest blow of all. I loved Chris. It was never like what I feel for you, and some days I just want to sink right down into the earth.

I am sorry for everything that I've done to you. I'm sorry that I made your first experience bad. I'm sorry that I've ruined your hopes and your dreams. If it's ever in my power to do something to bring you closer to happiness, please let me know.

Sam stared at the letter for a long moment, and then he folded it up and put it into an envelope. If he tried to edit it, he'd wind up burning it.

The next morning, he slipped Oliver's letter into his mailbox, and Jake and Joey's letters into Jake's mailbox. He didn't have any other way to get Joey's to him. Then he headed to his own office, where the DNA results from the Marsten swabs awaited him.

Chapter Twelve

Oliver walked into his office with a big smile on his face. He greeted the receptionist. He shook hands with the janitor, who was mopping up after what looked like a rookie cop's failure to reach the barrel after a visit to the morgue. He high-fived Javier, and took his seat with enthusiasm.

"Tell me that's just hormonal," Jake groaned from his seat.

"Nope." Oliver passed one of the two coffees he'd brought in over to his best friend. "I've decided I'm not going to let anger and bitterness rule my life. I meant what I said yesterday. It was turning me into someone I don't want to be. I *am* that happy guy at the office who loves his job and is there because he wants to be. Sam doesn't get to take that from me unless I allow it, and I'm stronger than that." He drummed his hands on the desk for a moment.

"And what's not to be happy about, huh?" He threw his arms out wide. "Look around you. Every one of these files is a question. Every one of these questions can be answered. By us, us people sitting here in our white coats, with our computers and our machines and our big and beautiful brains." He smiled even more widely, until he thought that his head might fall off. "Out there, beyond that door, there are problems. I've got problems. You've got problems. Javier's got problems, Molly's got problems, Deepika's got problems. But once that door is closed, all we have are questions and answers. If we just do our jobs, put one foot in front of the other, we can put the questions and answers together and everything will make sense."

Javier, Molly, and Deepika all applauded. Jake just raised an eyebrow at him. "Very inspiring," Jake said, as the others turned back to their tasks. "This does explain the number of days you forgot to come home and stayed at the lab all night. Did you get a letter in your mailbox this morning?"

"I did!" Oliver kept his huge, manic grin plastered on his face. He booted up his computer and stared straight at the screen. He wasn't willing to look at Jake. That might have put a crack in his cheer.

"Did you read it?"

Oliver logged in. "I did not! That letter was likely to contain Problems, and Problems need to stay outside the lab." He kept his voice light and cheerful.

"Okay, but Oliver, I think he's really trying to fix things. I'm not sure what your letter or Joey's letter said, but he admitted that he has some issues that he's trying to work through. He's trying to get better. Maybe you don't want to make a hasty decision before you read it."

Oliver put his hands flat on his desk. "Jake," he said, and he let the cheer fade from his voice, "I feel like I've given him so many chances to explain himself that I might as well be a daytime talk show. Nothing changes. It's all about him. Everything is all about him, and how he knows what's best. It's all an excuse. And it's fine—I mean, he has the right to make decisions for himself, that suit his needs and everything, but he doesn't get to sit there and decide what I really want or need.

"Every time that I interact with him, I get hurt. Every time. So sure, I love him. I don't know why at this point, because he's not half the man I thought he was, but I'm in kind of a crap situation here and I don't have time to wait for him to come around. I don't have time to hold his hand or tell him how special he is. He's decided, whatever excuse he wants to slather over it, that he's not going to be with me or this kid." He snapped his fingers. "Okay, fine. Done. He's out, but now I have to focus on what comes next and how to get to what comes next and still keep my identity."

Oliver picked up his head. "My life is crap right now. But you know what?" He slathered that smile back onto his face. "I've still got the lab. I've got this place, where I don't have to sit around and think about how I might cheerfully kill to wake up in someone's arms, just once, but I'll never get that chance. Or how, assuming that I keep this baby, if something happens to me it will go directly into the foster care system because I'm all it has. Or how if I lose my job I'll be homeless with a baby on the way, or with a baby. Or how there isn't anyone around who can take me to the hospital when the time comes, because it's no one else's job. Just mine, because I was stupid." He blinked back tears.

"I can't do anything about any of that right now. But you want to know what I can do something about?" He picked up a file. "I can test these samples for the presence of heroin. And if there is heroin, I can contribute to keeping it off the streets. That will keep it from messing up hundreds of lives. I have to keep my head on straight in order to do that. So—problems stay outside the lab, the damn letter stays in its box, and I get to be the happy guy in the lab who loves his job and is here because he wants to be."

Jake blinked back tears too. "I wish it could be different, bro."

"I used to." Oliver bowed his head. "Now I just want to get through it."

Oliver tested the samples with the GC-MassSpec. Just as he'd thought, the substance was in fact heroin. It wasn't pure heroin, though. The drug had been cut with a lot of filler, to include quinine and rat poison. That made Oliver raise his eyebrows. Quinine was a toxic, but not uncommon, filler for street heroin. Rat poison might cross the line into murder.

Of course, it wasn't his place to prosecute. All that he did was write up the report. It was up to the detectives from whatever jurisdiction had submitted the samples to pursue the dealers, and up to the prosecutor to get the conviction. Oliver would testify in court when they'd done their jobs, months or even years after he'd run the tests. That was the extent of his involvement.

He wrote up the report and started to prep the samples for another piece of the backlog when he got a message. This one was from Ray Langer. *We just arrested Isaiah Marsten for the 1992 Cooper Block fire. You want to come and take a gander?*

Oliver blinked at his screen. Who said *take a gander* these days? He declined the invitation. *Thanks, but my place is here.*

The truth was, he wanted to go. He wanted to at least watch the interrogation. He'd been there for the beginning of the case. He should get to be there for the end of the case, too. It was only right.

He couldn't trust the guys from Cold Case. Who knew if they'd been in on this whole plot? Maybe they had, maybe they hadn't, but Oliver couldn't be sure. That meant that he couldn't be sure that this invitation wasn't part of a setup to try to get him and Sam back together.

Something else Sam had cost him.

He wasn't going to think about that. He was going to be the happy guy in the lab. He turned back to working on his samples, and kept working on them until he left for the day.

On his way out, he saw that letter sitting in his mailbox again. His hand hovered over it. He could take it out and bring it home. At home he could read it and get as angry as he needed to, and then he could let it all go away by the next morning.

He walked away, leaving the letter where it was. He didn't owe Sam anything, certainly not his attention. He couldn't move forward if he let Sam keep tugging him back, and there would always be part of him that would want that letter to be something it couldn't. He'd want it to be a love letter, or an apology. He'd want Sam to ask him to come back, which Sam would never do. He'd want Sam to admit that he was wrong, which would happen only after the world ended.

He went home, grabbed some food, and considered his options yet again.

He ran a quick budget. He might be able to afford to have this baby, if he could find a comparatively inexpensive daycare facility. Of course, that wouldn't cover all of the times he got called in to deal with sudden finds or emergencies. The baby would just have to deal with growing up at crime scenes.

What a life. Shuttled from crime scene to crime scene, stuck sitting in a car or at Oliver's desk while Oliver worked. It wasn't like Oliver could afford to quit his job, either. Maybe sometimes Joe or Jake would be willing to watch their little sibling, but that wasn't something he could ask of them all that often and they both had jobs that involved being on-call themselves.

Then there was the apartment situation. Oliver couldn't afford to buy yet. If he tried to upgrade to a bigger apartment, he wouldn't be able to afford daycare at all. Sure, they could share the bedroom. That would be fine until school started, he guessed, or until they were both trying to get dressed independently of each other.

None of that had any bearing on the mental or emotional toll of parenthood. People liked to pretend that having a child was just a few sleepless nights and then all cuddles and giggles. Oliver knew better. Kids got fussy. They got whiny. They got demanding. They threw tantrums. In Oliver's case, there wasn't going to be anyone else who could step in when things got to be too much. It was going to be all him, twenty-four-seven, forever.

Rebellion welled up in his heart. Why in the hell should it be all him, anyway? He hadn't been the only one to make this baby! Why should Sam get away without any consequences while Oliver had to suffer?

He forced those thoughts away. He knew why. That was just the way that things were. He could probably go after Sam for child support, which would ease some of the financial burden, but that wouldn't help with any of the other issues.

Abortion was one option, but it wasn't viable. Omega abortions were technically legal in Massachusetts, but few doctors would perform them. It wasn't so much a moral decision as a matter of risk. An omega didn't develop an opening for a fetus to emerge from until the point of birth, so an abortion had to involve risky abdominal surgery with a long recovery time. Most doctors wouldn't accept that kind of risk unless the omega in question's life were in immediate danger. He might be able to find someone who would do it, but the long recovery time was daunting.

That left adoption. Oliver could always have the baby adopted by someone who couldn't give birth themselves. The thought alone gave him chest pains, and for a moment he wondered if he should go to the hospital. They subsided after a moment, and he returned to his contemplation.

He didn't necessarily want to give up his baby. He didn't want to be a parent, either, not alone, but the thought of carrying the baby under his heart, going through birth, and then having nothing to show for it made him cry. He'd already lost his alpha, his hopes, his dreams, and even his innocence. This baby was his only chance to have anything like a family. Now he had to seriously consider giving it to someone else.

At the same time, what kind of a life could he offer this child? He was in no position to raise a child alone. He wasn't suited to it. He might be able to scrape by financially, but only if there were no surprises. That didn't take into account the physical, mental, or emotional toll on him.

Let people call him selfish. He'd seen how it could be for a kid, to grow up with a parent that had no support at all and just couldn't cope. He'd been there, he'd done that, he had the damn tee shirt. He couldn't justify doing that to any child, never mind one that he had carried under his heart for nine months. Not one that he loved.

He dropped his hand down to his belly. He wasn't showing yet; that was a long way off. He couldn't feel the baby either. He could admit, though, deep inside, that he loved this baby. He might not want it, but he loved it. He loved it too much to subject it to the life he'd had growing up.

He headed off to bed. He knew what he had to do. He hated it. Something inside of him screamed out in pain at the thought, and he couldn't do anything to stop it. He was an omega, damn it. He needed connections. He needed a family of some kind, any kind. He had Jake, but Jake would have a family of his own soon. He had a few casual friends, but no one he could lean on. This baby was his one chance, and he couldn't take it and still look at himself in the mirror.

Oliver was going to die alone and forgotten. It was an omega's greatest fear. As he passed himself in the bathroom mirror, he imagined that he could see his whole life stretching out before him. The lab moved around him as he sat at his workstation; head graying as he bowed over his work. On the day that he finally collapsed, eyes sightless and staring, the lab moved on around him, like no one had even noticed.

Oliver headed to bed. At least he had the lab. It would probably be a different lab. He didn't think he could sit and watch other people move on and be happy while he rotted. It was a shame. He liked it here. He liked the seasons, he liked the people in the lab, and he liked his friends.

He couldn't live with their pity, though. It was bad enough now. After the baby was born, it would become intolerable. Once he'd recovered, he'd start his job search and hope that Nina understood.

***

Sam went through all of Tuesday on tenterhooks. He expected to get a message from Oliver in response to his note, surely by lunchtime if not mid-morning. "All is forgiven, you're awesome" would probably be a little much, but "Child support would be great, thank you" didn't seem unreasonable. When Oliver declined to come along to see the culmination of his hard work with the arrest of Isaiah Marsten, he knew he had a problem.

Wednesday rolled around. Sam had heard from Joe, who said that maybe they should talk. It was progress. He met for lunch with Jake, who accepted his hearty hug and told him that he was strong for getting help with his issues.

At the end of the meal, Sam bit the bullet and asked Jake about Oliver. "How is he? Is he doing okay?"

Jake looked away. "He's as well as can be expected. He's doing the best he can, you know? Making the best of things."

"Hmm." Sam forced himself to keep his expression neutral and to not get mad. "I was curious. He hasn't replied to my letter."

Jake winced. "Look, Dad, I don't want to fight here. You're my dad, but you kind of did him wrong and he has a right to feel his feels."

Sam tried to figure out what *feel his feels* might mean. "Okay, but he could at least reply."

Jake bit his lip. "He hasn't read it."

Sam lifted his eyebrows. "He hasn't read it?"

Jake's shoulders slumped. "Look, Dad, it's... okay. I did ask him, and I did urge him to read the letter. And he said that it was physically painful, at this point, to have contact with you. He pointed out that it doesn't matter what you guys say when you talk, because nothing actually changes. And he's right, Dad. I understand why you aren't going to keep him and the baby in your life, but they aren't really reasons that are for him. They're your reasons." He held up a hand. "They're valid for you, okay? I'm not pretending that they're not. I'm just... He's still holding the bag. And he's got to go on, while holding the bag. So hearing you dismiss him, again, isn't going to make anything better for him. It's only going to make him hurt worse. Okay?"

Sam bit down on the inside of his cheek. It wasn't his place to get angry about Jake's words, because they were right. If he had the right to reject Oliver's arguments, then Oliver had the right to reject his. He could admit that when he didn't have Oliver's scent right there, conflicting his heart and mind.

He hadn't realized that he'd spoken aloud until Jake scoffed. "Dad, no. He's not even making arguments. He's seeing through yours. If you wanted him badly enough, you'd be together. You don't. And you're going to lose out on this kid."

"If he would open up that letter, he'd see that I'm giving him child support." Sam scowled. "He can't keep me from the kid if I'm paying child support."

"First of all, I don't think he'd take it from you at this point. Secondly, I'm not sure that he's keeping the kid." Jake bowed his head.

"What are you talking about?" Sam waved a hand. "Omegas only give their kids up when they're young and poor. He makes more than I do, in that lab, with his degree."

"There's more to raising a kid on your own than just money. You know this, Dad." Jake chuckled. "He doesn't have any family, and even if he did they'd be in someplace weird like Indiana. What's he going to do with the kid when he gets called out to a crime scene, huh? Hand it a trowel and tell it to pretend it's a sandbox?"

Sam shook his head. "He'll reconsider. Omegas don't just give up their kids. It doesn't happen. He'll come around. It'll be a little weird, but it'll all work out for the best. Trust me here, Jake." He scratched his beard. "I do want him to find someone. Someone good."

"He doesn't want to." Jake shrugged and poked at his fries. "Remember? Anyway, this is something that we should probably stay away from. I have to support him."

Sam snorted. "You should support your old man."

"So do something I can support." Jake raised an eyebrow. "Joey said he called you, and you're going to get together sometime soon."

"Saturday." Sam nodded. "Someplace public, because we're still trying. It's been a long time."

"Too long. But I'm glad you're both willing to make the effort." Jake flashed one of his brilliant smiles, and the subject changed.

Sam tried to take his mind off of the Oliver problem with work. Just because they'd placed Marsten at the scene of the crime didn't mean that anyone was going to prove that he'd been behind the fire. Marsten could afford any number of high-priced lawyers, the likes of which would make Langer's sleazy omega's hair turn white.

There was nothing for it. He was going to need help with this. He grabbed Langer to act as a chaperone and dragged him down to the lab.

Langer grumbled the whole way down. "You did get the memo that I'm not part of your love life, right?"

"Yeah, yeah. I got the memo." Sam rolled his eyes. "Look, we need to nail this guy before he croaks or something, okay? And they're not even going to let me in the door of the lab without someone else holding my leash. That has to be you."

"Why me?"

"Because everyone likes you, Langer." Sam gave Langer a brilliant smile.

Langer cursed, but agreed to be the first person through the door.

The receptionist was having none of that. "Can I help you detectives?"

Langer gave the receptionist his most winning smile. "Look. We're not trying to harass anyone. We're just trying to get someone with a more scientific mindset than we have to help us puzzle out the best way to go. We knew, from the outset, that we were going to need a lot of the lab's help with this. We're just trying to follow up on that."

The receptionist crossed her arms over her chest. "You guys have a lot of nerve. You do realize that we don't have a bunch of scientists hanging around on hooks, right? They're not just waiting for some detective to ask for their expertise. They're working. On cases. That's why we have a system." She shook her head. "Go and use the system. Send your request in and it will be routed through appropriate channels."

Langer sighed and put his hands on her desk. "Look, Rebecca. I'm really sorry to have to bother you on such a nice day, but this is really important. We've got an arsonist who's likely to walk if we don't get some help with this. Now, I know you don't want that. This guy, assuming that we're right about this, has already killed at least sixty people to include two firefighters. Do you want that on your conscience?"

Sam thought that was a pretty good speech, as these things went. Rebecca, on the other hand, did not. "You guys work in Cold Case. Your boy's been inactive for a minimum of five years. The rape kit backlog that never gets smaller has cases drop off every day because we can't get to them fast enough and the statute of limitations expires. We've got drug convictions to re-process thanks to that one scandal, and if we don't get them done we're going to have thousands of people walking the streets who shouldn't be. Or, conversely, thousands of people locked up who shouldn't be. We've got two active murder investigations, an arson that turned into a homicide, a string of arsons from the South Shore, and an honest to God case of organ theft. That's what the day shift has going on, right now. You barging in there would disrupt any one of those cases. Are you honestly willing to look back on your life and have *that* on your conscience, just because you in your eternal alpha arrogance were too pigheaded to follow the established procedures?"

Langer pressed his lips together. He couldn't argue any of those. Sam couldn't either, even if he wanted to. He did wrinkle his nose. "Organ theft?"

"Actual organ theft. We're hoping that the victim survives." Nina Burton appeared in the other doorway, the one that led from the vestibule into the workers' area. "I heard the raised voices. Detective Nenci, you're not supposed to be here."

Sam threw his arms up into the air and let them fall. "Don't you think that's a little ridiculous? I mean, it's kind of unprofessional to ban an entire department from the lab just because of an after-hours fling between one of your guys and one of ours—that was manipulated by someone else."

He could see Oliver peering around the corner. If he could just reach out and put his hand on his mate's shoulder for a moment, just half a second, he could buy some time.

He shook his head. Oliver was not his mate. There was nothing to buy time for, unless it was to sway his decision toward parenthood.

Nina glowered down at Sam. "I can ban whoever I want from my lab, thank you very much. I can absolutely ban people who insist on going around the established protocols. If I let you ignore them, then I have to let everyone ignore them, and it would just be a free for all. Now get out."

Sam looked beyond her and over at Oliver. "Look," he said. He addressed himself to Nina, but he pitched his voice so that Oliver could hear it. "I get that the whole idea of putting Oliver into the field was a setup, but Devlin was right. This case does need more science than most cases. All that I need is for someone to tell me which way to go, to make sure the bastard can't walk. It shouldn't take more than a few minutes and everyone knows that Oliver's the best at that."

Nina crossed her arms over her chest and glanced back at Oliver. Oliver looked ashen, but he nodded. "Fine," she said, "but after hours. And he gets a chaperone."

"Fine. Good. Whatever he needs, he gets." Sam held his hands up. "I'm really sorry to have bothered you."

"Don't let me see you in here again." Nina turned on her heel and walked back into her lab.

"I'll make sure you know exactly which case went out the window because of you," Rebecca told Langer with a sweet smile.

Langer glowered at Sam as soon as they left the lab. "Seriously, I knew that we were on the lab's list but tell me that I didn't just make myself public enemy number one because you screwed up with your omega so badly that the lab's declared war on us."

"I'll send Doug flowers." Sam massaged his temples. "I'm sorry. I didn't think that it would be that bad."

"Well, it was worse." Langer ran a hand through his dark, curly hair. "How do you think you're going to dig yourself out of this one?"

Sam clenched his jaw. "I don't think I can. I'll have to retire once this case is finished, maybe. I've got my twenty years in, and then some, so that won't be a problem." He rubbed the back of his neck. "I don't think anyone will be sorry to see the back of me as it is. But it would probably solve the problem with the lab."

Langer snorted. "Don't you think that's a little melodramatic? You have one negative encounter and you're ready to hang it up?"

"Langer, I literally hobbled us all. Devlin tried to do something nice to me and I was so bad at it I destroyed our working relationship with the single most important ally our department had. And I imploded my relationship with my kids to boot." Sam stopped in the middle of the hallway.

"So fix it, Nenci." Langer rolled his eyes. "Try actually being nice to your omega and treating him like a person, Jesus. They really like that sort of thing. Trust me. Sometimes they'll even let you into their office and not throw shoes at you."

"He's not *my* omega, for crying out loud. He was never going to be *my* omega." Sam grabbed Langer by his arms. "He's too young to hitch himself to me, for crying out loud."

"It's not ideal." Langer gently freed himself from Sam's grip. "But you can't help who you love, man. Especially alphas and omegas. It's all chemical. It's fate. Do you think that I went out looking for a defense lawyer? Or do you think that Robles sought out someone like Tran? No. But once you stop fighting it, and accept your love for your omega, it works out."

"Yeah, until you die of old age and take your omega with you while he's still got a full life ahead of him." Sam scoffed and headed back toward the Cold Case squad room.

"You don't know what'll happen." Langer kept up with Sam easily. It was those damn long legs of his. "And I honestly think it's kind of crappy of you to make the decision for him, like he's too young to know what risks he's willing to take. I mean look, he's obviously been crazy about you since he got here. And you're just as besotted with him. What's really holding you back?"

"Why does everyone think that there's something else holding me back? That's it. I'm not willing to take such a guy out of the world." Sam stopped again.

Langer snorted. "If that was all, you'd still have treated him decently while you were together. Plenty of people can be together without a claim. You chose not to. I think you need to take a look at yourself and figure out why." He kept on walking toward Cold Case.

Sam sat down and considered the question. His instinct was to bristle and lash out, of course. Anyone's would be. With no one to rail against, though, he had to look deeper.

He hadn't meant to treat Oliver badly, but he had. He could see where Oliver had gotten a bad impression, time and time again. He wasn't going to get another chance with Oliver, and he wasn't sure how he felt about the idea of living together without a claim, but he knew that he'd done wrong by Oliver and that he loved him.

He called Trujillo's office and changed his appointment for an earlier one. He was going to need it before he went in.

Chapter Thirteen

Oliver sat down at the table. Ryan Tran sat next to him. He'd never been all that close with Tran, but he appreciated the efforts Tran had taken on his behalf during this whole mess. He wasn't sure if Tran was doing it for Oliver's sake or to get at Sam in some way, but right now he was pretty sure he didn't care.

Sam looked like he was sitting on a pile of thumbtacks. It was what it was, Oliver guessed. Part of him wanted to reach out and give Sam some comfort, but he didn't have anything to offer that Sam would accept. He folded his hands on top of the file in front of him and kept his eyes down.

Tran nudged him. "Dude. You have the information. You've got all the power here," he whispered.

Oliver nodded. Tran was technically right, but Oliver couldn't feel it. Not the way he should, not in his bones. After all, Tran wasn't the one who was going to have to leave town come March. He cleared his throat. "Yeah. Yeah, okay." He swallowed. "So, I heard what it was that you needed. You're looking for some additional technical information that would prove that Isaiah Marsten was at the Cooper Block fire and had some sort of altercation, beyond the image on the video and the blood on the objects at the scene."

Sam tugged at his collar. "Yeah, that about sums it up." He shifted to the left. "I mean yes, I'm positive that he's guilty. I'm not trying to cast aspersions on the quality of your lab work." He twirled his pen around in his hands. "I'm just concerned that he's going to have some fantastic lawyers, you know? The guy's loaded. He could afford to buy and sell Langer's omega six times over."

Tran buried his face in his hands for a second. "Can you maybe phrase that differently, considering present company?"

Sam rolled his eyes. "Sorry. Anyway, you know what I mean. I need there to be no wiggle room for his lawyers, no wiggle room for that jury. I mean, I'm putting a seventy-five-year-old man up on trial for multiple homicide and arson. I need to make it stick."

Oliver nodded slowly. "Yeah. I can see that all right." He bowed his head. "Fine. Okay." He opened his folder. "After you left I reached out to someone at Manchester PD. It took some digging on their part, but they found a record of a Manchester resident by the name of Isaiah Marsten who brought himself into Addison Gilbert Hospital in Gloucester. He presented with a stab wound to the knee that required surgical intervention and a head wound. The date is the same night as the Cooper Block fire."

"And he does use a cane to walk." Sam took the printout that Oliver passed him. Their hands brushed against one another during the exchange, which made Oliver's breath catch in his throat. How was he supposed to get through this meeting?

Oliver looked down again. "It says here that the attending physician noted that Marsten claimed that the injuries were the result of a kitchen accident, but these injuries don't line up with any kitchen accident I can imagine. Very few kitchen accidents involve stab wounds to the knees. The officer noted that Marsten had a strong smell of smoke about him, but he explained that away by saying that he was using an outdoor cooking area. The officer couldn't disprove the statement, and Marsten appeared to be the victim, so he had to step away."

"Is there any possibility that we could track down that officer?" Sam perked up a little, and Oliver warmed up to see so much life in his alpha. *Not your alpha*, he reminded himself.

Tran cleared his throat. "Mr. Wesson is not a detective. He can't be expected to do that type of leg work in place of his actual lab work."

Sam lowered his eyes. "Of course not." He bit his lip. "Is there anything else I can use? Any more nails for the coffin?"

Oliver rolled his eyes. "You're not asking for much here, are you? Only that I drop everything I'm working on, for literally ten other cases, to focus on one I've been pulled off of." He shook his head. "I'm such a sucker."

"Look, I'm sorry that it's inconvenient, but you started the job, Oliver." Sam sat up a little straighter. "Don't you think that it's only right that you see it through?"

Rage burned through Oliver then. "You've got a lot of nerve talking to me about not seeing things through."

Sam snapped a rubber band that hung around his wrist. "I thought this was supposed to be a strictly business meeting."

"It's not like you'd have bothered talking to me if it weren't." Oliver closed his eyes and tried to find his center. Tran's hand on his back helped. "There are additional notes in the back of the file, small details that might help and might not. There isn't a lot of physical evidence this far removed from the date of the crime. There aren't any clothes to examine; he's already gotten rid of the car. We have the surveillance photos, we have the blood evidence. We have motive. You get to come up with the corroborating evidence for all of that. This isn't television. I don't go knock on doors and talk to people. You do."

"You're angry." Sam sat back.

"Yes, Sam, I'm angry. I think I've got a right to be angry. I'm pregnant, I have no one to help me or support me, and you've decided I'm something you can throw away. My life in Massachusetts is essentially over. Yes, I made the decision to have sex, and it's on me. I should have expected all of this, and I'll never expect better from anyone again, but God damn it I am still angry."

Sam stood up. He looked like he was trying to calm himself. His chest heaved, and his hands clenched by his sides. "If you'd read the damn letter that I wrote, I poured my heart into it. I'm giving you child support. I'm willing to play a part in the baby's life, as like a great-uncle or something. I just can't be the kid's father. I mean, think about it rationally for a minute, would you? I'll be seventy when it turns twenty-one!"

"So what?" Oliver shoved the folder across the table at Sam. "Is your child support going to make sure that someone's there to watch the kid when I get called out to a crime scene at three in the morning? Or are you just okay with your crime scene being contaminated by dirty diapers and Cheerios? Is your child support going to help me when I've just gotten home from a fifteen-hour day and there isn't a goddamn other soul who can soothe that crying baby with another tooth coming in, because I'm the only one it has? No. It isn't. And that *uncle* it sees once a month is cold comfort, Sam. I know you think you're being generous there, but in reality it's a slap in the face. Another one." He stood up. "The thing is, you don't even know you're doing it. And when I tell you, you don't care."

Sam reached over the table and grabbed his arm. "How can you say that I don't care? Being apart from you is killing me! I'm doing this for you!"

Tran's voice cut through the misery like a knife. "You're going to take your hands off Oliver, Nenci, and you're going to do it now. This is your only warning."

"Oh come on." Sam stood back, hands raised.

Oliver supported himself on the back of a chair. "Look. I think the solution is pretty clear. I'm not going to raise a kid alone. Some people might be cut out for it. You did just fine with Jake and Joe. I'm not that guy. I've seen what happens when someone who's not suited to single parenthood tries to do it. It's constant recrimination, constant self-doubt. *What did I do to make Mommy angry today?* Nope. I'm not putting my kid through that." He picked his head up. "I'm putting the kid up for adoption."

"You don't get to do that." Sam leaned forward again, but he didn't try to touch Oliver.

"Excuse you." Ryan stepped forward again. "It's his body, his choice."

"It's his body, but that baby is part of my family. It's not a big family and you can't just scatter my family, my progeny, over the country all willy-nilly!" Sam's eyes shone with unshed tears. "I mean, for crying out loud, Oliver, you can't just take my kid away from me!"

Ryan sneered at him and crossed his arms over his chest. "I think you'll find that the law says something different, Nenci. Weren't you just saying that you weren't willing to be a father?"

"Be reasonable here. I'm old!"

"Not too old to make a baby. You want to talk about being reasonable, try not expecting Oliver to suffer the consequences alone." Ryan pinched the bridge of his nose. "You know what? In a good and loving relationship, it's not necessarily suffering. It's still hard. I mean, me and Nick, we still have our troubles, and having a kid is one of the most frustrating things in the world sometimes. I don't think that I could do it on my own. I love DJ, but I'm like Oliver. I think I need a partner to be a good parent to him."

Sam tore at his hair. "Would you two listen to yourselves? I raised not one, but two boys by myself and I did just fine."

"You did. And you managed. Good for you." Oliver tossed his head back. "You also had a lot of support from their dad's family. I don't have that. I'm alone. I'm always going to be alone, because no one wants used goods, and I can't raise a kid by myself like that. I'm sorry. I know you were looking forward to being an uncle and spoiling the kid rotten or something, but you're going to have to wait until one of your own kids takes a mate.

"And by the way." Oliver walked toward the door. He'd never been this aggressive before, and he wasn't sure if he liked it, but the words needed to be said. "I notice how your responses are just dismissing my issues without offering any actual solutions. Classy, Sam. I'm not your brood mare. I'm not just an incubator for your spawn, here to bring it by to your house once a month so you can feel good about the choices you made.

"I'm going to give the baby up. I'm not doing it because of you. I'm doing it because of me, because I can't be a good parent alone. And then, once I've recovered from the birth, I'm going to start looking for a new job. I'm going to move far away, because I don't want to be angry and hurting anymore. I just want to be left alone. I want to forget that I ever met you."

"You hate me that much?" Sam staggered back.

"I should. I should absolutely despise you, for how you've treated me. I don't hate you. I even love you, after everything. But I need to not be around you, because I don't like who I'm becoming." He left the lab.

Ryan followed him out to the bicycle lockup. "That was pretty powerful," the tall detective told him. "Are you going to be okay?"

"No." Oliver looked down. "I'm not. I haven't been okay since that first night with him, to be honest. I don't think I'll be okay for a long time. But I want to be."

Ryan sighed and leaned against the bike rack. "I wish it didn't have to be like this." One corner of his mouth twitched up. "I've always been a sucker for a happy ending, you know? Do you really want to give your baby up for adoption?"

"No." Oliver unlocked his bike. "I don't. I cried. I cried a lot, and I'm not some weeping statue kind of guy, you know? It hurts. Just the thought makes that empty, aching place inside me even bigger. But I don't feel like I have an option. My mom was a single mother, and we're a lot alike. And yeah, there are a lot of single parents who do a great job. She wasn't one of them."

Ryan pursed his lips and nodded. "I see. Do you ever hear from her?"

"Nah. She wanted me out as soon as I turned eighteen. She stopped by to visit a couple of times when I was in college, but that stopped." Oliver rubbed his arm. "It's okay, you know? I don't really mind. It's just between knowing that she's my only example, and not having someone else right there to help me learn to be better, and the job, and everything else—"

Ryan put a hand on his shoulder. "I get it. I was a foster kid myself. When I found out I was pregnant, I can't say I was happy. Me and Nick were a little volatile at that point. I had to think seriously about what to do. Whatever you decide—and it sounds like you've made a pretty rational decision—I'll back your play." He grimaced. "It's going to be rough either way, though."

"I know." Oliver hung his head. "I don't think there's any other option."

"Well, it does look bleak." Then he grinned. "The great thing about pregnancy is that it can't be rushed, though. Something could change. Don't polish off the old resume just yet, okay?"

Oliver chuckled. "Yeah, we'll see. I'm not going to leave the lab on short notice. We're down too many people as it is."

"See? You can't leave. We need you." Ryan patted his shoulder. "Give me a call if you need anything."

Oliver smiled and hopped onto his bike. He rode home feeling both saddened and lighter than he had before. He'd told Sam what was in his heart, and what his plans were. They couldn't be changed now. Everything was set in motion, he had a course of action, and all that was left now was to follow through.

He would miss the Mass. State Police. He liked this lab. Nina had been good to him. He had friends here, for a given value of friends. They weren't close enough to help with this problem but they were still good people, folks he liked to see every day, and it would be weird to not see them every day.

He would miss the apartment, too. It wasn't huge. But it was safe, and it was close to his lab. Would he be able to find a place like this so close to his next job?

He shouldn't think about the negative qualities. It was going to be the start of a bold new adventure.

***

Sam scanned and forwarded the entire file that he'd gotten from Oliver before he remembered to check his email. Sure enough, Oliver had forwarded him an electronic copy of everything related to the case, and cc'ed his boss. He decided that he could forgive himself for the slip up. It wasn't like he'd just been cut off from his youngest child or anything.

He didn't say a word to anyone that night. His phone rang, but he ignored it. Maybe it was Oliver, calling to say that he'd changed his mind, but who was Sam kidding? Oliver had no reason to change his mind. Oliver had every reason to stick to his guns and move on. Why would he want to raise Sam's baby? Sam was just Sam—decrepit, old, nothing to offer.

He got through the next day on autopilot. He didn't pay much attention to anything outside of the case. The small part of his brain that was still awake and functioning figured that the case had destroyed his life; he might as well finish it off.

Well, the case hadn't actually destroyed his life. He'd reached a point where he could make tentative overtures with Joey again. He and Jake were communicating better than they had in years. He was working toward getting along better with his colleagues and he'd even managed to keep from blowing up at Devlin about the manipulation. On all fronts but one, this case had improved Sam's life a thousand-fold.

The only thing that it had destroyed was his relationship with Oliver. Before the case started, Sam's relationship with Oliver had consisted almost entirely of little sighs and fantasies he didn't talk about outside of the privacy of his own bedroom, and sometimes the shower. Now, though, he'd had a chance and he'd blown it so spectacularly that it looked like Atlanta after Sherman got done with it.

His last session with Dr. Trujillo had been enlightening. He'd convinced himself that he was avoiding a relationship with Oliver, whom he adored, because of the age difference. Trujillo had deeper suspicions about his motives, and after some probing questions she leaned forward. "I don't think that the age difference has much to do with it. I think you are concerned about it, but I don't think that you'd be quite so dismissive of his acceptance of the risks if it weren't for your own opinions about yourself."

He wanted to argue with her about that, but he couldn't. "He can't love me," he said, after several minutes of stunned silence. "I'm the official department troll. I was thinking that I might retire after this case is over. It's not like anyone there would miss me, or even notice. I'm literally the office troll."

Trujillo shrugged. "That's a decision you have to make. But you came in here to work on that, right? And your boss cared enough to try to do something to bring you some happiness, even if it was misguided. So let's talk about why you're sabotaging your chance for happiness. Or, why you've sabotaged it."

Now, sitting at his desk and typing away, Sam had to admit that the past tense was key. It had very little to do with the age difference, even though that had played a role. No, Sam had blown things up with Oliver because he was afraid. He couldn't be vulnerable, and instead he'd ruined something that could have been—should have been—beautiful.

Their baby would have been amazing. It would have been beautiful, and smart, and if they'd been together it would have gotten Oliver's sweet temperament. Now even Oliver was losing Oliver's sweet temperament, because Sam poisoned everything that he touched.

Maybe Oliver's decision was the right one. Sam shouldn't be allowed near a kid, not anymore. Sure, Joey and Jake had turned out fine, but he could see that he was too messed up.

He stared at the screen. Families were weird. He'd never been all that close with his own family, but he'd built one with Chris and now that was gone. He had his sons but they were grown, and the jury was still out on how things were going to be with them going forward. Oliver, apparently, had no family either. They were both kind of screwed up guys, but they were functional. Mostly.

Then there were the Marstens and the Couchers. The Marstens were pieces of work. Sam knew, just by looking at the timeline he'd built, that taking Isaiah down had just been cutting the head off of a hydra. Another would spring back in his place, and they'd start all over again. If Sam were a gambling man, he'd put money on another spectacular fire on a Coucher property sometime within the next two years.

Of course, the Couchers weren't saints. The past couple of generations had gone clean, but the ones before that had been just as bad as the Marstens. They'd just been subtler about it. Now that they'd "gone legit," they limited their predation to the corporate world. To be honest, if Sam had gotten screwed the way that Bill Coucher screwed the Marstens, he'd probably want to set something on fire too.

Come to think of it, he didn't have the expertise to say anything about white-collar crime one way or the other. He thought he might know one or two people who did, but was it worth it? There would be subpoenas, and hassle, all for something that he just thought had probably happened because Sam himself couldn't quite understand how real estate law worked.

The Marstens did. They had lawyers to fight on their behalf, to shout and fuss and wave their fists. If there had been a problem, it would have been the Marstens themselves who would have found it.

He went home at quitting time. He hadn't said anything to another soul all day, and he found he didn't mind. No one else seemed to have noticed, which only cemented his own belief that retirement might be the best option for him.

When he got home, he found that he wasn't going to get the same privilege. Both of his sons' cars were in his driveway, front and center this time. Well, at least they were up front about it. There weren't going to be any surprises this time.

He steeled himself for the inevitable and headed into the house. Joey and Jake sat on the couch with identical looks on their faces. Sam recognized that look. He'd given it to Jake the time Jake had begged and pleaded to be allowed to enter the Academy. He'd given it to Joey the time that Joey had informed him in no uncertain terms that he would not be attending the Academy, thank you very much.

Chris had given it to Sam, the time he'd accidentally dropped Jake.

Sam took off his jacket and hung it on the peg next to the door. "All right, boys, let me have it."

The twins glanced at one another. "We're having a brother," Joey said, turning his head back to his father.

"Or a sister." Jake put his foot on the coffee table, which he'd never been allowed to do. Sam let it slide. "A sister would be kind of awesome. Think about the cute dresses we could put on her, man."

"I saw the most adorable little onesie at the mall today. You know, where I went when my little brother called me up." Joey turned flinty eyes over to his father again. "I even bought it. And then he calls me back and tells me that Oliver's choice is made."

Sam's eyes filled with tears, and he looked down and away. Of course, the twins weren't finished. Not by a long shot.

"Yeah, I spoke with Oliver. He's already spoken to a few agencies. He's really going with adoption." Jake dabbed at his eyes, and it wasn't a feigned gesture either. Sam could see the way that his eyes shone in the light. "I mean, I can't exactly blame him. It's a lot to ask, you know? *Hey, Oliver, raise my little sister all by yourself, when you have no idea what proper parenting looks like and will be lucky to get a sitter once every couple of months.*"

Sam sat down in the old lounger. This had always been his chair. Back when Chris had been alive, this had been his chair. After Chris was gone, this chair had held him long after the kids had gone to bed, when he could cry with impunity. "I want to say, *We don't need another kid, we're fine the way we are.*" He blinked to force the tears away. "I'd be lying, but I still find myself wanting to say it to put a good face on it for you kids."

Joey shook his head. "There's no way to put a good face on this. Never mind that Oliver is our friend. That's got its own issues. But that baby, that's ours. Part of our family."

Jake nodded, as Sam's heart sank. "I mean, like I said, I don't fault Oliver for the decision. I'm just… Dad, I'm trying real hard not to be confrontational here. I am. But it's hard, you know? Because I'm having a hard time not getting excited about this baby, and I can't get excited about this baby. I know that he loves you, and I know that you feel something for him."

"I love him." Sam interrupted his son without hesitating. "I love him more than I can say, all right? He's a good guy. He's the best. It might be disloyal to say that here, in Chris' house, but I do love him."

Jake pursed his lips. "See, it's not disloyal. It's been a long time, and I only knew Daddy as a little kid knows his dad, you know? But he adored you."

Joey nodded. "He did. I know that your claim was arranged, but it worked well. You guys were happy together, and you loved each other. The thing is, because you loved each other, you'd never want the other one to be unhappy. He'd never want you to be miserable, Dad. And, I have this on good authority, he'd be pissed as hell that you were making another omega unhappy."

Sam turned his face away. "Does no one care about my feelings here?"

Jake stood up. "You're conflicted. It's natural. You've got some issues, and they're all kind of valid for you. The fact is, though, you love him. You love him, but you're letting him do this to himself."

"At this point, I'm not sure that I can stop him." Sam bit his tongue. "I mean, you do realize that I never had any intention of building a life with him?" He shook his head. "I couldn't do that to him, I couldn't do that to you boys."

Joey snorted and thumbed his nose. "There's no 'doing that to us boys.' We want you to."

"He's younger than you are!" Sam dropped his jaw.

"By a couple of months, come on. But we want you to be happy. We think you deserve to be with someone who loves you as much as Dad loved you." Jake stepped toward him, hands out and palms open. "We know you're worth it, Dad."

There was that term again. Jake had picked up on the same thing that Trujillo had, seen through the same BS. How he managed to be that discerning, Sam didn't know. It had to be the detective genes. "He doesn't want me anymore."

"You two were built for each other." Joey stood up now too. "He's always going to want you. You tell me that I should claim him. I would. Honestly, he's a great guy, he's handsome and smart and he smells good. But he's always going to want my father. I'd do it if he needed it, like if he was in omega distress or something, but not otherwise."

Sam buried his face in his hands. "He doesn't want to see me anymore, guys. He says it hurts him." He pulled his hands away. "I honestly don't know what the right thing to do is here. I mean, he said to go away. That's something I have to honor." He sighed. "And I'm not the man I was when I claimed your dad. I don't have anything to offer anymore. I'm old."

"You're forty-nine, Dad." Joey rolled his eyes. "That's hardly old."

"I don't see you making a play for any forty-nine-year-old omegas." Sam glowered at his son. "I've only gotten worse with time. I have no community to offer him, no family besides you two. And you two should be thinking about your own futures, not fussing around about your old man."

"That's a separate issue." Jake snapped his finger. "Stay on task here. Are you seriously willing to just let your youngest child walk out of your life forever, with no hope of ever knowing them?"

"I don't have a choice!" Sam wailed. "I tried to talk him out of it. I did!"

Joey snorted. "Probably with more of that *for your own good* crap."

Sam sat up straighter. "Someone has to think of what's best for him. An alpha's job is to protect omegas. Even when it's painful, even when it's ugly, even when it makes them cry, we have to keep them safe. Even when it's from us. That's what we're for."

Both of his sons stared at him. "Oh my God, Dad, do they have air conditioning in your cave?" Joey shook his head and turned his back.

Jake sighed. "Yeah. Chivalry is a nice idea, but it's kind of based on this idea of a helpless omega that isn't really justified. You do get that both Oliver and I could kill you and make it look natural, right? Like it wouldn't be a problem."

Sam scowled. "That's not the point. He's being led around by his hormones. Someone has to be the levelheaded one and think rationally. He can do better, and I don't have anything to offer him or this kid."

"He thought that you did, once." Jake stepped in. "You've done your best to make sure he doesn't care what you have to offer. He blames himself, you know? It's on him, for not recognizing that all alphas are basically scum." He shook his head. "I honestly resent you for that. He thought you were some charming, wonderful guy."

"I'm not." Sam turned away so his sons wouldn't see his shoulders shaking.

"You are. That's the thing." Joey spoke from just over Sam's left shoulder. "You are a wonderful guy. You're attentive to the needs of a victim. You're sweet to kids, you're good with traumatized people. He had every reason to believe that you'd be good to him. He never said anything about a claim, but I think he was reasonable to expect more than a quick screw. You gave him every reason to expect it."

"One more person I've let down." Sam hung his head.

"You have the chance to fix it." Jake stepped back, shaking his head. "But you won't. I'm not sure what to say to you right now, Dad. I'll call you later."

Both boys left, and Sam was left to cry in his chair.

Chapter Fourteen

Oliver looked at himself in the mirror. He had a handful of "going to court" suits. None of them were particularly exciting, or expensive. They did the job and were distinctly lacking in chemical stains, but they'd need to be replaced soon enough. Maybe Nina wouldn't want him to go up in front of a jury, though. An omega who was pregnant outside of a proper claim wasn't exactly a credible witness, no matter what his qualifications might be.

Oh well. That didn't matter right now. He wasn't showing yet, and he could still fit into the suit.

He checked his hair. He checked his waistline, even though he couldn't even be six-weeks pregnant yet. Had it only been that long? Did he really have another thirty-four to go?

"You finished primping?" Jake stuck his head into the bathroom. "Everyone's ready to go to the courthouse."

"Primping." Oliver snorted. "Yeah, you know I'm still finding containers of hair gel in the bathroom? How does one man manage to go through so much product in three weeks?"

"Hey. Looking this good doesn't just happen, bro. It takes effort." Jake preened. "Seriously, though. Nina's going to give you a ride."

Oliver followed Jake out into the hallway. "I can drive myself."

"She wants to make sure that you've got some protection, just in case someone tries to give you a hard time. You know." Jake looked away. "I mean, I'm not taking sides or nothing, but I think she's right in this."

Oliver rolled his eyes up to the ceiling. Someone had thrown a wad of bubble gum up there. He looked away. "I can handle being around an alpha. I'm not some kind of orchid. I'm not going to wilt just because someone's yelling at me." He made himself grin. "I'm over that. Trust me."

Jake shook his head. "Her job is to have her people's back. And I think she wants to talk to you about staying with the lab in the long term." He tugged at his collar. "You didn't exactly make a secret about wanting to go."

Oliver made a face, but he didn't rise to the bait. Jake got it, insofar as anyone could. Oliver couldn't put all of his issues onto Jake.

Nina was indeed ready to go. They took her personal car, a Toyota, instead of one of the state vehicles. It was an act of rebellion, and one that gave Oliver pause. How much trouble had Oliver's issues with Sam caused Nina with the higher-ups? The lab was already having issues. He should have been more considerate of her.

The ride up took an hour. Nina waited ten minutes, during which they made small talk about cleaning bones for analysis, before she turned to the subject of the baby. "So," she began. She sat up a little straighter and gripped the steering wheel a little tighter. She kept her gray eyes straight ahead and her mouth tight. "I'm not sure what your decision will be with regards to your baby, and you've got time before you have to really commit to a choice."

"I don't need time." Oliver looked at the carpet. He saw a variety of different hairs, and a broken fingernail. What story would that trace evidence tell, if he were to try to analyze it? "I'm giving it up. I can't raise a kid on my own."

She gripped the wheel a little tighter. "He's not going to stand up?"

Oliver shrank in his seat. "He wants to be some kind of creepy old uncle. He's willing to pay child support, but it takes more than money to raise a kid."

"Damn straight it does. I mean, there are people who can do it, and more power to them, but it's not something that everyone can do." She sighed. "Damn it. Anyway. I've heard you want to leave us after the baby's born."

Oliver closed his eyes. "I don't, actually. I like the lab. I like the area. I just don't think I can cope with the pity."

"Could you cope with it for a raise and a promotion?"

Oliver blinked slowly. "That... that doesn't make sense. I mean, I screwed up. I screwed up a lot, Nina. I couldn't keep control of myself. I got myself pregnant, I got into it with a colleague, and now we're in a cold war with the guy's whole department. I have terrible judgment. I should be demoted, if anything else. I should be busted back to Analyst I."

Nina chuckled. "Okay, you should have used protection, but these things happen. And you didn't get yourself pregnant, unless you've got some very interesting mutations that I never want to hear about ever. Oliver, everyone makes a mistake sometimes. You're no different. You're trying to do the right thing for both you and that baby, making the right decision knowing your own personality and history." She patted his hand. "That shows amazing judgment, frankly."

Oliver licked his lips. He couldn't find it in himself to believe that he'd be rewarded for his monumental lapse. "Why would you promote me?"

"Because, Oliver. You're one of the best in the country, and you're definitely the best in the lab. We need you. We don't just need you doing what you do now. We've lost a lot of people, and we need to replace them." She risked a glance over at Oliver. "If we're going to avoid repeating the mistakes of history, we need to have someone leading the way who can teach the new hires the way to do things right. I need a second-in-command who loves the job, who has a passion for the work, and who wants to be there. I need someone teaching those new hires that it's okay to think outside the box, it's okay to be smart, and it's okay to do the right thing. That's you, a hundred percent."

"I want to say yes." Oliver's stomach twisted. "But I don't know. I mean, everything's already so different, you know? Everyone knows my business now. Everyone. They know how bad I—"

"They know how bad you were treated." Nina's jaw clenched. "And that it wasn't just by Nenci. And they see how high you're holding your head. There might be a little bit of pushback about the adoption. I can't lie. People get more judgmental about choices people make regarding not having children than anything else." She paused. "When it was me, the overt comments lasted for about a year. I mean, I'm not an omega and the father wasn't a co-worker. It did suck, and it was hard, but it wasn't the end of the world."

Oliver choked back a sob. He couldn't go into court with a face like he'd been crying. "Really?"

She gave him a kind smile and shook her head. "It really isn't. It just feels like it when you're going through it." She grabbed his hand and squeezed it. "You don't have to make up your mind right now. I just wanted you to know that you don't have to leave the lab, and no one wants you to leave the lab. You're a great scientist and a respected colleague, and we want you to stay."

"Thank you." They felt like weak words to convey the depth of Oliver's feeling, but he couldn't think of anything else. He'd have to let the look on his face and the tone of his voice do the work for him. "Thank you."

"Also I put a mackerel in the back seat of Nenci's car this morning." She put her hand back on the wheel and replaced her kind smile with a nasty smirk. "It's under the floor mat in the back seat. It's July, his car is black—this is going to suck for him."

Oliver threw his head back and laughed. The prank was juvenile and petty, but it gave him exactly the kind of pick-me-up that he needed to get himself together before the ordeal of court.

Nenci and Devlin were in court, of course. The prosecutor sat at the table on the left, and the defense team sat at the table on the right. Bill Coucher sat amongst the spectators in a somber black suit. Isaiah Marsten sat with his lawyers, looking like one of them in an expensive Italian suit. His sons sat in a row behind him.

Oliver looked away. Everything had been for this, and the smirking jackass in the suit still thought he was going to get away with something.

Well, Oliver had done his part. That part hadn't been insignificant. He knew, deep in his heart, that Isaiah Marsten was guilty.

The judge arrived, and opening arguments began. Oliver tuned them out. Legal arguments were of little interest to him. They had their place, of course. Oliver just didn't care about them. He dealt in facts, not in weasel words. Nina's words in the car burned like fire in his heart. He was a scientist. Science didn't care about doubt. It only cared about facts.

Sam testified about how he'd come to look at Marsten as a suspect. He explained that while Coucher had given him the Marsten name right away, he'd been dismissive until he'd looked into the history between the families. He'd still dismissed the thought of a single arsonist for both fires until he'd seen Oliver's re-creation of the fires.

His voice stumbled over Oliver's name, only a little.

When he explained that he'd asked for DNA to rule out Isaiah Marsten, that he hadn't expected the head of the family to be the one to get his hands dirty, Isaiah smirked. His lawyer frowned, though, and looked troubled. "Nothing could have surprised me more," he said, "than when that DNA came back as a match. There are plenty of six-foot-two guys in Massachusetts, but to have that DNA come back knocked me back."

The defense lawyer made a halfhearted attempt to cross-examine him, but Sam was like iron up on that stand. He wouldn't bend, and he wouldn't be swayed. Oliver squirmed a little bit in his seat; all he needed was to have to get up onto the stand with a hard on.

Finally, Sam was allowed to sit down, and the prosecutor called Oliver up to the stand. A screen was brought to the front of the court, so that Oliver was able to show the animations he'd created. He was sworn in, and then the prosecutor asked him about how he'd gone about investigating the crimes on his side of the fence.

Oliver explained that he'd been brought into the case because of his strong background in arson investigation, which he then described. He spoke about his research into the history of the building, and about finding the jewelry on site. "That led Detective Nenci to investigate the family history a little more thoroughly, while I tried to focus on the science." He managed not to stumble on his former lover's name. "I'm better at that."

The prosecutor chuckled. "And what did you find?"

"Well, after so many years, I couldn't go back and re-analyze old samples. I created a program to give me a visual representation of the fire, based on the original data and known information such as building materials and sprinkler information." He showed the animation for the 1967 fire. "Now watch as I show the 1992 fire." He split the screens and ran both animations at the same time. "As you can see, the human factors are identical. Even the pour factor is the same.

"The only differences are here." He paused the program. "Here, in the 1992 fire, we have video of the arsonist at work. Image analysts were able to isolate an image of the killer. It was grainy, but it allowed us to rule some people out. In the evidence from the 1992 fire, we found some DNA evidence that came with someone who had fought with people who were killed in the fire. That was corroborated in the historical record.

"As you can see, the same person had to have set both fires. The pour pattern is identical, right down to the splashes on this northern wall here and here." He pointed to the wall in question. "We have DNA evidence tying Mr. Marsten to the scene of the crime, and evidence that the victims fought him to get that evidence. We have him on video at the scene. We have motive." He spread his hands wide.

The defense lawyer approached, but he was pale. "You said yourself that the video image was grainy."

"I did. The image analysts who worked on the image were able to get a general description using techniques also used by the FBI, which are detailed on page thirty-seven of the evidentiary report you were given." Oliver gave the lawyer a bland smile. "It's not enough for a positive ID, but it was enough to get a warrant to rule Mr. Marsten out. He wasn't chased down. Detective Nenci expected to exonerate him."

The attorney returned to his bench. "No further questions, your Honor."

The judge, unsurprisingly, found plenty of evidence to proceed to trial. Marsten was sent to jail to await that trial, and court was adjourned. Reporters mobbed the scene as people left the courthouse, and Oliver shrunk back. He'd never had people shove cameras or microphones into his face before.

A skeletally thin blonde, with a cameraman looming over her, stepped into his personal space. "Mr. Wesson, how does it feel to be the one who solved the murder of sixty people?"

Oliver stepped back and blinked. He wasn't authorized to speak to the media, and who knew who this woman even was? "The case was just held over for trial, ma'am," he told her. "The science is solid, but we have to see what the jury finds. And Detective Nenci's hard work made everything possible."

Sam was there, a suave and menacing presence slipping between Oliver and the cameras. He could breathe again, even if those breaths involved Sam's scent. "Mr. Wesson needs to get back to the lab now," Sam said with a thin smile. "Lots of crime to solve, and with everything that's been in the papers there's less people to do it. Excuse us. Have a great day." He put his hand on Oliver and Nina's backs and escorted them through the crowd until they got to the Toyota.

Oliver's cheeks blazed. "Thanks for that." He couldn't look up. Just that little hint of Sam's scent made him want to plaster himself to the alpha's side. "You did well up there."

Sam chuckled. "It's part of the job." He opened the door for Oliver. "Goodbye."

Oliver slid into the car and buckled himself in. Sam closed the door behind him and tapped the top of the car twice.

Nina started the car up and drove away. She didn't say anything about the tear tracks on Oliver's face.

***

Sam tapped Nina's white Toyota on the roof and watched it drive away. He didn't challenge Nina on the fish in his car. He'd picked up on it right away. It hadn't caused any damage and he'd honestly deserved it. Oliver turned back to look at him, and tears escaped the omega's eyes before he turned back to stare out the windshield.

How was Sam supposed to live with that?

He'd made his omega cry. Oh, sure, Oliver wasn't really his omega. There was no claim. They weren't even speaking. Oliver had given up on him. Sam had done his best to chase Oliver away, and it had worked. But by God, Oliver was Sam's omega. Sam's sons knew it, Sam's therapist knew it, Sam's colleagues knew it, and Sam's boss knew it. Sam wouldn't approach him, and he would respect his decision, but he wasn't going to pretend anymore.

Oliver had been the one for him.

He left the courthouse and went back to the office. He had paperwork to do in order to officially close the case. That would take up the rest of the day. Next week he would help Tessaro with his messy case until Devlin assigned him to something new, or he came to a decision about hanging it up, or until he and Tessaro came to blows, whichever came first. His money was on coming to blows with Tessaro, but anything could happen.

He busied himself with the minutia of paperwork until he'd crossed every *t* and dotted every *i*. By the time he was finished six o'clock had come and gone, and he could congratulate himself on successfully numbing the pain for another day. When he looked up from his screen, though, he found Tessaro looking at him. "What's up?" he asked his colleague, scratching at his beard. "You looking for a cheap barber? Because I've got a set of clippers left over from when the boys were younger, I can get rid of all that in like five minutes."

Tessaro snorted and pushed himself back from his desk. "You know, the hair is actually pretty popular. You might want to think about growing yours out a little." He got up from his chair and walked around his desk, finally coming over to sit on Sam's desk. "It might help you out a little with the omegas, you never know."

"I'm pretty sure that you've got a little more going for you than hair that belongs in a shampoo commercial, there." Sam glowered. "My desk is not a chair."

"Nope. It's a desk. But I figured it would be a good idea for us to talk, and maybe this would be better than shouting our business over the squad room like hood kids back in East Boston, you know? I mean, we can do that if you want. It's not like I give a crap." Tessaro pressed a hand into his chest.

Sam leaned back and groaned. "Is anyone ever not going to sit there and get into my business?"

"I don't know, Nenci." Tessaro smirked at him. "We're detectives. All we do is get into other people's business. All day, all night. That's kind of our thing. I tried to hook up with a Boston cop last week but we got sidetracked when we busted a drug mule."

"Seriously?" Sam shook his head. "You're making that up."

"Talk to Devlin. Or don't, if you're still pissed at him." He tilted his head to the side and looked up at the ceiling. "I mean, I'm kind of pissed at him."

"Are you really?" Sam pulled back in surprise. He wouldn't have looked to Tessaro for backup, not on this.

"Hell yeah. The guy might have meant well, but how many of the people we deal with mean well? Most of 'em, am I right? What he did was wrong, end of story. Of course, the problem now is that he messed up your life, and Oliver's life, and now there's a kid on the way and all of our cases take six times as long because we can't cut in line anymore. But hey."

"We can't blame him for all of that." Sam closed his eyes and leaned back. "I screwed it up, every time. It's a thing I do. My therapist says it's called *self-sabotage*."

"You seeing Trujillo?" Tessaro grinned and toyed with Sam's stapler. "She's pretty good, huh? And yeah, she's right. You're totally self-sabotaging. You've been self-sabotaging a lot of things, for a long time. It's about time that you stopped, don't you think?"

"It's a little late." Sam picked himself up and opened his eyes again. "I mean, his choice is made, right? He's giving the baby up. Says he's going to move away, although my guess is that Nina would move heaven and earth to keep him here. And I've been awful, with every chance I had with him. I didn't just shoot myself in the foot. I burned down every bridge, and half the city to boot. He'd be ridiculous to take me."

"Yeah. He would." Tessaro picked up a paper clip and untwisted it as he spoke. "Honestly, if it were him I was talking to instead of you, I'd tell him to run. But I'm talking to you, because I know you. I've known you for a few years now.

"And I've watched you try to push each and every one of us in this department away. I think all of us has had a *bury Nenci* plan going at some point. And then something happens, and you pull it out and you show us just who you really are. You stand by us. You stand by the victims, who are usually people who have no one else to stand for them. You handle cases with so much dignity and compassion that I've actually cried, Nenci. And I don't cry.

"So yeah. I care about Oliver. I do, and I'm pissed about the way that you've treated him, but I know that you can do better. And I want to see you happy. I want to see you both happy,

Nenci. I know that you don't want to miss out on that baby's life. I know Jake doesn't want to miss out on that baby's life. And Ryan's told me that he doesn't think that Oliver wants to give the kid up either."

Sam bit his lip against the rage that filled him. This wasn't any of Tessaro's business. Tessaro hadn't had a relationship last longer than two nights, at least not that anyone knew about. He had no business giving relationship advice to anyone, much less a man who had claimed an omega and raised two sons.

At the same time, what he was saying was the truth. Sam wanted the baby. More than that, he wanted Oliver. He wanted the family back together. "It's hopeless though." He turned away. "I'm not even allowed to go near him, on threat of pain."

"Where do you think he is right now?" Tessaro jumped off of the desk and forced himself into Sam's line of sight.

"It doesn't matter! He won't see me!"

Tessaro leaned into his personal space. "Listen to me, you son of a bitch. That omega needs to know that he can count on you. He needs to know that you'll be there for him and he needs to know that you *want* to be with him. You haven't shown him that you're capable of any of that. You've just gone on about your day, wrung your hands and said woe is me. Come on. Are you an alpha or not?"

Sam leaped to his feet and shoved Tessaro back. "Excuse the hell out of you?"

"Oh good. You can do something. I thought you were going to merge with your chair and become one with it." Tessaro tossed his head. "What would happen if someone decided to go after Oliver, huh? Or the baby? Or Jake, or even Joey?

Would you sit there and sigh pathetically at your screen or would you get up off your ass and do something?"

"You'd best watch your tone." Sam clenched his hand into a fist. "I don't care if you're eight inches taller than I am, I'm not going to hesitate to take you down. I'll punch you in your knee if I have to; I've done it before."

"How about you put some of that energy into getting your omega back, hot shot?" Tessaro stepped back, just out of range.

"What am I supposed to do?" Sam roared. "He won't see me!" How many times was Sam going to have to repeat himself before Tessaro listened?

"So go see him!" Tessaro threw his arms up into the air. "Grovel, if you have to. Beg. Be contrite. Be honest. Explain the truth and tell him that you need him. Tell him that you want him, you want the baby, and that you want to make it work. Buy him a damn ring, like the one in the evidence locker, only don't cut it off of a dead guy because that's creepy."

"The mall will do just fine." Sam blinked and shook his head. "Wait, I can't believe I'm even considering this."

"It's your only goddamn shot at not spending the rest of your life trying to fill an empty space where your omega should be." Tessaro stepped back in and grabbed Sam's arm. "Do you want this or not?"

Sam swallowed. Panic rose up in his throat. "I want this," he said, forcing the bile down. "I have no idea how it's going to play out."

"At least you'll know, by the end of tonight." Tessaro gripped his arm tighter and dragged him out the door. He was only barely willing to give Sam time to reach for his wallet or car keys.

The mall wasn't far away. They found a suitable ring. It was probably easier for them to find a ring given that they rushed into the store demanding "a ring, for omegas, make it nice," and didn't hem and haw over the decision. Neither Sam nor Tessaro was an expert on marital jewelry, and so they were able to get out before the sun started its descent.

They didn't ring Oliver's bell. Instead they rang Jake's. Jake was not the one who answered, though. "Hello?"

"Is this Jake Nenci's apartment?" Sam asked, exchanging glances with his fellow officer for a moment.

"Yeah, hold on, let me grab him. Jake, isn't that your dad?" The voice disappeared.

Tessaro turned away from Sam, shoulders shaking with laughter.

Jake's voice came through the speaker next. "Uh, Dad, not a great time."

"Okay, Jake, it's not even dark out, put some pants on and we'll talk about this later." Sam clenched his hands into fists.

"My house, my pants, my rules." Jake sounded smug. "And my rules are no pants. Why are you here?"

"For reasons that I'd rather not discuss in a public lobby." Sam turned to look at Tessaro, whose face was bright red. The taller cop was trying to stifle a laugh in his hands. It wasn't working.

"Ugh. Fine, but you owe me. Take your sweet time coming up; I can't find my shirt."

The door leading to the building's interior buzzed.

Tessaro doubled over, gasping. Sam kicked at his foot. "Yeah, yuk it up. Someday it's going to be you, interrupting your kid's shenanigans, and I'm going to be the one laughing at you."

"You're kidding me, right?" Tessaro made a face. "No. Not me."

"What, you're so good at telling other people how to handle their kids, you're not planning to have a baseball team of your own?"

"Nah." Tessaro stuffed his hands into his pockets and followed Sam to the elevator. "Not my thing. I had my chance and I blew it." He glanced over at Sam. "Why do you think I'm on you guys so much about not screwing things up with yours so badly that it can't be fixed?"

The elevator doors opened. "I had no idea." Sam stepped inside. "I figured you were just a busybody."

"I am. Professionally, remember? So are you." Tessaro leaned back against the elevator wall. "Now remember. You're being conciliatory. He made his choices, but you shot yourself in the foot."

Sam nodded. "Right."

Jake apparently couldn't find his shirt, and rather than find another one and greet his father in some semblance of order he just threw a hoodie on and left it unzipped. He wasn't being subtle about what had been interrupted. At least Dinesh had the good grace to get fully dressed again, and look sheepish.

Huh. Dinesh was still in the picture. That was something, anyway. Hopefully they'd do things in the right order.

Tessaro explained things to Jake. Sam almost interrupted, but then he decided to keep his mouth shut. Tessaro was doing a perfectly good job of explaining the situation, and Sam knew that if he tried to justify things to his son he'd probably lose his temper.

Jake shook his head. "I don't like this. You've had plenty of time to try to be better. Joey and me, we showed up and begged you to do better by Oliver, and you just sat there like a toad. Why is it different now?"

Sam grimaced. "Because Tessaro isn't my son, and because he sat there and insulted my masculinity until I got up and shoved him?"

Jake crossed his arms over his bare chest. A bare chest that bore several hickeys, Sam noted, and choked back his anger. "If that's all it took I'd have been happy to insult your masculinity all night."

"It's different." Tessaro tightened his jaw. "Just—look. Nenci has to at least try to make it right, okay? If Oliver says no then fine, I won't blame him a bit, but at least Nenci will have tried. He needs to have the chance to try."

Sam hung his head. "I don't want to spend the rest of my life not knowing what he would have said. I know what he should say, but if I don't ask him I won't know for sure. I just—I'm trying, here. I'm learning how to be a better man."

Jake's lip curled, but he grabbed his phone from the coffee table. "Hey, Oliver? You home? Yeah, it's me. I've got a visitor here for you. I think you should at least try to hear him out. No, no, I mean, if you don't want to you don't have to, but he brought a chaperone. I think he wants to try and be reasonable. I don't know, if he starts acting like a dick have Tessaro shoot him or something, that's what he's *for*."

Tessaro pulled his head back and blinked at Jake. "Seriously?"

Jake waved him off. "Yeah, sure. Call me if you need me." He turned to his father. "Do not make him need me. Do I make myself clear?"

"Crystal." Sam paused for a moment, surprised by the role reversal, and then he headed down the hall toward Oliver's apartment. Tessaro hurried along behind him.

Chapter Fifteen

Oliver's heart beat a wild tattoo against his ribcage when he opened the door. He knew that he shouldn't do this. He shouldn't waste so much as three seconds on Sam or his words. Oliver had set a course, and he needed to stick to it. That was all that there was to it, or at least it should have been.

His hand trembled as he unlocked the door, and Oliver couldn't tell if it was from need or anger. He wanted to reach out and touch. He wanted to yell and scream. He did neither. Instead, he pulled back and gestured to the couch. Then he sat on the chair. There would be no succumbing to proximity here. He might want Sam, but he wasn't going to give in to that.

Sam hung his head and stuffed his hands into his pockets. He shuffled over to the couch and took a seat. Tessaro walked at a more normal pace, with his head up. "Thanks for seeing us," Tessaro said, with a flash of a grin at Oliver.

Oliver didn't return it. He just sighed and pulled his knees up. He hadn't bothered to dress up. After work, he'd come home and put on sweats. He felt underdressed, but he couldn't muster up enough passion to be bothered by it. It wasn't like he could impress Sam anymore. "I have to admit that I'm a little confused. I'm not sure what else is left to say."

"I know you're not." Sam leaned back and melted into the couch. "I haven't given you much of a reason."

"No." Oliver shook his head. He looked over to the side and at the floor. "You haven't."

Tessaro elbowed Sam. Oliver wasn't sure what was going on there, and he wasn't sure that it mattered.

Then again, maybe it did. Sam jumped a little when Tessaro's elbow connected. "Well, see, it's... Okay, look." He took a deep breath and toyed with the corner of his shirt. "I told you I've been in therapy. I started therapy because you made me want to be better, Oliver. I realized that I had a problem. I couldn't be what you needed, and there was no one that I could even talk to about it. I needed to be better. It's taken me time to realize, though, that I was sabotaging myself. With everything, not just you, but yes, with you too. I was pushing you away because I was scared. I am scared."

Oliver closed his eyes. He couldn't look at Sam. Of course, with the element of sight removed, all that remained was scent. That was no help to him. Sam's scent was warm, alluring, and all but pulled him to his feet. He wanted to give in so very badly, but there was nothing to give in to. "Sam," he said. He gripped the arms of his chair. "Sam," he said again, "I'm not sure why you're here. I mean, you've come to try and 'explain,' or whatever, before, and it hasn't gone well. I don't know what you want or what. It hurts. I've told you that before. I need to just make a clean break."

Sam made a choked off sound, like a kicked dog, and Oliver turned his head away again. He couldn't let himself feel bad for Sam here. He had to protect himself.

Tessaro cleared his throat and leaned forward, elbows on his knees. "What if you didn't have to do that?" He folded his hands together. "What if you didn't have to back away? What if there was an option that let you keep your baby, and be with the man I'm pretty sure you want to be with?"

Sam held his breath, and Oliver glowered at both of them. "I'm pretty sure it would have come up by now, don't you think?" He bit down on the inside of his cheek. "I mean, I might not be perfect. Sure, I slept with him before a claim, but you know what? Thousands of omegas do that and they don't suffer. I didn't even ask him for one. I just... I put his needs first, and this is what I got for it." He bit down on the first knuckle of his thumb.

"I know you did." Sam stood up from the couch. "And that's on me. I was wrapped up in my own stuff and I convinced myself that I was doing right by you. I wouldn't listen to anyone else when they told me I was wrong. Until now. Oliver, I was wrong."

Oliver stopped biting on his skin. His heart quivered in his chest, unsure how to respond. "What are you trying to say here?"

Sam stepped closer. "Oliver, I'm sorry. I was pushing you away because I was afraid of success. I want to be with you. I'm still afraid of claiming you, because of the age difference, but I want to be with you. We can work out the other issues— the claim, or not—later. If you're willing. But I want you to be with someone who loves you, and who loves you with his whole heart. I want you to have the family you deserve—a child you love, or even more than one, and a partner who will support you and give you what you need to make it work. I want to be all of those things for you."

Oliver couldn't move. All he could do was stop and stare at his alpha. "This isn't real," he decided after a long moment. "This is a hallucination; someone at the office dosed me or something."

Tessaro frowned. "Does that happen often?"

"No. But it's more plausible than Sam suddenly deciding that he wants to be a father again after putting me through all of this." Oliver buried his face in his hands and tried to fight off his tears.

Sam stroked Oliver's hand with a finger. "Oliver. I'm so, so sorry that I've done this to you, that I've made you lose this much faith in me. Please let me try again. Let me be your alpha. Let me show you the alpha I've wanted to be for these three years and counting, Oliver."

Oliver pulled his hands away from his face. "How do I know that you're not just going to flake out again in the morning? Or an hour from now?" The question was mostly rhetorical. Oliver's body might be completely on board with everything that Sam was saying, but his head and his heart knew better.

"Look." Sam reached into his pocket. Oliver's eyes were glued to his hands. "I couldn't claim you right now anyway. We can talk about that a little bit later, maybe. But there's a solution that doesn't put you in danger for now." He pulled out a small box, and with a shaking hand he offered it to Oliver.

Oliver couldn't move.

Sam handed the box to Oliver. "Here. It's a ring." He opened the box.

Sam swallowed. "I want to be with you, for the rest of my life. I want to raise our child together. I don't want to lose that chance, Oliver. I don't. I love you. I love that baby, even though it's really not more than a bunch of cells that looks kind of like a bean right now. I want to be yours, if you'll still have me."

Oliver's hands were shaking too much to pick the ring up. It wasn't some kind of ostentatious thing, but a simple gold band with a few small diamonds set into the band. It was clearly designed for a man, a man like Oliver. "I'm scared," he admitted, once he found his voice again. "I don't know what to think. I'm afraid. I want to say yes, but it's such a risk. It's not just me that I'm risking here."

"I know it's not." Sam took the ring and slipped it onto Oliver's finger. "But I have people watching my back. They're not going to let me let you down. They care about you too. Ryan Tran, Tessaro, Jake and Joey—they're all going to hold my feet to the fire and keep me doing the right thing by you, even when I get scared."

Oliver looked up into Sam's eyes and saw desperation, and honesty, and love. He knew that he should pay attention to the lessons that he'd learned. He also knew that he couldn't turn his back now. He reached out and touched Sam's face, letting the light catch the small diamonds in the ring. "Sam," he whispered.

Tessaro bolted for the door. "That's my cue." He grimaced. "I'll be at the bar if anyone needs me."

Sam helped Oliver to his feet. Oliver needed the help; he couldn't remember the last time he'd felt so unsteady. His alpha's strong hands held him up and let him get safely to the bedroom. Sam even paused to make sure that the door was locked as they passed it.

When they got to the bedroom, Sam undressed Oliver slowly and carefully. Oliver felt like a present being unwrapped, and that was enough to make him giddy. Sam's care in peeling off Oliver's shirt made Oliver's breath catch in his chest. The softness, the gentleness with which Sam took off Oliver's sweatpants brought a surge of heat to Oliver's entire body.

He leaned back against the pillows on his bed as Sam's eyes looked over his naked form. "I thought I'd never be able to have this again," Sam murmured. "To be with you again. God, Oliver. Thank you." He unbuttoned his shirt and took it off almost violently. His undershirt went next, and then his trousers and underwear. Socks and shoes were the last to go, and Oliver could drink Sam in.

Sam approached the bed and ran his hand down Oliver's chest. "So beautiful," he whispered. He reached into his trouser pocket and pulled out a small bottle of lube.

Oliver licked his lips as his alpha crawled into the bed with him. Just his scent was enough to make Oliver weak, but pressing their flesh together brought a moan to his lips that he couldn't contain. Was sex like this with all alphas? Oliver didn't know, and he wasn't ever going to know. Sam was it for him, and he'd known it since the day they met.

Sam's hands, and Sam's lips, ran along Oliver's skin to warm him and get him ready. Each caress and every kiss had a purpose. They pushed away the lingering sadness and soothed Oliver's fears. His issues were still a factor, of course. The lessons of the past wouldn't disappear simply because Sam said some pretty words and lay down with him again, but he could feel a change already.

This time their coupling was deliberate, purposeful. Sam took his time opening him up, drawing out the pleasure for Oliver instead of treating it as a means to an end. He rocked his way into Oliver with short, shallow thrusts that built in intensity until he finally bottomed out, and then he set up a slow, romantic rhythm that drew things out even further. Oliver's pleasure built as he rocked his hips, meeting his alpha thrust for thrust, and when he finally came it was without any touch other than his alpha's careful thrusts.

Sam lost the rhythm after that. He collapsed with his head against Oliver's shoulder and panted for a few long moments before he pulled out and got something to clean them up with.

Oliver held his breath when Sam walked away. This was usually when Sam left. Granted, a sample set of two was hardly statistically significant, but he couldn't shake the memories.

Sam pulled the covers back and slipped beneath them. He took Oliver into his arms. "Is it all right if I stay?" he asked in a small voice.

Oliver rolled over and kissed his alpha. "I want you to," he said, and rested his head on Sam's chest.

Part of Oliver expected to wake up alone, a pillow shoved into the space where Sam had been. In the morning, though, his arms were still full of Sam. He smiled, almost giddy with relief. Maybe things could work out for them after all.

***

Sam and Oliver packed Oliver's clothes up that day and brought them to Hopkinton. They moved the rest of his things over the next few weeks, not that he had much. His apartment wasn't all that huge, so he couldn't afford to accumulate all that much.

There was some furniture, and Sam and Oliver had to discuss that furniture's fate. The furniture was new, or at least newer than the furniture in Sam's place. It was stylish and in great shape, as opposed to Sam's dated and kind of beat-up furniture. Sam liked Oliver's things better, but the older things had been chosen by Chris. He didn't want to get rid of them.

Oliver, being Oliver, had a solution. "The finished basement is empty now. Why not move the older furniture into the basement, and we can turn it into a playroom? That way we're not getting rid of the things you shared with Chris. He's still part of your life." Oliver took Sam's hand. "He's part of our life, and our baby's life. We're growing instead of replacing."

Sam's heart swelled when he heard that. The nagging suspicion that he was somehow being disloyal to Chris' memory was minor, but it hadn't left. He could only love Oliver more, knowing that Oliver was ready and willing to welcome Chris' memory into his heart. Joey came over to help move the heavy things, and that was all there was to it.

Both of Sam's sons were ecstatic about the new arrangements. Joey demanded that his old room become the new baby's nursery and helped to paint it and get it ready. Jake insisted on helping out too, and he brought Dinesh with him to lift, carry, and paint. Oliver blushed at all of the fuss, but he let the alphas do their thing and stayed in the kitchen with Jake to cook.

They got married on the Thursday after they agreed to try again. They didn't have a huge ceremony and they didn't make a fuss. They brought Jake and Joey as witnesses, as well as Ryan Tran and Pat Tessaro. They simply went to the Justice of the Peace, said their vows, and signed the right paper. It didn't take much, and they didn't need much. All that they needed was that commitment.

Their reunion and marriage didn't soothe all ruffled feathers. Ryan Tran had a few private words with Sam about treating Oliver right, and Sam didn't object. He'd earned that, and he knew it. Nina Burton had the same talk with him, which was somehow scarier. Tran might hesitate to hurt a fellow cop. Nina wouldn't.

Either way, Sam wasn't going to draw their ire. He knew that he'd screwed up badly. He was going to do better now. He was going to make Oliver feel like a king.

Of course, it wasn't easy. Sam knew that it wouldn't be easy when he went into the marriage. He was scared, and he knew that he could be overbearing sometimes. Oliver was still sometimes hesitant and he was always going to be young in Sam's eyes. They'd chosen one another, though, and Sam had made a commitment to himself. He was going to do this, and he was going to do it right.

As Oliver's belly grew, the Cooper Block case wound its way through the court system. Very little of that had anything to do with Sam, and even less of that had to do with Oliver. They paid attention, because it was the case that had brought them together, but they didn't need to get involved until the trial itself started.

The trial started six months after Marsten had been arrested. During that time, the Marsten family laid low. They didn't want to make things worse for their paterfamilias, who had been released on his own recognizance provided that he wears a GPS monitoring anklet. Sam couldn't help but shake his head at that. The man had killed sixty people and he got to await trial in the lap of luxury.

The trial started out with interminable opening arguments. The prosecutor talked about the dead, about vendettas, about change and about hewing to old patterns. He spoke about science, about the different ways that technology made it possible to prosecute this type of crime. He spoke about justice, and about the horror of death by fire.

The defense team, led by a man that made Sam's fists itch, countered with arguments about Isaiah Marsten's devotion to his family. He spoke about prior scandals at the crime lab, and about how anything that came out of the lab had to be discounted now due to what had happened in the past. He questioned the value of cold case investigations at all, given that "the perpetrator, whomever he may be, has been quiet for over two decades. Should we waste time chasing after someone who no longer poses a threat?" He harped on his client's age and on his client's generosity.

Sam had to testify, of course. He knew what the prosecutor would ask, and he was able to answer those questions without a problem. He described the facts of the case as he knew them, and detailed the timelines of both fires and how he'd come to determine that Marsten was the culprit. The defense attorney tried to trip him up on cross-examination on the basis of his earlier statements that he hadn't thought that Marsten would be a likely suspect at all, but Sam stood firm. That only made Marsten a more solid candidate, he told the court. He hadn't had any kind of bias that might lead him toward Marsten.

Oliver was next in line, and by the time that he got to testify he was eight full months pregnant and as big as a house. He looked physically uncomfortable as he made his way up to the witness stand, and the judge himself offered Oliver a cushion for his back.

Sam couldn't be sure if the gesture would get Oliver sympathy with the jury or not.

Oliver's testimony took a full day. He had to explain the science behind his findings, and he had to give the details on how he'd created the program that re-created the fires. He then had to show the re-creation for the court, and describe both what was happening and his conclusions.

The defense attorney was vicious on his cross-examination. He tried to attack the science behind Oliver's conclusions, based on the issues that had gone on at the lab in earlier times. Oliver successfully defended all of the science behind his work, so the defense attorney attacked Oliver's personal integrity. He lashed out about Oliver's pregnancy, taking place as it did outside of a claim, and attacked his ethics for sleeping with a detective with whom he'd been working.

Sam heard the lawyer's attacks, and he clenched his fists. He rose in his seat, ready to rip the lawyer limb from limb, but Langer held him back.

Oliver on the other hand heard the lawyer out and then leaned into the microphone. "Your questions are entirely based on beliefs centered around a set of cultural values. My testimony here has been based around science. Science doesn't care what you believe. Science doesn't care who you are. Science cares about facts. If stimulus x is applied, reaction y will be the result. In this case, if kerosene is applied to the walls of a building and splashed onto the carpeting here, and ignited here, the burn pattern will always display like this, regardless of the person who is examining the evidence." He folded his hands and rested them on his belly. "That's how fire works."

Sam could not have been prouder of Oliver than he was in that moment.

The defense called a few witnesses to the stand, but no one could provide an alibi that the prosecution wasn't able to disprove. The defense tried to call some forensic witnesses, but they stated that after viewing Oliver's testimony they were unable to refute it.

The jury came back with a guilty verdict. It wasn't justice, not exactly. Isaiah Marsten had lit the match, and he'd almost certainly ordered the 1992 fire. He hadn't acted alone, and he hadn't named his accomplices. His oldest son had stepped into the headship of the family as soon as the trial began. Nothing would really change, but at least this one man would pay some kind of penalty for his crime.

Sam wasn't in court to hear the verdict. He was notified by text, while he stood at the head of Oliver's bed in the hospital and encouraged him to push.

The birth wasn't an easy one, and Sam ultimately had to leave the room because he couldn't handle seeing Oliver in pain. Once Amelia had been safely delivered, however, Sam could be re-admitted and view his daughter and his husband with the adoration they deserved.

Amelia was perfect. She was tiny, but neither Sam nor Oliver was all that large. She had a full head of wild, dark hair, and an imperious cast to her tiny face that Sam fell in love with immediately. She disliked being put into her bassinet and had a strong preference for being held by one of her fathers or brothers.

Oliver was exhausted and uncomfortable after the birth, but he was happy. He loved their daughter, and he could barely bring himself to part with her long enough to let Sam hold her.

Sam stared down at his husband and child. Maybe he would overcome his fears and claim Oliver, and maybe he wouldn't. What he knew was that he would give them the world.

Bonus Chapter Sixteen

Oliver strapped Amelia into her car seat. She waved her little arms and let out a little squeal of delight. "Daddy!" she shouted, and stared at him with her wide gray eyes.

"That's right, Amelia!" He dropped a kiss onto her button nose, which earned him another squeal and several giggles. "I'm your daddy!" His heart swelled with pride. Maybe someday he'd get tired of hearing her incessant chatter, but that day hadn't come yet.

She pointed over at Jake, who was busy strapping his own daughter, Chandra, into the other car seat. Chandra was only six months old, able to look around and show an interest in her surroundings but not to do much else yet. "Jake!" Amelia identified, kicking her little feet with glee. "Chandra!"

"That's right, sprout." Jake winked at her as Chandra grabbed his tie and pulled it into her mouth. Chandra was getting a new tooth, and that meant everything was fair game right now. Fortunately Jake was a scientist, and science had taught him to do his research. He only wore machine-washable ties these days.

"No sprout! Mel-ya!" Amelia put her hand on her chest. "MEEL-ya!"

Oliver shook his head with a rueful grin. He couldn't believe how forward his daughter's language development was. She was only fifteen months old, but she had plenty of words and she was more than happy to use them. She always wanted more words, too, demanding to know the identity of everything she could see. She might not be able to pronounce everything yet, but she was getting there. He adored her curious mind. "That's right, honey. You're Amelia."

Amelia settled into her seat with a satisfied grunt, and Oliver was able to finish strapping her in. Jake looked up at Oliver. "Is that seriously what I'm in for?"

Oliver closed the door and walked around to the driver's seat. "I don't see why not. I mean you guys are smart guys, you read to her often, there isn't any reason why Chandra wouldn't be an early talker." He started the car while Jake buckled himself into the passenger seat. "For real, though, everyone's wired differently and she's used to hearing two different languages so she might not. Bilingual kids talk later."

"That's true." Jake glanced into the mirror, so that he could get a glimpse of their kids. Amelia had reached across the seats and taken Chandra's hand.

This had become a daily ritual, ever since Jake had returned to work. The babies shared a daycare. They spent most of their time together when they weren't at daycare too, with one of their fathers always being at the other one's house. Oliver and Jake always provided babysitting services when the other needed it, whether it was because one of them got called to a crime scene in the middle of the night while their mate was unavailable or for more pleasant reasons. Chandra had even inherited a healthy portion of Amelia's clothes, as Amelia outgrew them and Chandra grew into them.

Now that Joe's omega knew that he was also expecting a girl, those dresses, pajamas, and onesies would get recycled again. Oliver's heart swelled with joy at the knowledge that they'd be able to keep the happiness going around the family, and that the adorable mouse onesie with the tail wouldn't disappear.

Ordinarily, Oliver would drop Jake and Chandra off at their place on his way home, or they'd drop him off at his. Tonight, though, Amelia was going to be staying with Jake. She was going to stay there for a few days while her dads took a little drive down to Newport. She'd come down with her brothers and the rest of the family in a few days.

When they pulled into the driveway, Oliver had a hard time separating from Amelia. He knew that it was for the best. They'd been planning this trip for a while, and they'd been planning this vacation for almost two years. Oliver just couldn't quite reconcile that purely-theoretical *we'll leave her with Jake for a few days* with walking away empty handed, and knowing that he wasn't coming back for her.

He kissed her goodbye, not once or twice but three times, and told her to be a good girl for her brother. Then he got back into his car and drove the whole ten minutes to his own house.

Sam was waiting for him when he got there. He'd changed out of his work clothes and wore khakis and a polo shirt. He looked incredible, but then again, he'd always look incredible to Oliver. Maybe there were a few more gray hairs in his beard than there had been two years ago, but that was okay. It just made Sam look more distinguished. Oliver greeted him with a kiss when he walked in the door.

Sam lifted their suitcases like they weighed nothing. "Are you ready to go?"

Oliver looked into his husband's gray eyes. "Yeah. It'll be a long drive." He bit his lip and glanced at the playpen. "I miss her."

"I do too." Sam gave Oliver a little smile. "We'll see her in a few days, though."

"Yeah." Oliver followed Sam out to the car, and tried not to think too hard about what was going to happen between now and then.

Would Amelia be able to tell somehow?

They hit some traffic on the way down to Newport, but it wasn't bad. Oliver was in Sam's car, wrapped in Sam's presence and Sam's scent. He could have been in bumper-to-bumper traffic and not cared. Things weren't perfect, of course. They both had their own insecurities, but they'd made a commitment and so far they'd done a good job of honoring it.

They pulled into the parking lot at the hotel and checked in. The hotel was a true indulgence, something that was so far out of the ordinary for them that Oliver would never have thought of it for himself. It was in one of the old Newport mansions, now converted into a luxury hotel, and their room overlooked the ocean. It had been decorated with the French Renaissance in mind, had a jetted two-person tub, and dripped opulence.

Sam had found it. All three couples had saved for a long time to be able to afford it, but they were worth it.

Once they settled into the absurdly fancy room, Oliver locked the door and turned to his husband. Sam was staring at him, pupils blown with lust. His jaw tightened. "Are you sure that you still want this, Oliver? Because if you're having second thoughts, or even hints of second thoughts, we'll call it off. I won't mind. We can still do the vacation; we'll still be together forever. We don't have to do this one part if you have any doubts at all."

Once Oliver would have been offended or bothered by that. Now he just smiled. "What do *you* want, Sam?"

"I want you to be safe." A couple of tears escaped from his eyes. "I want you to be safe, and healthy, and happy."

Oliver stripped off his shirt. "And?"

Sam grinned. "And I want you to be mine." He hung his head, but kept his eyes on Oliver as Oliver continued to take his clothes off. "I've wanted you to be mine since the day I met you. I can't fight it anymore. I just can't, Oliver. I want to see my claim on you."

Oliver had gotten rid of all of his clothes by now. "I want to be yours." He stepped closer to his alpha. "I want people to look at me, to see that mark on my neck and know that I'm your omega. I want to be tied to you forever. One life between us, Sam. That's it. I want you to know that I'm yours, every minute of every day, because of the way that we're tied together."

Sam put his hands on Oliver's bare shoulders. "We can't undo this once it's done."

"I don't want it any other way."

Sam got rid of his own clothing and grabbed onto Oliver. Oliver let his mate pick him up and carry him off to the giant bed and lay him down. Sam's muscles trembled with the effort of holding himself back even now. Oliver could have been perfectly happy to draw this out, or even try to seduce Sam a little bit, but Sam didn't seem to need that right now. He lay back and stretched himself out, making himself as accessible as he could.

It seemed almost as if someone had flipped a switch in Sam's head. Now that they were going to perform this claim, Sam seemed downright frantic with need. His hands were everywhere, and his mouth followed in short order. Oliver, with the small part of his mind that was still capable of rational though, knew that this was normal. Now that Sam had given into the urge to claim, his instincts would be pushing him further and further until he'd done exactly that.

And he knew that he was no better. Oliver was not typically a submissive lover, but right now every muscle in his body demanded that he bare his neck and yield. He rolled over when his alpha demanded it, and he parted his legs to give Alpha better access. He let Alpha work him open quickly, instead of drawing it out the way he usually liked, and he mewled his pleasure without shame.

Alpha entered him in one slow, patient thrust that must have been ten times as difficult given the white-hot need burning through him. Oliver didn't ask him to wait. As soon as he felt that he'd adjusted to the intrusion, he told his alpha to move.

Sam complied. He set an almost brutal pace, one that had Oliver gasping almost immediately. He wasn't about to complain. He wanted this, exactly like this. He let himself cry out in his pleasure, and he didn't hold back. He rocked back to meet his alpha's thrusts and gave himself over entirely to his instincts.

He had no idea how much time had passed when Sam's bite descended, but the effect was instantaneous. Oliver shouted into the pillow as he spilled his release up onto his body. Sam spilled into him, and it was over. The haze left him, and all that remained was the post-orgasmic bliss that he so treasured.

Sam collapsed on top of him for a moment, and then he got up and staggered into the bathroom. Oliver thought he was just going to get them a cloth, but then he heard the bathtub running. After a moment, Sam came back and helped Oliver to his feet. "Mine," he said, touching the spot on Oliver's neck where he'd left his mark.

It was still tender. It should have been. It was a bite wound, after all.

Oliver blushed and rested his head on his alpha's shoulder. "Yours," he murmured. "Forever."

Once the tub was full, they both slipped into the hot water and each other's arms. It was a nice, freeing feeling. They couldn't do this at home. The tub wasn't jetted, for one thing. It wasn't big enough for two people. It wasn't even big enough for one person to fully lie down in, and there was a guarantee that if someone tried to take a proper bath there would be a tiny person hammering on the door to be let in right away.

"Happy?" Sam shifted and squeezed Oliver a little closer.

"Yeah." Oliver relaxed into his alpha's arms even more fully. "I feel like I've been waiting for that—with you—my whole life." He stroked across Sam's hairy chest. "Nothing can keep us apart now."

Sam chuckled. "No. It can't. I'm always going to be here for you. And Amelia, of course." He stroked Oliver's hair. "I'm glad we finally did this."

Sam washed them both, and he even dried Oliver before bringing Oliver back to the bed. Oliver was perfectly capable of walking himself by this point, but his happiness had given him a certain degree of lassitude. He climbed into bed, and Sam tucked him into bed before slipping in beside him.

The next day, Oliver and Sam woke at the same time. That wasn't something they'd ever done before. Usually Oliver woke up first, to work out and take care of Amelia, while Sam slept a little bit later. Today, though, their eyes opened at the same instant. Oliver laughed when he noticed, and that brought a smile to Sam's face. "I'd forgotten about that," he said with a rueful shake of his head.

Oliver squirmed a little. "I'm sorry. I don't mean to bring up bad memories."

Sam kissed him. "It's not, not really. When we first got together, the whole waking up together thing was weird as hell. Especially since we were still basically strangers to one another. But we got used to it, didn't even think about it anymore after a few months." He sighed and sat up. "I didn't think about it at all until he died, actually. Then it was, you know. Difficult. It's been a long time. I forgot how beautiful it was, to wake up next to someone like this."

Oliver pulled himself into a reclining position. "So what's on the agenda today, Alpha?"

"Mmm. I love it when you call me that, by the way." Oliver could see Sam's reaction, from the little flush on his skin to the way that his dick gave a little twitch. "I thought we might be able to go and explore Newport a little bit, grab something to eat. Then I thought we could come back here and make a mess of the hotel a little more. I was kind of tired last night after a full day of work." He wrapped his arm around Oliver's shoulders. "You know, I could get used to this."

Oliver laughed. "We'll see how you feel about this whole one-room living thing when Amelia gets here on Tuesday night!"

They found breakfast in a little coffee shop downtown, and they took a cruise around Newport Harbor. They did a little bit of shopping, and they hit the beach for a little while. They bought some food to bring back to their room, though, because they had no intention of leaving it.

By the time Tuesday morning rolled around, Oliver felt rested and sated. "I think this is something we both needed," he said, as he and Sam lay in bed and watched the ocean.

"The claim? Of course." Sam kissed Oliver's scar. He could barely keep his mouth off of it.

"That too. I'm beyond happy about that. Which you know," Oliver added with a mock glare. "I meant this." He gestured around the room. "This is the first time we've had to be alone together since we met, and I mean truly alone together. No one interfering. No one pushing, or pulling, or doing things for our own good."

Sam hummed. "It's true. Of course, I don't think we'd have ever gotten together if it weren't for people pushing, or pulling."

"There's that." Oliver leaned over and kissed his alpha's lips, morning breath notwithstanding. "I love you."

Sam carded a hand through Oliver's hair and kissed him back, harder and longer. "I love you too. And I always will."

<<<<>>>>

Preview Chapter: Look Back

Elias shook hands with Agent Fredericks. "I'm glad that we could resolve this case so quickly, and so well," he said. Maybe "well" wasn't the right way to put it. The parents were getting back a traumatized kid who was going to be scarred for life, mentally and physically. At least they were getting the kid back, he supposed, and he'd met the Wilkersons several times. If there had ever been a family with the heart and strength to help a kid heal, they were it.

Agent Fredericks shook his hand. "Honestly, we couldn't have done it without you and HomeSafe. You guys are absolutely top of the food chain when it comes to missing kids." She shook her head. "How do you guys manage it?"

Elias grinned. "To be honest, it's because it's all we do. We only work on missing kids, day in and day out. It's a grind, don't get me wrong, but it does allow us to help law enforcement in ways that they might not be able to do on their own." He stretched. The hotel bed hadn't been kind to him.

"So where's home for you?" Fredericks walked out of the building with him.

"I have a place in Providence. I'm not there very often." He chuckled. "I should probably sell it, to be honest, but I have to have some address to put on my tax returns, right? Seriously, though. I'm all over the place."

"That sounds…" She made a face but bit her lip; clearly stopping herself before she could say too much. "I mean I travel a lot, but I do come home first." She wrinkled her nose. "You must not have kids, then."

Elias could see his car in the distance. He focused on that, instead of on his memories. The last thing that he needed right now was to remember the smell of his own blood, or his own insides, in the hospital. He still remembered those, sometimes. "No. I don't. Can't, actually." That wasn't necessarily true. The doctors had slipped a "probably" in there somewhere, but that wasn't important right now.

"I'm sorry." She put her hand over her mouth. "That was incredibly callous of me."

He waved a hand. "Don't worry about it. It was a long time ago." That wasn't a lie. It had been a long time ago, ten years, and yet he could still remember every detail. "Anyway, you have a safe trip back to Quantico."

"You drive safe now! Where exactly are you headed to next?" She knit her blonde brows together.

Elias opened his mouth to respond, and then he scratched his head. He never worried about where he was going, until he had to be there. "I have no idea," he admitted. "I got a message while we were in that press conference, but I haven't had a chance to sit down and listen to it yet."

"Oh. Well, drive safe!" Fredericks waved goodbye, and Elias slipped into his car.

He pulled out his phone and called his boss back. "Hey, Dagmar, what's up? I saw you called while I was in that conference with the locals."

Dagmar cleared her throat. "How do you feel about taking on another case so soon?"

Elias rolled his eyes. How was he supposed to feel about taking on a case? His title was investigator. That was what it said on his business cards—*Investigative Analyst*. What else was he supposed to do, sit around for a week and do yoga or something? "I feel fine taking on another case, Dagmar," he told her. He tried to keep his voice from sounding condescending. "That's why I'm here."

She chuckled at him. "Glad to hear it, Elias. If it makes you feel any better, this one's in Boston. You can stay in a hotel on-site if you want, or you can work from your own place back in Providence."

Elias choked on his own breath. "Boston, Massachusetts?"

Dagmar laughed, just a little. "Uh, yeah, tiger. Where did you think I meant, if you had the option to work out of your place in Providence?"

For a moment, just a moment, Pat's face sprang to mind. That was absurd, of course. Plenty of guys went into the police academy. That didn't mean that Pat would even be in the same jurisdiction as this case, never mind have both made detective and be assigned to this case. "Sorry. I lived in Boston for a while."

"I know. That was part of the appeal, to be honest. You're familiar with the area, and you speak both Spanish and Portuguese. I think that's going to come in fairly handy. Are you okay with going back?"

"Yeah. Yeah, of course. There's nothing I won't do for a kid, you know?" He tugged at the collar of his shirt. "What should I know?"

"Well, for starters, we're dealing with a dead kid here. I'll send you the case file. It's—well, it's weird, Elias. You'll be working with the State Police on this one. Their Cold Case unit is working with the Abused Persons unit together on it. It's too weird to explain over the phone, you have to read it to believe it."

He pinched the bridge of his nose. "Yeah. Okay. I'll head out tomorrow morning, it'll be about a fourteen-hour drive."

"Take the day after off, do some laundry or something. Or don't try to do a drive like that in one day all by yourself. The cops will still be going over tape and everything. Read the file, Elias. This isn't going to be a quick job."

"No." Elias wouldn't be that lucky. "I'll call you with any questions, Dagmar."

"Talk to you later, sweetie." Dagmar hung up.

Elias headed back to his hotel. He had a lot of driving to do tomorrow; he might as well read the file now.

It took him about five minutes to realize that this case wasn't going to be like any other case that he'd ever seen. The body of a ten-year-old boy had been found, neatly wrapped in a white sheet, just inside the doorway of an abandoned hotel in Boston. While the boy was naked under the sheet, there was no indication of sexual trauma; the sheet appeared to be something more along the lines of a traditional shroud than anything else. The child appeared to have been well cared-for, although not overfed by any stretch of the imagination. He'd been found yesterday.

Today, the medical examiner found that John Doe had died from diphtheria.

Someone from the State Police Crime Lab had taken the initiative to scan not only the boy's fingerprints, but his footprints too. Elias wouldn't have asked for that. Diphtheria was easily preventable, with vaccines. He wouldn't have expected someone who had neglected to vaccinate their child to have bothered to register his footprints in any kind of database. Of course, he'd hardly have expected people who let their child die from a perfectly preventable illness to have wrapped their kid up in a shroud like that. He wouldn't have expected people who wrapped their child nicely in a shroud to dump the body in an abandoned hotel, either.

So many contradictions. Or maybe Elias was moving too quickly to judgment. It was an occupational hazard.

The footprints had, in fact, been stored in a database, which had provided an identity for the child. That identity was of little help.

Scott Gilbert, five months of age, had been snatched from his mother's shopping cart in a grocery store in Shrewsbury, Massachusetts, ten years ago. He hadn't been seen since, not until he'd turned up dead from something that had been curable since the turn of the last century.

A chill ran over Elias' body. Someone had taken him and raised him up, and then dumped him like trash.

He pushed the thought from his mind. He had to stay objective. He couldn't let his anger cloud his judgment or he'd never find the culprit. That wasn't an acceptable outcome. If the perpetrator had stolen a child, for whatever reasons, they would do it again. Elias had to stop them before it was too late.

He packed up his things, leaving out only what he would need before leaving in the morning. He even slept in the nude, so that he wouldn't have to worry about packing up his pajamas. Someone else might have laughed at him for that, but it had been a while since there had been anyone to laugh at his travel habits.

He wasn't going to think about that. Instead, he was going to pack up his computer. He'd turn on the TV and try to think about just about anything else—anything other than the case, anything other than the life he'd left behind in Massachusetts. He drifted off to sleep while watching a documentary about ancient Roman engineering feats, and dreaming about aqueducts and coliseums.

When he woke up, he dressed quickly and hit the road as soon as he could. Bardstown was nice enough. It wasn't so nice that he wanted to linger, especially not with a fourteen-hour drive ahead of him. He found a place to get breakfast and coffee, and then he hopped onto the Bluegrass Parkway heading east.

Even all of the coffee in the world couldn't keep his mind from wandering as he drove north and east. It would have been impossible under any circumstances, but to ask it when he was heading back to Massachusetts was just absurd. He knew that there was no chance of running into Pat again. How many cops were there in Massachusetts? The odds that Pat had become a State Trooper, and was now a detective, were so small as to be minuscule.

But what if?

Elias wasn't a "what-if" kind of guy. He dealt in facts. The only "what-if" he liked to see was hypothesis testing. What if the child didn't run away, but was taken? What if the child wasn't taken, but got lost? When he was stuck in a car for fourteen hours, with no companion and no hope of distraction, he couldn't fight the pull of his brain.

What if he and Pat hadn't split up?

What an absurd question. Elias and Pat were always going to split up. They would never have lasted. Pat's ego couldn't tolerate being with a partner who had more resources than he did. His masculinity, and his identity as an alpha, had been too threatened. All that Elias had ever wanted to do was to help him, but Pat couldn't allow that.

Anger lanced through him, like a stab wound. Why would it have been the end of the world for Pat to just let Elias help? It wouldn't have been more than a drop in the bucket, for crying out loud. Had Elias really meant so little to him?

He snorted as he passed from Kentucky into West Virginia. He truly hadn't meant much to Pat. They'd gone their separate ways. Pat hadn't even taken long to move his stuff out. He'd told Elias that he was leaving, Elias had replied with some choice words before class, and by the time he came back Pat's stuff was just gone. He hadn't called to talk or to check in or anything. He hadn't passed on a forwarding address, either.

Not that Elias had wanted him to. Elias hadn't reached out either. Pat had meant the world to him, but he hadn't reached out and hadn't tried to bring him back. The breakup had happened, and that was it. When Elias' world had sent him reeling a few weeks later, he hadn't called, even though he should have.

And when his world came crashing down, he hadn't called him either. Why bother?

He wasn't going to see Pat again, and most of him didn't want to see Pat again. Sure, he'd loved Pat, but that chapter of his life was over. Too much had happened in the years since, and he wasn't that naive young man who thought that love would be enough to bridge everything that divided them.

Part of him, though, would not stop asking, *what if*?

What would he do if he saw Pat? How would he react? What would Pat see? Would he see a bitter, broken-down old omega that no one wanted now that he couldn't give them children anymore? Or would he see a tall, strong, confident man who didn't need Patrício Tessaro, and never actually had? Which version did Elias want him to see?

And how would Elias cope when Pat refused to be moved by either one?

The thought weighed him down as he cruised through Maryland, and Pennsylvania. Elias had always been the one to need Pat, never the other way around. Hell, Pat probably didn't even remember him.

As he crossed the border into New Jersey, Elias rolled his shoulders. He wasn't here to moon around over lost love. Elias did good work, damn it. He saved lives. He brought families closure. Maybe he was still alone, but he was going to leave a legacy behind him that outshone the sun itself. He didn't need to go mooning around after some guy whose middle name was probably Pride.

He pulled into his parking spot at the condo complex and hauled his bags upstairs. He hadn't been home in over a month. Nothing looked any different; he didn't expect it to. The whole condo looked like a large hotel suite. For a moment, the emptiness got to him.

Then he roused himself out of it. He had tomorrow off. He would call the Cold Case and Abused Persons units in the morning, and schedule time for a meeting. Until then, though, his time was his own. The fact that a certain someone hadn't wanted to share it with him just meant that he was at complete liberty to do as he pleased.

He ran himself a bubble bath, because he could. He opened himself a bottle of champagne, and after a moment's thought he brought the bottle into the tub along with a flute. He got himself a book from his shelf, a popular biography about Alexander Hamilton, and tossed his laundry into the pile in the corner. Tonight was for him, and he was going to unwind.

He pulled himself out of the tub when his mood had improved enough, and when he started to feel the danger involved in getting too attached to his bottle of champagne. He rinsed himself off, got dry, and headed for the bedroom.

Outside his window, the city of Providence bustled on in the blustery autumn night. Providence was a good place to be, he figured. It was far enough away from Boston that it had its own identity, but close enough that he could get into the larger city if he wanted to. Hell, he could get into New York if the mood so took him. He liked it here. He'd chosen it as a base for a reason, after all.

Maybe there were some good sides to getting assigned to a job in his home area after all. He rolled over and closed his eyes, a little smile playing across his face.

***

Pat sat and watched as Robles and Nenci verbally sparred over the Montague case. He knew what was really going on there. Neither one of them wanted to work the dead kid case, so they were trying like hell to work any other case that Devlin might see fit to open up for them.

He guessed that he could see their point of view. He didn't want to work the dead kid case either. The fact of the matter was, though, that someone had to work the dead kid case. *Scott Gilbert*, he reminded himself. He couldn't just think of the victim as some random dead kid. They were victims, they had been people, and they deserved respect even in the privacy of his thoughts.

They deserved names, damn it.

Someone was going to have to work the Scott Gilbert case, and none of the guys on the squad were going to have the first thing to say about it. Devlin was going to assign who he was going to assign, for reasons of his own, and that was all there was to it. He wouldn't assign Robles to it, because Ryan Tran from Abused Persons was already on the case and Robles and Tran were mated. They also couldn't work a case together without needing to be forcibly separated, so that meant that Robles got a pass this time.

Nenci turned to look at Pat. "What's up with you, Tessaro?"

Pat leaned back in his chair. "What do you mean, *what's up with me*? Nothing's up with me. My life is profoundly dull."

Robles snorted. "Dull my ass. Didn't you go home with two omegas last week?"

Pat scoffed. "Okay, maybe *dull* has more than one meaning. What does that have to do with anything?" He shook his head. "Besides, you know I'm not going to kiss and tell. You're the one with the lifetime commitment; you don't get to live vicariously through me."

Robles flipped him off. "Someday you're going to fall, and you're going to fall hard. And I'm going to be right there to laugh my ass off."

Pat chuckled. "You keep watching, Robles. You keep waiting. Never going to happen."

Nenci winked at him. "Ah, so the big man around town is too cool for love, huh?"

Pat folded his hands behind his head and closed his eyes. "That's exactly right, Nenci. Too cool." Nenci knew the truth, or some of it. That didn't stop him from teasing, and Pat didn't expect it to. Nenci didn't get it though, not really. Pat didn't want to fall in love, not again. It had hurt too much the first time, and Pat knew damn well that he wasn't going to find someone he cared about as much as he'd loved Elias.

Too bad it hadn't been mutual.

Whatever. He wasn't going to sit around and waste time and energy whining about what could have been—especially when there never was a "could have been."

"The consultant will get here when they get here. We'll find out who Devlin assigned then. Robles, you already know it ain't you. Why don't you find your chill and go do a crossword puzzle or something? You don't need to fight over the Montague case. It's a messy and ugly one, and there's no reason to try to get yourself stuck on it if you don't have to."

"An excellent point." Devlin walked out of his office. "The consultant is here. Why don't we all head into the conference room over near Abused Persons?"

Pat got up, folding his mouth shut. He had so many questions that he wanted to ask, but Devlin wouldn't answer them until he felt that the time was right. Manipulative bastard. The odds that HomeSafe would have sent Elias as a consultant were slim to none anyway. The guy never did cases in Massachusetts.

Pat had checked.

Morris stepped forward. "Uh, sir, our conference room is bigger. Why don't we just sit in there?"

Devlin glanced at him. "Because, Morris. The conference room we're using has better projection capabilities. Also, it has more exits. We're six alphas walking into an enclosed space. The consultant should feel as free as possible to run if he needs to."

A pit of dread spun itself into existence in the middle of Pat's stomach. His boss' words strongly suggested that the consultant was an omega. That didn't necessarily mean that their guest was Elias, but it did increase the odds. This was not good.

At least Pat wouldn't get stuck with the Scott Gilbert case. He hated working on cases with dead kids.

He followed the rest of the team into the empty conference room and sat between Nenci and Langer. Now that he'd built up that ball of dread, he just wanted to get the meeting over with. He needed to get this out of his system. He just had to get away.

The door from Abused Persons creaked open. Ryan Tran walked in first. He glanced around the room, spared a curl of the lip for Nenci, and sat down at the other end of the table. The man who followed him in, however, was someone that Pat didn't need to see to identify.

Elias looked good. He'd gotten older, in the ten years since they got done with undergrad. That only made sense. He still had that long, curly brown hair. This time it was tied back into a ponytail with a little black elastic. His brown eyes widened when he saw Pat, and he stopped moving.

Pat tried not to breathe too deeply. He hadn't smelled the lilac scent of the man he loved in over a decade. For half a second, everything fell away, and all he could think about was getting Elias back into his arms.

Nenci put a hand on Pat's arm. "You okay, buddy? You look like a ghost walked over your grave."

Elias' lip curled. "I can't do this."

Of course he couldn't. Elias had walked out of Pat's life without so much as a goodbye ten years ago. Why would he be anything but disgusted to see him now? He'd been repulsed at the thought of being with a cop. Seeing Pat here, with cops, must have made him want to vomit.

"I'll just go." Pat got up from his seat and headed for the door.

"Of course you will. It's what you're best at." Elias sniffed.

Words welled up in Pat's throat, but he choked them back. Words hadn't helped then, and they wouldn't help now. Besides, the last thing that he needed was to have his dirty laundry aired in front of the rest of the Cold Case Squad. Those guys were vicious. Pat should know; he wasn't any better. Instead, he brought up his right hand and extended his middle finger.

"Sit down, Tessaro." Devlin's voice cracked like a whip over the silence of the room.

Tessaro froze. If he ignored his boss' orders, he could be kicked off the force. Considering that he'd lost Elias in part because he'd chosen to join the force, he couldn't get kicked out now. He knew his movements were stiff as he returned to his seat, but he couldn't do anything about that.

"Mr. Salazar, do you have a problem working with the alphas from my team?" Devlin raised an eyebrow and stared Elias down.

Elias wouldn't be intimidated. Why would he? The guy could have bought and sold Devlin ten times over back when they were undergrads. Who knew what he could do now? "I had a relationship with Mr. Tessaro a very long time ago." He shrugged, the very image of supreme indifference. "It's hardly relevant. I apologize, Lt. Devlin. I was simply surprised to see him again." Elias closed his eyes and gave a full-body shudder before sitting down beside Ryan.

"Shows how much you know, buddy." Morris snickered. "Tessaro doesn't do relationships."

"That's probably for the best." Elias managed a thin, polite little smile and pulled out a notepad. "If we could perhaps keep ourselves to the case, instead of to Mr. Tessaro's shortcomings, this will be a much shorter meeting."

Pat's cheeks burned with humiliation, but he bit down on the inside of his cheek and kept his mouth shut. He could sit there and analyze things later. Right now, they had a mystery to solve.

"Okay." Ryan glanced from Elias to Pat and back again. "Now that that's clear as mud, let's look at what we do know. We do know that the state medical examiner, the assistants who loaded the body into the van, and the lab tech who initially processed samples from the body have all had to be taken to the hospital for treatment and isolation. Tests confirm that the disease is diphtheria, which is a terrible way to die, and that Scott did die from the disease."

"So what are we looking at here?" Devlin turned his eyes to Elias. "Have you ever seen a kid come back after ten years, when they've been kidnapped that young?"

"Actually, yes." Elias managed a smile. It didn't reach his eyes. "We have had cases where abductees have come forward and recognized themselves, sometimes well into adulthood. It's not usually accompanied by nudity and easily preventable diseases, though."

Pat scowled. He shouldn't engage, but this was too much. Elias was putting the cart before the horse, and they'd never solve anything that way. "If you can put your judgment aside and maybe get a picture on the screen—thanks, Langer. Look. The ME's report says that the kid doesn't seem to have had a lot of variety in his diet, but that he had food to eat. There are no signs of trauma—no sexual, no physical. No bruising."

Elias glared at Pat, clenching his pen so hard Pat thought it might break. "Your point?"

"He also found that the sheet was wound in a certain, very specific way. There were remnants of certain oils and resins on his body, items mentioned in old texts as appropriate for use in burying a corpse." He gestured up at the screen. "I'm not saying that the person was right to abduct baby Scott. Far from it. I'm saying that in their way, they cared for him. We're not looking for some child trafficking ring here."

Elias pursed his lips. He looked like he'd been sucking on a lemon. "You're probably right. It might still be a possibility, but those types of organizations don't usually show this level of care for their victims." He relaxed, although he still looked like he'd bitten into something foul. "Something still seems off here."

Tran chuckled softly. "Yeah, all we do is *off*. And these guys? Their *off* is even more *off* than ours. That's why they're here too." He shook his head. "What can you tell us about cases like this, Elias?"

Elias took a deep breath and put a hand on the table. He almost looked as if he were steadying himself. "Well, I can't tell you much. We do see some cases where a person will steal babies, but they'll usually be stolen when they're smaller. They'll usually be sold to a desperate childless family that couldn't adopt for whatever reason. Sometimes the perpetrator will keep them, but they won't usually refuse to vaccinate."

Pat kicked Nenci under the table. He wasn't going to contribute anymore, not if it meant risking being assigned to this case, but he could egg others on.

Nenci jumped and glared at Pat, but he spoke up. "There's a clue right there. Our perp might be a vocal anti-vaxxer."

"Or too poor to afford vaccines." Robles twirled his pen in his hand. "That could explain why they couldn't adopt by normal means."

"Why dispose of the body in that way, though?" Elias' face twisted. "I mean that's just wrong. It's just plain wrong. He was thrown away like an old carpet!"

"It seems that way." Langer scratched at his chin, his eyes far away. "What are some alternative explanations? Morris?"

Morris shrugged. "When I was in the service, I knew a woman who brought the bodies of her relatives to an old, bombed-out place—I think it was a tomb of some kind, but I'm not entirely sure. She wasn't in great shape, physically, thanks to the war. She couldn't dig graves for them, but she couldn't just leave them lying around." He pursed his lips in thought. "She brought them to that place in the hopes that someone would find them and bury them decently. Just a thought."

Pat cleared his throat. He didn't want to intrude and cause Elias more disgust with his presence. "The Hotel Alexandra was kind of a landmark in the area. People are always around it. Someone would have found the body eventually." He tapped his pen against the table. "I don't think that the way that the body was anointed and dressed is consistent with a careless disposal. Hey Nenci, is Oliver working on the rest of the trace evidence that came in with the body?"

"He most certainly is not." Nenci crossed his arms over his chest. "Oliver is four months pregnant. He's not going anywhere near something with diphtheria exposure. Once that Sheedy kid gets out of isolation, Oliver can supervise him in getting that trace evidence."

"Okay, is there no one else in the lab who can examine evidence?" Elias sighed. "I mean you guys are paying for my services, so I'm going to stay here for as long as you need me, but the clock is ticking. Someone who will steal a baby once will do it again." He bowed his head. "The trauma of losing one, especially if they've gotten attached, can unhinge them."

"I'll see if I can talk someone into it," Ryan inserted smoothly. "No promises, though. Oliver lets us cut in line because he's married to Nenci." The corners of his mouth twitched in something like a smile. "The rest of the lab is a little less enthusiastic about line cutting."

"I see." Now Elias did smile, or at least smirk. It was the first real expression, other than disdain, that Pat had seen on his former lover's face since they'd gotten here.

"You're already working on this with Ryan." Devlin cleared his throat. "I realize that this might be an unpopular decision, but I want Tessaro on this case."

"What?" Pat squawked.

"No!" Elias recoiled.

Devlin held up a hand. "I said I recognized that it wasn't going to be a popular decision. It is, however, final. This case is messy. Tessaro's good at messy. He is, in fact, the best detective we have when it comes to messy. I don't know what your beef with him is, and I honestly don't care. This is about that little boy now. You're both professionals. Act like it, and get the job done that much faster."

Pat rose to his feet. "I guess I'll see you bright and early tomorrow morning."

Elias glowered at him. "I'll be lodging a formal complaint."

"Get in line." Pat left the room without waiting to be dismissed.

Devlin had gotten one thing right. Pat was the best at messy.

<<<<>>>>

Made in United States
North Haven, CT
31 December 2023